My Fair Godmother

Also by Janette Rallison

My Fair Godmother

Janette Rallison

Walker & Company
New York

First published in the United States of America in 2009 by Walker Publishing Company, Inc.
Visit Walker & Company's Web site at www.walkeryoungreaders.com

For information about permission to reproduce selections from this book, write to
Permissions, Walker & Company, 175 Fifth Avenue, New York, New York 10010

Library of Congress Cataloging-in-Publication Data
Rallison, Janette.
My fair godmother / Janette Rallison.
     p.   cm.
Summary: High school sophomore Savannah wants to find the perfect prom date after her
boyfriend breaks up with her to date her older sister, but when a godmother who is only fair
becomes involved, Savannah finds herself in trouble in the Middle Ages, along with a boy who
would like to be her charming prince.
ISBN-13: 978-0-8027-9780-3 · ISBN-10: 0-8027-9780-6 (hardcover)
[1. Fairy godmothers—Fiction.   2. Magic—Fiction.   3. Sisters—Fiction.   4. Dating (Social
customs)—Fiction.   5. Middle Ages—Fiction.   6. Self-esteem—Fiction.]   I. Title.
PZ7.R13455My 2009   [Fic]—dc22   2008013361

Book design by Daniel Roode
Typeset by Westchester Book Composition
Printed in the U.S.A. by Quebecor World Fairfield
2 4 6 8 10 9 7 5 3 1

To everyone who still believes in the magic of reading

A special thanks to Emily Easton, my editor,
for helping me to make this a better book

My Fair Godmother

For Master Sagewick Goldengill

Dear Professor Goldengill,

Thank you for allowing me to raise my semester grade through this extra-credit project. First off, let me say that I was a little worried about the whole thing. When I went into the Fairy Godmother Affairs office to get my assignment, the lady behind the desk wouldn't even tell me which of the sisters, Jane or Savannah, was supposed to get the wishes. She gave me a condescending look and told me that as a fairy godmother my first task was to figure that out. Then she handed me this huge report to read and said, "I do hope this mission is more successful than your last."

Personally, I think the main problem I had with my last assignment was the leprechaun assistant FGA gave me. I mean, I know we have a lot of free time during these projects, but halfway through the job he wandered off to play poker with card sprites and I never saw him again. So I told the lady that I wanted to work with, you know, some really hot elf guy or at least a unicorn, but she flipped through her papers and said, "You've been assigned Clover T. Bloomsbottle."

Which is the same leprechaun I had last time.

I asked the lady, in a very calm manner—despite what she might tell you—"What in the world is FGA thinking?"

She told me, "FGA is aware of Mr. Bloomsbottle's shortcomings on the last mission. That's why he's been relegated to twenty-first-century America until he can prove he's willing to use his magic in accordance with the Unified Magical Alliance guidelines. FGA believes in giving everyone a chance to redeem themselves."

So let me say right now that this would have gone a lot smoother had I been given an assistant who actually assisted with something.

Here is the sixteen-page report I put together about the troubled teenage souls involved, so you can see how I used my magic to solve their problems, thus proving I have mastered the magic necessary to pass apprentice level and pursue my education at God-mother University. Where, I might add, I will totally apply myself.

I've also added side notes to this report in order to show you how much I've already learned about human culture.

Sincerely,
Chrysanthemum Everstar

HOW I USED MAGIC TO GRANT WISHES, MAKE MORTALS HAPPY, AND RESCUE THEM FROM THEIR DREARY LIVES

by Chrysanthemum Everstar

Subject One: Jane Delano, eighteen years old
Place: Herndon, Virginia, early twenty-first century

Boys weren't a problem for Jane. They only paid attention to her while asking for help with homework. She always knew the answers. See, no problem at all.

It wasn't because she wasn't pretty enough. She was. She had long dark hair the color of milk chocolate, hair that she usually wore pulled back into a ponytail because it took her two minutes to do and didn't fall into her face while she looked down at her schoolwork. Her eyes were warm and large, even behind the glasses she always wore. It was, unfortunately, her air of extreme competence that scared boys away. In fact, she didn't seem to be a teenage girl at all. She was somebody's mother, just waiting to happen.

Fairy's side note: Many perfumes promise to lure men to women. None of them smell of motherhood. None of them proclaim the wearer to be tidy, thrifty, and sensible. At least not in high school. Those traits become attractive much later on, when guys finally realize they're not living somebody else's life.

So there was Jane, walking out of the school building with a backpack, which was heavier than it needed to be, because it couldn't hurt to read over her Shakespeare assignment one more time. As happens with most life-changing events, she was not thinking about anything important at all. If she had thought of Hunter Delmont that day, those wishes, those half-formed sighs of longing had faded as soon as calculus ended. He had picked up his books and tucked them under his arm without a glance in her direction.

Not that she'd expected otherwise. Her seat was at the back of the class. He sat in the front. He had no reason to turn around. Which was why it was so odd when she looked up and saw him leaning against her family's Taurus in the school parking lot.

She stopped midstride, looking like a Jane statue someone had created on the edge of the sidewalk. Not really such a far-fetched idea, actually. The way the teachers loved her, they could have erected a statue in her honor. They would entitle it *The Student the Rest of You Should Have Been.*

Jane forced herself to take another step. She analyzed the situation. He was either resting against her car because . . . she couldn't fill in the blank. He must want to talk to her. Her. HER.

It didn't matter that she already knew it would be about homework. What mattered was he knew she existed. This was clearly a gift from the universe. A whiff of magic and hope that had suddenly blown in.

As she walked to the car her steps gained bounce. He was one of the smartest guys in the class. He didn't need help with homework. He wanted to talk to her.

She smiled as she approached him; a greeting started to form on her lips, waiting for a kick of courage to spring it into action.

Hi, Hunter. What can I do for you? Actually, let me answer that question. In fact, let me send you a résumé.

Only she didn't say it. Courage is a fickle creature. Just as you need it, it often makes excuses and rushes out of the room.

He looked at her and stood straighter, his expression friendly but unreadable. Jane tried to read it. She tried to read her entire future in that gaze. What did the arch of his dark eyebrows signify?

"Are you Savannah's sister?"

"Yes." Her footsteps faltered, but not enough to be noticed, at least not by a guy who'd never glanced at the back of the calculus classroom.

"Jane?" he asked, as though it might have been Jenny or Jamie.

She said, "Yes." But her mind said, "What does Savannah have to do with anything?"

His attention shifted to something behind her and he smiled, a sudden dab of sunshine reflecting in his expression. She turned and saw her sister striding toward the car.

Vision is also a fickle creature. You can see an object a hundred times, a thousand times, and it remains unchanged. Then in one swift second you realize it has been changing all along and your eyes hid it from you.

Savannah wasn't just the little sister who left her clothes strewn on the bathroom floor, who always needed help with her geometry homework, and who misplaced the car keys with such regularity that she ought to have them stapled to her purse. Until then Jane had never realized—Savannah had become beautiful.

Subject Two: Savannah Delano, sixteen years old

Even though Savannah was only a sophomore, she was an inch taller than Jane. Her chocolate brown hair—the identical color of Jane's but with lustrous highlights that their mother painstakingly applied once a month—swung around her shoulders. Not only had Savannah long ago switched to contacts, but the eyeliner and smoky eye shadow she wore gave her a glamorous air.

Her walk was fluid, filled with confidence, and her clothes looked like they'd been torn from a fashion magazine.

Fairy's side note: For mortals, it is almost as tempting to hate beautiful girls as it is to love them, and Savannah had felt her share of both emotions from her peers. But she had only experienced love from her sister until that moment. Often, it only takes a moment to change everything.

Savannah glanced at Jane, then smiled at Hunter.

"I see you found my car."

"It's just the hot rod you promised."

She threw Jane a longer gaze. "And you've met my sister."

"We were just getting around to that." Hunter turned his attention back to Jane. "I'm Hunter. Savannah and I are . . ." He shrugged. "You know . . ."

Savannah laughed, a tinkling sound of happiness, and nudged into him.

Neither one of them noticed Jane for a moment, which was for the best, as Jane looked like parts of her had been ripped up and flung into the wind.

While Hunter smiled at Savannah, little pieces of Jane fluttered down to the parking lot. She was able to put on a disinterested stare by the time they turned to her again.

"We stopped by to tell you that I'll be riding home with Hunter," Savannah said. "He's got a rebuilt T-Bird. How cool is that?"

"Cool," Jane said.

Hunter took hold of Savannah's hand casually and nodded in Jane's direction. "It was nice to meet you."

As they turned and left, Jane realized, with another rip to her heart, that he hadn't recognized her. He didn't even know she sat in the back of his calculus class.

She waded through the litter of her old self and climbed into the battered Taurus.

Fairy's side note: An amateur might think that Jane had need of a fairy godmother at this point. I wouldn't make such a mistake, though. Jane is the type that, even had she believed in fairies, wouldn't have asked for our help. Jane was too self-reliant for that.

For the next few days all of Savannah's happiness came in hues and shades of Hunter. Love kept her drifting around the ceiling, too far up even to notice the usual high school popularity drama that envelops most teenage girls. We will not dwell on her now. Happy people are rarely interesting.

Jane buried herself in her schoolwork, silently mourning with differentials and integrals. Sometimes when the mood struck her, she would lash out with Shakespeare or grow haughty with Spanish verbs. Occasionally she tortured herself by asking Savannah questions about Hunter.

"Where did the two of you meet?"

"He's on the track team," Savannah said. "At first I was sort of intimidated by him because he's a senior and he's so—you know—to-die-for gorgeous, but I went up and flirted with him and it turns out he's really down-to-earth. Very smart. He reminds me of you sometimes."

Savannah went up and flirted with him. That was it? That was all it took to get Hunter's attention?

Why hadn't Jane joined track? Her father had suggested it, after all. Since he was a lieutenant colonel in the marines, he jogged four miles a day. He said jogging could become a family affair. Jane, however, had insisted that it was irrational to run on a track. You didn't actually go anywhere, so what was the point of getting there the fastest? That was the problem with being smart. Sometimes you overlooked the obvious points—like the opportunity to flirt with jocks.

Not that Jane really knew how to flirt anyway.

Besides, how could such a smart guy like Hunter have been captured by mere flirting? Did he not care that Savannah doodled her geometry proofs into abstract art instead of finding out the area of the angles? Did he not know that Savannah's definition of "taking notes in class" meant passing pieces of paper with messages scrawled on them back and forth with her friends?

Four days after their meeting in the parking lot, Hunter noticed Jane in calculus. He walked into the room and, in an apparent visual aberration, his gaze wandered toward the back. His head jerked slightly in surprise and he walked over to her desk. "Hey, I didn't know you were in this class."

Yes, she had realized that already; every day and every moment since he'd first spoken to her. She'd worn that knowledge like clothing. When he'd taken Savannah's hand in the parking lot he might as well have said to Jane, "Here is your invisibility cloak."

She smiled back at him like it was a surprise to see him too. "Yeah, I sit in the back."

"Do you like calculus?" he asked.

"Yes."

She hadn't meant to sound offended by the question, but she must have because he laughed uncomfortably and said, "It's just that for Savannah's last pop quiz she gave the definition of an isosceles triangle as 'one that was lonely.' Scalene was one that suffered from skin disease."

It gave Jane a wicked sense of satisfaction that he'd noticed that aspect of her sister's personality, but she tried not to sound too arrogant. "Savannah doesn't worry about homework.

Apparently they don't care about your GPA when you apply for beauty school."

"Beauty school, huh? I would have thought she'd already graduated valedictorian from there."

Jane blinked at him in frustration.

Fairy's side note: Adults are constantly telling teenagers that it's what's on the inside that matters. It's always painful to find out that adults have lied to you.

Hunter shrugged. "I guess I shouldn't have assumed you'd be like Savannah where math is concerned."

Meaning: After all, you aren't pretty like she is.

Jane let out a small inner gasp, but before she could crumple or rage or decide between these two actions, he added, "We'll have to get together and study some time."

She gripped her pencil, but it wasn't really a grip, it was a hug. "Okay."

"We've got that test coming up next Monday. Do you understand L'Hopital's rule?"

Now that they were on familiar terrain, a glint appeared in her eye. "Well enough to explain it to you."

A grin spread across his features. "What did you get on your last test?"

"A ninety-eight," she said.

His smile grew. "I got a hundred."

And that's how their friendship started, over differential calculus and chain rule and winding through limits that approach infinity. Sometimes at lunch—sophomores ate before the seniors—they'd study together. She enjoyed the look of concentration that came over him as his eyes scanned the numbers. She adored his small block print that couldn't decide whether to slant or stand tall. She liked to watch his lips as he said the word "maxima."

Fairy's side note: Love makes even smart people act like idiots. For example, even though Jane knew Hunter was dating another girl— in this case, her sister—she began to believe he had feelings for her.

Her list of rationales:

1. Hunter started picking up Savannah in the morning and inviting Jane to come along. "There's no point in both of us driving there," he told her, but what were the chances that he was actually environmentally conscious?

2. Since Savannah was often running late in the morning—coifing your hair to perfection can't be rushed—he would turn around in his seat and talk to her while they waited in the car. He never seemed to mind that Savannah was late. And what were the chances that he was actually patient?

3. Hunter also looked at her while they spoke, cared about what she said, and smiled at her.

4. But most important, Jane willed him to like her, and that had to have some impact on his feelings.

Fairy's side note: Even people who don't believe in magic really do.

And then one day, three months after he first leaned against her Taurus, things changed.

Again she was walking with no thought that anything important was about to happen. This time she walked downstairs in worn gray sweats that doubled as pajamas. She had come in search of a book because she couldn't sleep. It was Friday night and Hunter and Savannah had gone to see a movie, which bothered her slightly. The movie had ended an hour ago and they still weren't home, which bothered her more. So she walked into the family room and discovered that she was wrong. They were home. They were on the couch kissing.

She let out a gasp, and then blushed furiously when they both turned and looked at her. She didn't say anything, just rushed from the room. All the way back up the stairs she chastised herself for being so stupid. Why shouldn't they be kissing? Had she really thought Hunter didn't kiss Savannah because he was friends with Jane? She didn't mean anything to him. He was just a guy, who, it turned out—disappointingly—was also environmentally conscious and patient. He hadn't been nice to her with any ulterior motives at all.

Jerk.

Savannah's laughter followed Jane up the stairs. "At least it wasn't my dad."

Jane couldn't hear what Hunter answered. He probably laughed too. He was probably thinking what a pitiful figure Jane made in her cheerless gray sweats. He didn't want someone who could discuss calculus as easily as she discussed life. He wanted someone who looked like she'd graduated from beauty school.

Jane didn't go to sleep for a long time. She went into Savannah's room and with shaking hands took the stack of teen magazines from her sister's closet. She retreated to her bedroom, sat on the edge of her bed, and studied every single one of them.

The next day Jane made an appointment with the optometrist for contacts. She also went shopping with Savannah, who was thrilled her sister wanted to update her appearance. Savannah helped her with the zeal of someone administering life support.

As they flipped through the racks at Forever 21, Savannah put together outfits and handed them to Jane. If Jane balked because something was too bright or too flashy, Savannah quickly brought her around again with a gentle reminder. "Clothes say a lot about a person. Right now yours say you're on the fast track to becoming an eccentric cat lady." Then she would shove the outfit at Jane and say, "Now go try this on and show everyone how beautiful you really are."

Jane didn't feel guilty about accepting Savannah's help. She wasn't trying to steal Hunter. She was trying to punish him. She wanted Hunter to notice her so she could ignore him.

After Jane had spent enough money on outfits and accessories to ensure that she would need a scholarship to go to college, she had her mother, who'd worked as a beautician for years, cut, highlight, and shape her hair until it was the mirror image of Savannah's.

Savannah, who was almost as good a stylist as their mother, made the finishing touches and applied the hairspray. "Now we look like twins again."

They had often been told this growing up, back before their styles had detoured.

On Monday, Jane drove her own car to school. By the time calculus rolled around she was in good spirits. She had received a lot of approving gazes from the guys. Flirting would be a problem for her, she knew. But she'd seen Savannah do it enough times. You looked into the guy's eyes, smiled, and complimented him. She could handle the first two tasks on this list. She just needed to come up with some generic compliments that would work on a variety of guys.

"You're so smart."

"You're so funny."

"You have really great biceps."

She'd have a boyfriend in no time.

Hunter walked into calculus, did a double take, and strode over to her. "Savannah, what are you—" He stopped as though pulled back by a leash. "Jane?"

"New haircut," she told him. "Don't feel bad. People have been doing it all day."

"Oh," he said, and continued to stare at her.

"Don't you like it?" she asked.

"It's exactly like Savannah's."

"Right," she said. *You're so smart.*

He broke his gaze away from her for a moment, seeming to come out of a trance.

"I'd better say yes or I'll have both you and Savannah mad at me, won't I?"

"Right," she said and laughed along with him. *You're so funny.*

He went back to staring and didn't say anything else. Oddly, the silence didn't make her feel awkward. She owned this silence, not the other way around.

"You're wearing makeup," he said.

"I was ready for a change." *You have really great biceps,* she thought, *and I will never let you put your arms around me.*

They didn't eat lunch together that day. She said she didn't feel like doing homework. While he ate with guys from the track team, she talked to football players in the hot-lunch line. She laughed and flirted, her inexperience making her too obvious and nearly drunk with desperation, but she didn't care. This was not something she had to do well, just something she had to do.

Fairy's side note: Guys can smell desperation. It triggers an instinct in them to run far and fast so they aren't around when a woman starts peeling apart her heart. They know she'll ask for help in putting it back together the right way—intact and beating correctly—and they dread the thought of puzzling over layers that they can't understand, let alone rebuild. They'd rather just not get blood on their hands.

But sharks are different. They smell the blood of desperation and circle in. They whisper into a girl's ear, "I'll make it better. I'll make you forget all about your pain."

Sharks do this by eating your heart, but they never mention this beforehand. That is the thing about sharks.

The sharks at the school began to take notice of Jane. Over the next few days one after another slid up to her, stopped by her locker to talk, measured her with hungry gazes. "What's your phone number, Jane?" "Who are you hanging out with this weekend?" "My friend is throwing a party. It's going to be a lot of fun." All of them swishing about her, humming, "Come swim with me in the deep water."

Jane didn't know enough about guys to recognize a shark when she saw one. But Hunter did. He grew more upset every time he saw her wading farther away from the shore, every time he saw her smiling as the fins circled around.

Finally Hunter and Jane had lunch together again. They had a test on Friday and Jane was not so reckless as to abandon her grades in the pursuit of revenge. They studied as they ate, then went to the library to study some more. As they walked there, a sharp-toothed jock sauntered up beside her. "You never got back to me about the party on Friday. Are you going?"

She smiled at him. "I haven't decided yet."

"What's to decide? I can pick you up if you need a ride."

Another smile and a toss of her hair. "I'll let you know."

He swam off, and Hunter's glare followed him. "You're not really going to go anywhere with that guy, are you?"

"Maybe," she said.

They walked into the library, but instead of sitting down at a table he took her arm and pulled her behind the history section. "What's gotten into you? Why are you doing this?"

"Doing what?" she asked, but she knew. She just wanted him to say it.

He held out one hand, waving it in front of her. "The way you're acting. The way you're suddenly carrying on with complete jerks." More hand waving, as though he were trying to erase something in the air. "You've stopped being you."

She tilted her head at him in accusation. "Why shouldn't I change? You never liked the old me."

His head snapped slightly backward. "I did too."

"No, you didn't." She swept her hand in front of her, presenting herself. "You like this. This is why you're dating Savannah and not me." There, she'd said it, and she hadn't even meant to.

He looked at her without speaking, realization saturating his expression.

She turned to go. She did not want to be there when he found the words to speak.

But he never did. Speak, that is. He reached out, took her arm, and moved in front of her to block the way. She stopped and looked at the belt loops on his jeans, waiting for him to say something. Still, he didn't.

She watched his chest move up and down with each breath. Some sort of emotion made the breaths come faster, but she was afraid to find out which emotion that was. She stared at the bookshelves around her, at the books lined up in perfect, tidy rows. Her life had been like that once— perfect, tidy.

"Jane," he said.

She looked up to decipher his gaze, but didn't see much of it. He bent down and kissed her.

Somewhere in her mind a row of books went flying. Pages flapped by like birds in flight. She kissed him back and felt them flutter away in a reckless scramble. *Don't think*, she told herself and then, *don't let him go*.

But of course both happened eventually. He stepped away from her and ran his fingers through his hair, watching her breathlessly.

"We shouldn't have done that," she told him.

"No—we should have done that a long time ago." He leaned down then and kissed her again.

In Jane's defense, it took her a while to process what he'd said. It was hard to think while he kissed her. Finally she gave up trying to sort it out and pushed him away. "What do you mean? Do you think I want to betray my sister?" She took a step away from him. "What kind of person do you think I am?"

He looked at her as though just realizing it himself. "I think you're the perfect person for me."

Jane shook her head. At last she remembered Savannah—but you can't blame her. You haven't thought of Savannah in pages. Savannah was, at that moment, ignoring her English assignment in favor of a prom dress catalog. She was wondering if Hunter could set up Jane with one of his friends. That way they could double date.

But back to Jane and Hunter. The taste of his kiss had turned to bitterness on Jane's lips. "You already chose Savannah."

"And that was a mistake."

They looked at each other silently, each one weighing the past against the future. "I'll break up with her," he said.

"Not yet," she said. "We have to think of a way to do it gently."

Jane thought over this particularly difficult equation for the next week. The ride to school in the morning became an exercise in awkwardness. Lunch was better and worse. After they ate, they walked the rows of the library. Biographies and poetry. General fiction and mysteries. At some point Hunter would take her hand and say, "There is no way to do it gently. We just need to tell her."

Jane would lean into him, stand close enough to hear his heartbeat, and want nothing more than to keep her arms around him. But she always said, "Not yet."

Hunter grew more silent and distant toward Savannah during their car rides. Occasionally he sent heavy, questioning looks in Jane's direction. He never took Savannah's hand or put his arm around her.

Savannah should have known then, but she didn't. Sometimes love not only lifts you to the ceiling, it also keeps your eyes there.

One day as the three walked across the parking lot, Savannah told Hunter that he'd become gloomy and really, he should stop worrying about finals—hadn't he already been accepted to George Mason? She took hold of his hand and gave him a knowing look. "Seriously. We're going to have to refresh your fun skills." She gestured toward her sister. "Even Jane is loosening up—look at her."

He did.

"She's going to be a total hunk magnet when she goes to college. She'll probably have so much fun that—I don't know—she'll let a grade or two slip to an A minus."

He kept looking at Jane. She blushed.

Savannah nudged Hunter because his hand had gone limp in hers. "Let's go do something fun tonight."

"We'll go out tonight," he said. "It's time we did."

Then his eyes found Jane's again. Right or wrong, the equation was written.

Jane nodded. Watching the way her sister possessively took hold of Hunter's hand had momentarily blocked out thoughts of loyalty.

Fairy's conclusion: In ten years Jane wouldn't have let things unfold that way, but eighteen years old is too young to understand that things that are easily done are often much harder to undo. Sometimes impossible. And when you invite a grudge that big and vicious to come and sit between you and your sister, well, let's just say it will be keeping you company for a long, long time. I've seen grudges half as small scare off trolls and goblins. Large grudges make dragons shiver. But there it was, grumbling with hunger and stretching its claws between the two of them.

All those years of sisterhood were about to be chewed to pieces.

This is why mortals need magic.

Of course, they don't realize it. Never has a fairy godmother been called upon to vanquish a grudge. Instead they settle for jewels, kingdoms, handsome princes, that sort of thing. It was this reason, by the way, and not laziness, disinterest, or time spent at too many Pixie dances—as some of my magic professors asserted—that I concentrated my studies on jewels, kingdoms, and handsome princes. In fact, as you have seen from my final reports, I spent more than the required time studying handsome princes. This was due to the extreme importance mortals put on royalty, and not, as Headmistress Berrypond suggested, that I am an incurable flirt.

I hope you will see from the Wishes Granted budget report that I used my magic to the best ends and took on this project following fairy godmother protocol ensuring that the subjects, Savannah Delano and her sister, Jane, lived happily ever after.

From the Honorable Master Sagewick Goldengill
To Mistress Berrypond

Dear Mistress Berrypond,

 I am in receipt of Chrysanthemum Everstar's
report, yet it seems quite a bit has been left unsaid
about her time as a magical godmother for the mortal
Savannah Delano. Can you please have the Memoir
Elves elaborate so that the academy and I can more
accurately assess her project?

 Yours,
 Sagewick Goldengill

From the Department of Fairy Advancement
To the Honorable Sagewick Goldengill

Dear Professor,

As you requested, we sent Memoir Elves to the mortal Savannah Delano's home. Madame Bellwings, Memoir Elf Coordinator, was not at all pleased with this request, because elves who write the memoirs of teenage girls have the unfortunate habit of returning to the magical realm with atrocious grammar. They can't seem to shake the phrases "whatever" and "no way," and they insert the word "like" into so many sentences that other elves start slapping them. They also pick up the bad habit of writing things in text message form (e.g., R U going 2 the mall?) and for no apparent reason occasionally call out the name Edward Cullen.

Currently the Memoir Elves who delved into Savannah's mind while she slept are in detox. They are doing well in their recovery process, although one still occasionally stands in front of the mirror and asks, "Do you think I look fat in this?"

Savannah is none the wiser and the elves were able to compile a thorough report. You should be able to find out exactly what part Chrysanthemum Everstar played in granting wishes and whether she did indeed follow all fairy/mortal protocol.

The memoir report follows as told to the elves by the subject Savannah Delano.

Chapter 1

Here's my definition of a bad day: your boyfriend of four months—who, until twelve seconds ago, you thought was the most perfect guy to set foot on earth—breaks up with you.

My definition of a truly horrible day: the aforementioned boy dumps you for none other than your sister.

The definition of my life: he does all of this right after you inform him that you blew your last dollar buying your dream prom dress. He asks if you can get a refund. It turns out he'll be taking your sister.

• • •

I stared at Hunter across the restaurant table, so many thoughts shooting through my head that I didn't know which one to pick first and aim in his direction.

"I'm sorry," he said. "Jane and I didn't mean for this to happen."

"Really?" How do you not mean to ask your girlfriend's

older sister to prom? Do the words just trickle out by themselves? Was someone else in charge of your lips when this happened? I didn't say any of this, because there wasn't a point. What he meant was: I didn't mean to like her better than you.

I wanted to ask him why he did—like Jane better than me, that is—but somehow I couldn't bring myself to ask the question. The answer would hurt more than not knowing.

Almost as if he'd read my mind he added, "It's just that Jane and I have more in common. We're both more..." He moved his hand in a rolling motion as though trying to catch the right word somewhere over the tabletop.

During the pause, I thought of my own adjectives. Smart? Talented? Good-looking? No, it probably wasn't looks. Jane and I look too much alike for that. She's pretty, true, but I always get noticed first. Jane always has been content to be known as the quiet, studious one. The quiet, studious one who had now stolen my boyfriend.

"Organized," Hunter said.

"Organized?" I repeated. "You're dumping me because I'm disorganized?"

"I guess 'responsible' is a better word," he said.

"So I'm disorganized and irresponsible?"

He leaned toward me but his eyes distanced themselves. "Don't take it the wrong way. You have lots of great qualities: you're fun and you're pretty, you're just..."—more hand rolling, as though this somehow unwound his tongue—"always late for everything."

I stared back at him, stunned. This was how guys chose girlfriends—based on their punctuality?

"I'm not late for everything," I said, even though I hadn't been ready when he came to pick me up that night. But I'd had a good reason. One of Mom's hair clients had needed an updo for a fancy night out and Mom hadn't finished with her perm appointment, so I'd stepped in to help out.

I nearly pointed this out, but then stopped myself. It hadn't been tonight's ten-minute wait that had decided my fate with Hunter. He'd only scheduled this date to break up with me. I should have sensed it by the way he'd hardly looked at me while he ate his dinner.

"Jane and I both want to go to college," he went on. "You don't even want to go to high school."

"What's that supposed to mean?" I have never said I didn't want to go to high school. I enjoy high school. Well, at least the socializing part. Geometry I could do without. Ditto for world history. And really, why should I care what the symbolism in *The Grapes of Wrath* stands for? Do employers ask those kinds of questions during job interviews?

He shrugged. "You don't take your grades seriously."

"I took us seriously," I said.

That made him flinch. "I'm sorry," he said.

I pushed my chair away from the table. "Take me home."

We drove back to my house in silence. Inside my head a whole orchestra of thoughts played out, competed with each other, blared so loudly I could hardly think.

He drove looking straight ahead and I caught a glimpse of his profile. I hated myself for still thinking his wavy black hair had the perfect amount of gloss to it, that he looked more like a knight preparing for battle than a high school senior. A girl shouldn't have thoughts like that about the guy who just dumped her.

My throat felt tight and I willed myself not to cry. I wanted to point out all of Jane's faults to him. She was the most unspontaneous person in existence. She had no imagination, no creativity. When we were bored as kids, could she come up with a decent game using a box of macaroni, a tube of toothpaste, and the kitchen table? I think not.

I didn't say anything though. I had enough pride not to beg him to reconsider. I just sat and listened to the orchestra in my mind playing loud and clear: your sister is better than you. Finally he pulled up in front of our house. Without a word I opened the car door, stepped outside, and slammed it shut.

I didn't walk across the lawn to our house; I walked down the sidewalk. I was not going inside. I didn't want to talk to Jane right now, or hear the same type of apologies I'd just heard from Hunter.

Instead of driving off, Hunter pulled up alongside me and rolled down the car window. "Where are you going?"

"I don't see why that concerns you."

"If you don't go inside, it will look like I never brought you home. Your family will wonder where you are."

What he meant was, Jane would worry where I was. Heaven forbid she experience any guilt over this. "Well, you know me," I told him. "I'm the irresponsible one."

He kept following me. The car inched along beside me going about two miles an hour. "Come on, Savannah, don't be this way."

I wasn't supposed to have a reaction to this? I was just supposed to smile and wish them luck or something? I didn't answer. I looked straight ahead and kept walking. I had meant to go over to my best friend Emily's house but I couldn't go there with this one-car parade following me. When I came to the corner of our street I walked straight instead of turning right.

Hunter leaned toward me, a mild reprimand in his voice. "It's dark and you didn't even look for cars before you crossed."

"I didn't have to. If a car was coming they'd have hit you first."

He let out a sigh. "Get back in the car."

I kept walking.

"I mean it, Savannah. I'm not going to let you run off and upset everyone at your house because they don't know where you are."

Which just goes to show you how arrogant he was. He just assumed I'd planned on turning the night into a big production where I disappeared and Jane got to worry that I'd run away from home or something. Well, okay, maybe that did sound like a good idea, but still, it was arrogant of him to assume that sort of thing about me. I didn't look at him. My purse thumped against my side in an angry rhythm.

"Savannah, get in the car."

The park came into view. I picked up my pace.

"You're being melodramatic about this."

Well, he could just add that to the list of my other faults he no longer had to put up with.

"I'm not leaving and I've got a full tank of gas."

Of course he did. Organized people always kept their tanks full.

I made it to the park and finally turned to him. "If you want to follow me, fine. Have fun driving through the swing sets." I left the sidewalk and walked across the grass. The park sat in the middle of our neighborhood, surrounded by houses, and more than a few streets ran up to it.

I didn't have to look back to know what Hunter would do. He would sit in his car and watch me walk across the park until I headed toward a street. Then he'd drive around and head me off on that street.

I strolled toward the first street opening on the right. Before I got out of sight I turned to check and see if his car had left. As soon as it had, I doubled back, walking the same way I'd come. Except that instead of walking home, I turned on

Emily's street. Really, Hunter was almost pathetically easy to lose. Which just goes to show you that college bound doesn't necessarily mean street smart.

I stayed at Emily's for the next three hours. Not really long enough to worry my parents. My curfew on weekdays is 10:00 PM. If Jane knew I wasn't with Hunter anymore and worried about me—fine. If she thought I was out with her new boyfriend until past 10:00—even better. I sat with Emily on her bedroom floor, cried, and ate Oreos. The whole time Emily told me what a great catch I was and how I didn't need Hunter. What kind of jerk hits on his girlfriend's sister? What kind of sister steals boyfriends from family members? They deserved each other.

I nodded at everything she said but couldn't agree with any of it. It felt like the people who knew me best didn't care about me. In my mind, Hunter's list of my faults kept growing. All of my popularity was a sham. I didn't really have anything going for me. I was disorganized, irresponsible, and didn't take my classes seriously. Which probably showed a lack of ambition, talent, and dependability. Obviously there was something permanently wrong with me, something too huge to fix.

And on top of all that I had a cream silk and chiffon prom dress hanging in my closet that cost me three hundred and fifteen dollars. I didn't want to return it to the dress shop. How humiliating would that be?

Emily must have sensed that her pep talk wasn't working— probably because I kept making Oreo skyscrapers and shoving them in my mouth. She finally took the package away from me. "Savannah, someone else will ask you to prom. Someone better, someone who appreciates you, and then you'll see Hunter was wrong."

I nodded. I still didn't believe her.

When I walked into my house at 10:15, my parents and Jane

sat in the family room talking in harsh, subdued voices. I knew they were talking about me because they stopped as soon as I walked in. Three faces turned toward mine. My parents' expressions were concerned. Jane's showed a mixture of worry and defiance. She didn't speak. I knew she was waiting for my accusations; I could already see her lips poised in defense.

"You owe me three hundred and fifteen dollars for a prom dress," I told her, then walked upstairs to my room.

· · ·

I ate oatmeal without sugar the next morning as a sort of dietary penance for my Nabisco sins. I imagined the little oat flakes "tsk-tsking" as they floated by blobs of fat that were headed straight to my thighs. It was the only reason I could think of to be happy that I now had to walk to school. I wasn't sure if Hunter would still drop by the house to offer me and Jane a ride, but there was no possible way I was going to get in the backseat and watch Jane sit beside Hunter. So it was just best to be long gone before he came.

While I ate, Mom tried to talk to me about the whole situation. She'd also tried last night, but I'd told her I was tired and just wanted to go to bed. Jane came into my room last night too and gave me her side of the story, which was pretty much like Hunter's side of the story, except that her eyes didn't look away from me as she told it. When I didn't comment she added, as though it should explain everything, "Hunter and I will both be going to George Mason in the fall. You didn't think that a freshman in college was going to keep dating a junior in high school, did you?"

Yes. But I didn't say that. I just added "immature" to my mental list and said, "Would you mind turning off the light on your way out? I've got to get up early in the morning."

She sighed and left.

So Mom gave me a concerned-parent pep talk as I ate my oatmeal about how she was disappointed in Jane's choices, but if it hadn't been Jane, it would have been someone else. Dating had its ups and downs. After all, at this point in my life I wasn't looking for a future husband. I should be dating for fun, to learn about relationships, to see what kind of qualities I liked in a guy. I would go through many more boyfriends before I found the right one.

Which, I can tell you, is not what you want to say to your daughter when you are trying to cheer her up. I wanted to say, "Really? You mean I get to feel like the bottom of my stomach has been manually ripped out with each relationship I go through? I can hardly wait to get back to the dating market."

But of course I didn't say that because none of this was my mother's fault, unless you count the fact that she gave birth to Jane.

Besides, I'd finished crying about it when I'd finished my last Oreo skyscraper. As Dad would say, I'd taken my losses, now I needed to regroup, rethink, and plan the next offensive. Which in this case involved getting someone even cooler to ask me to prom in order to show Hunter and Jane that I didn't need or care about them.

I nodded at Mom. "I'm fine. Really."

She reached over and patted my hand. "I know you will be. Just remember, boys come and go. Sisters are forever."

Jane swept into the room, walking by the kitchen table and scanning the counters. "Has anyone seen my chemistry folder? I left it on the coffee table and now it's gone."

I picked up my glass of milk and took a slow sip. "Nope."

She hurried out of the room, mumbling.

I ate my oatmeal. Mom watched me in silence. Finally she said, "Maybe after school the two of us can go out and do something. Would you like that?"

"I'm fine. Really."

Jane came back into the room, this time with her hands on her hips. "My brown shoes are gone too. They were in my closet last night and now they're not. What happened to them?"

I took the last bite of my oatmeal and shrugged. "Don't know."

She pulled her gaze from me and turned to Mom. "If I can't find my brown shoes, I'm going to have to change my entire outfit. They're the only shoes that match these pants."

I stood up to take my bowl to the sink. "Don't be too long. You know how Hunter hates to wait." Then I left the room.

Okay, so it was slightly evil to hide her stuff, but considering all of the things I could have done, I figured she got off easy.

Chapter 2

For the next week, I ignored Jane and Hunter the best I could and flirted with everyone on my possible-prom-dates-who-are-way-cooler-than-Hunter list. I had thought attention from any of these guys would fill the hole that had been blasted in me when Hunter dumped me, but it only made things worse. One by one, they all asked other people to the dance.

On Saturday morning, Hunter came over to pick up Jane for some sort of date. I wasn't sure of the details since I wasn't on speaking terms with either of them anymore. The two of them discussed something in low voices in the living room, darting glances in my direction. I lay on the couch flipping through a magazine and trying to ignore them. This went on for a couple of minutes until finally Jane walked up to me. Hunter reluctantly trailed her. She nudged him and he spoke, "So, um, you know Tristan Hawkins from track?"

I did know him, if you counted the three or four times we'd

spoken over the last two years as knowing someone. He was the quiet type that just sort of faded into the background most of the time. True, he wasn't bad looking, in a choir-boy sort of way. He had nice features and pretty blue eyes. But he looked more like a freshman than a senior.

He probably would have been completely overlooked in high school if he wasn't an extremely fast runner. This skill may have been acquired by running away from bullies during junior high. But at any rate, the track coach loved him.

I nodded, pretending it didn't feel like swallowing splinters to look at Hunter.

"Well, I was talking to him the other day and he mentioned he wasn't going to prom, but you know, he'd like to. And I told him you weren't going with anyone—"

I propped myself into sitting position. "Wait a minute, are you telling me you're trying to set me up with Tristan?"

Jane and Hunter exchanged a glance. She said, "Well, you already have a dress and it would be a shame not to wear it."

I glared at her.

"You'd have a fun time," she went on. "And he's smart so he could help you study for your finals."

This was how she was going to make up for stealing my boyfriend? She wanted to set me up with another guy—and not even a guy like Hunter, but a guy like Tristan? I stood up and tossed my magazine on the couch. "I don't believe the two of you. Now you're throwing boys at me like they're some sort of consolation prize." I stalked up the stairs to my bedroom, but still heard traces of their conversation behind me.

"I knew she wouldn't go for it," Hunter said.

Jane let out a sigh. "She'll probably go hide some more of my stuff."

Hunter said, "Well, I guess it's in Tristan's hands now."

Oh, I was *so* going to avoid Tristan from now on. I mean, the only thing worse than not going to prom was going to prom with the pity date your ex-boyfriend set up for you.

· · ·

That afternoon Emily and I drove to a swim party together. Alix Lorie, one of the senior track girls, was having an end-of-the-season party. Her parents had rented out her country club's pool, so the invitation was for the track team and whatever friends they wanted to bring along. Half the school would be there. As Emily drove I fingered my track bag. It held the new turquoise bikini I'd bought specifically for the party. Since we were twenty-two days away from P-day, I knew this might be one of my last chances to remind the guys on my possible-prom-dates list that I existed. And apparently I needed all the help I could get.

The problem was that I'd never worn a bikini before. My dad doesn't allow them. He thinks even one-pieces show too much skin and constantly suggests that Jane and I wear wet suits.

The bikini had seemed like a good idea when I'd been out trying to shop away my feelings of rejection. Jane may have told me I was too immature for Hunter, but the mirror begged to differ. Now driving to the club, I had second thoughts. Maybe I just wasn't a bikini type of girl. Besides, Jane might be there with Hunter. What if she told my parents what I'd done? How upset would my father be?

Emily pulled into the club's parking lot and I got out of the car. It was too late to turn back. We walked into the women's dressing room and changed. I took out my contacts so I wouldn't lose them while I swam and put them with the rest of the things in my track bag. Then I reminded Emily she'd have to point out the cute upperclassmen to me. Without my contacts, I can't recognize faces more than a couple of feet away.

I hesitated before leaving the dressing room. The smell of chlorine and sunscreen wafted toward me. It was the smell of possibility—both good and bad.

Emily had to take my arm and pull me out. "Come on," she said. "You're here to get noticed." As we walked to the pool chairs she gave me a rundown as to who the blurry figures around the pool were, emphasizing the eligible blurs. "James Dashner is by the diving board, Bill Gardner is next to him in the red swim trunks—oh, and Hunter and Jane are directly across the pool. Jane is staring at you and shaking her head."

I lifted my chin and refused to care.

"Let's swim for a while," I told Emily.

Emily took a running jump off the diving board and created a huge splash. I climbed onto the diving board after her. I would do a perfect, elegant dive. A dive that said, "Look at this girl's grace and beauty. Those of you who have just dumped her—you are obviously stupid."

I felt the breeze pick up strands of my hair and blow them around my shoulders. I sauntered to the end of the board, looking out at the blurs that surrounded me. I couldn't tell if any of them watched but I imagined they all did. I took a one-step bounce then made a smooth, effortless arc into the pool.

Actually, there would be some advantages to wearing a wet suit. Primarily, it wouldn't fall off your body after you dove into the pool. As soon as I hit the water I felt the straps of my top give way. I tried to grab hold of it, but the momentum of my dive pushed me farther away into the pool.

I needed air, but I needed the top of my bikini more. I also needed to shriek, but I couldn't do that underwater. Instead of surfacing, I turned around and tried to go after my top. I could make out a turquoise shape sinking in the water across from me. I swam toward it until my lungs ached, but it drifted off, just out of reach.

Finally I swam up for air, but only because I had visions of passing out and forevermore being known as the girl who drowned while wearing half a swimsuit.

I broke through the surface, letting my face pop out of the pool while I tried to tread water only using my legs. I wrapped my arms tightly around my upper body.

"There you are," Emily said. She waved at me to come over to the side of the pool. I shook my head.

"Help me," I mouthed to her. I didn't want to say it loud for fear the lifeguard—a tanned blurry guy sitting in a tower not far away—would think I was drowning and jump in to drag me to safety. I gazed around at the blurs in the pool. I still couldn't tell if any of them were looking at me, which at this point was a good thing.

Emily swam over. "What's wrong? Why are you . . . hey, where's your top?"

I looked toward the bottom of the pool. "Down there. I'm going to go get it. Don't let anyone else dive in until I do."

"How am I supposed to—," but I didn't stick around to let her finish. The faster I retrieved my top, the better. I took a deep breath and dove back in, pushing through the water with all my strength. I could make out the turquoise blob, swaying softly below me. Stupid bikini. Man, I hate it when my father is right.

I grabbed my top, then turned around and looked up. I could see a pair of legs kicking in the water above me. I swam toward them. I'd need Emily's help to tie the straps on once I reached the surface.

As I got close, I held the suit to my body, trying to reposition it as best I could. I was concentrating on this and not on Emily's legs, which is why I didn't notice that they weren't Emily's legs until I surfaced.

And then I was face-to-face with Tristan. I let out a short, startled scream.

Tristan spun around as though I must have seen something frightening behind him. He checked to see what, you know, just in case a giant squid was about to attack.

I searched for Emily. Which was useless since I couldn't see. In the pressure of the moment, I couldn't even remember what color swimsuit she had on.

Tristan returned his attention to me, still looking for the cause of my panic. "What's wrong?"

"Um, nothing. You just startled me. I thought you were Emily."

This seemed to add to his confusion so I said, "I don't have my contacts in and I can't see very well. Sorry about screaming." I waited for him to swim away, but he didn't. I wondered if he noticed that my bikini straps were floating untied around my shoulders, and if he would mention it. How does one casually explain to passing swimmers that you are half naked?

Instead of paying attention to my straps he looked in my eyes intently. "I didn't know you wore contacts."

"Yep, I do."

He still didn't swim away. Oh no. He wanted to make small talk in the deep end while both of us treaded water and I was clutching my swimsuit to my body. I let myself drift away from him but he followed.

"I've always had twenty-twenty vision," he said.

"That's great."

I wondered if he'd ask me to prom right here. I suddenly had the urge to tell him that I knew Hunter was trying to set us up and I didn't want any pity dates. But that would have encouraged him to say something along the lines of, "No, I really do want to ask you out," even if he didn't.

The lifeguard blew his whistle and called out, "You need to leave the diving area so the next person can dive."

Tristan took several strokes toward the ladder, effortlessly pulling himself to the side of the pool. I followed after him, in what I'm sure looked like a failed attempt to walk on water. I still wouldn't use my arms so only my legs propelled me slowly toward the side.

Tristan turned back and watched as I attempted to march through twelve feet of water. "Are you okay?"

"Yeah, I'm fine."

It was then I noticed Emily at the side of the pool holding my towel for me. As I got closer she said, "Sorry. The lifeguard made me leave. But I thought it might be best if I brought you a towel anyway, you know, just in case you couldn't find your . . ." She looked at Tristan and her sentence drifted off.

Tristan's gaze flickered between the two of us and then zeroed in on my straps, which, now that I'd stopped marching forward, hovered beside my shoulders like turquoise tentacles.

A flash of understanding went through his eyes and then he snapped his gaze back up to mine. "Um, do you want me to help you with that?"

I held the suit tighter to my body. "No."

He tried to hide his smirk. "No, really, I was a Boy Scout. I know how to tie knots that stay put."

I didn't move. "I can handle this myself."

"Okay." He pulled himself up the ladder and looked back down at me. "Suit yourself. Although the next time you do it in that one, you might want to try a square knot."

He and Emily both laughed. I glared up at them, then looked at the ladder.

The thing about ladders is that you really need, oh, a minimum of one hand to climb up them. And there was no way I was moving either of my hands.

I felt stupid to have to say it, but I didn't have a choice. "Okay, I can't handle this myself. Will one of you please get back in the pool and help me?"

Emily handed Tristan my towel. "It's a girl thing. I'll do it."

She climbed down the ladder, but as soon as she got back in the water, the lifeguard blew his whistle at us again. "Clear the diving area!" he called.

I turned so my back faced Emily. She held onto the side of the pool with one hand and tried to tie my straps with the other. She didn't have a lot of luck with this method. I should have stuck with the Boy Scout's offer. "Please hurry," I told her.

She let go of the side of the pool and, treading water, tied the top straps. It was loose, but at least it was attached. She moved to the one that went across my back.

The lifeguard blew his whistle again, sending a shrill reprimand in our direction. "You need to exit the pool now!"

Really, lifeguards are way too uptight.

"She'll just be a second," Tristan called back. "Her bikini top came off!"

Let me say right now that if you're planning to ask a girl to prom there are several things you don't want to do. Yelling "Her bikini top came off!" in front of an entire pool full of her peers is on the top of that list.

I gasped, and then shrank into the water. A chorus of hoots and applause went off around me.

Emily gave my straps one final tug. "It's not perfect but it will at least hold until you can get to the dressing room to fix it."

As if I was going to come back out here after I'd just become the poolside entertainment. I hauled myself up the ladder. More clapping followed my ascent. Tristan held my towel open for me and I wrapped it around my shoulders tightly. "Did you have to announce that to everyone?"

"I didn't want the lifeguard to yell at you again," he said.

Even though I couldn't see them, I could feel Hunter's and Jane's gaze on me. I could feel everyone's gaze on me. In a low voice I said, "I've never been so embarrassed in my life." Then I made a beeline toward the dressing room.

I heard footsteps behind me, then Tristan called out, "Savannah, wait a second!"

I didn't. I hurried faster. The dressing-room door was in sight. "Savannah, don't—," he called.

I ignored him and dashed through the door, but I figured out the rest of his sentence as soon as I set foot inside. It was, "Savannah, don't go in there; that's the men's dressing room."

Because, yes it was.

Which just goes to prove you shouldn't say, "I've never been so embarrassed in my life," as that just invites life to outdo itself on your behalf.

I screamed. The guys in the dressing room screamed. Although their screaming was more of an angry "Hey, you shouldn't be in here!" scream, whereas mine was a high-pitched, "There's a bunch of naked guys everywhere!" scream.

Blurry vision doesn't have a lot of benefits, but for a few seconds in the men's dressing room, I was grateful I couldn't see well. Because really, there is no one on the track team that I want to know that personally. I turned and stumbled back outside, where I was once again greeted with clapping from my peers. In fact, this time some of them gave me a standing ovation. I plunged into the women's dressing room, grabbed my things, and ran out to the parking lot. I waited in Emily's car until she came and climbed in beside me.

"Well," she said as she threw her things on the backseat, "I'll give you one thing—you know how to get noticed."

Chapter 3

As soon as I got home, I went inside, changed into an old pair of gray sweats and a T-shirt, then sat in my bedroom. On the plus side, I was no longer so concerned about going to prom.

On the negative side, I was now concerned about going back to school. I was always going to be known as some sort of men's-room crasher.

Eventually Jane came home. She walked into my bedroom and sat on the end of my bed. "Do you want to talk about it?"

I looked at the ceiling and willed her to go away. "Nope."

She watched me silently. "Look, I wish you'd just yell at me and get it over with. Then everything could go back to being normal."

"Sorry," I said. Normal didn't exist anymore. She really should have known that without me having to tell her.

"I've liked him all year," she said. "I liked him even before you knew who he was. I didn't give you the silent treatment when you started dating him."

"That's because I didn't steal him from you."

"But if you had known that I liked him, would you have dated him anyway?"

I knew Jane too well to get swept up in her theoretical situations. If I said yes I was no better than her. If I said no then she'd ask me why I couldn't find it in my heart to be happy for her now.

Instead I smiled over at her. "Well, after you and Hunter break up, you can tell me who you want to date next and then we'll find out."

She let out a sigh, sat there for a few more moments, then got up and left. I lay on my bed for a while longer and considered job possibilities for people who didn't graduate from high school. I could be a waitress. At least that way I wouldn't starve because I could eat the unwanted scraps from people's plates.

Which made me hungry. I went downstairs and got a Ding Dong. When I walked back into my room, I saw the thing. Since I didn't have my contacts in, I could only tell that it was about five inches tall, mostly green, and moving across the end of my bed. A huge toad, perhaps? A mutated rat?

I picked up a book and walked toward the thing, ready to clock it if it turned out to be rabid. As I got closer, the creature looked up at me and in a thick brogue accent said, "I hope you plan on reading that book and not throwing it. I'd consider you tossing something at me an ugly breach of hostess etiquette."

I gasped, stopped, then leaned closer. As it came into focus, I realized it was a tiny man.

I dropped the book. My hands went to my mouth, and I had to stifle the urge to scream. Instead I let out quick breaths. "I'm having a nervous breakdown, aren't I?"

He put his hands behind his back and looked up at me.

"I'm not qualified to comment on your mental health. I'm a leprechaun—not a doctor. Now, on with our business. Where is your Miss High-and-Mighty godmother?"

"What?" I asked.

"Chrysanthemum Everstar." He scanned the room. "She's here, isn't she?"

I shook my head. "I don't know what you're talking about."

He did a full turn on my bed and then let out a *humph*. "Aye, it's just like her to be late. She ought to take her own advice every once in a while and that's the truth." He shot me a dissatisfied look. "And I know what you're thinking—seeing a leprechaun and all—but you can't have me gold, so don't even ask."

That's not what I had been thinking. I was wondering how long nervous breakdowns lasted and what else was going to pop up in my bedroom. "Uh, did I understand you right? Are you meeting someone in my room?"

"When she gets around to it." He walked over to my pillow and sat down in a huff. "Do you have anything to eat around here? It might be a while."

I attribute it to still being in shock, but I handed him my Ding Dong. It was nearly as big as he was. For a moment I worried that it would fall over and crush him, but he handled it well enough. He ripped the plastic, broke off a piece, and put it into his mouth. Then he nodded, smiling. "Not bad for Yankee food."

I watched him and resisted the almost overpowering urge to pick him up for a better look. I sat beside him on the bed and tilted my head down toward him. His clothes were so intricate. Tiny golden buttons lined the front of his jacket. It had a subtle pattern of dark green leaves I hadn't noticed before.

"So who is this Chrysanthemum Everstar and why are you meeting her in my bedroom?"

"I'd tell you," he said between mouthfuls, "but I'm just the *assistant*. Not supposed to overstep my bounds. A glorified errand boy, that's what I am. Stupid Unified Magical Alliance. We never should have unionized." He took another bite and wiped cream filling off his beard. "Relegated to America. A fierce awful place to be—hardly a magical creature around except for the fairies and computer gremlins."

"Computer gremlins?" I repeated.

"And a bad-tempered lot those are. Not much for company."

I looked over at my computer and shook my head. It was at this moment that I stopped thinking I'd lost my mind and believed him. "I knew it," I said.

I didn't have time to say more because just then a poof of light, like a hundred sparklers going off at once, filled my room. The next moment a life-size teenage girl decked out in a tank top, miniskirt, knee-high boots, and sunglasses stood before me. She had long cotton-candy-pink hair, which matched not only a small sequined purse on her shoulder but also her immaculate nail job.

I stood up in surprise, then blinked at her, trying to adjust my eyes after the intense light.

Without so much as a glance at me, she turned to the leprechaun. A pair of incandescent wings fluttered in agitation. "What are you doing here?"

"You said to meet here at 5:30 mortal time. I knew you'd be late so I came at six, and I still beat you here."

She put one hand on her hip. "I said to meet me at the edge of the rainbow and we'd come here together. You've not only ruined our dramatic entrance"—she glanced down at her wristwatch—"you've seriously cut into my shopping time with my friends."

He waved a piece of Ding Dong at her. "We're a leprechaun

and a fairy. We can't make an entrance without it being dramatic."

Still looking at her wristwatch she said, "I will say this
much for you, you're getting more efficient. We're just minutes
into this assignment and you've already made a mess of it."

"That's it." The leprechaun stood up and brushed off his
jacket. "I'd rather walk to Ireland than help you."

"Fine," she said. "It's a long trip. You'd better get started."

He raised his chin, took a few steps down my bedspread,
then turned around, walked back to my Ding Dong, and broke
off another piece. "Now I'm going." With one last *humph*, he
completely disappeared.

I stared at the spot on my bedspread, trying to see
something—some sign that he was still there.

The fairy walked over to me. "You don't need to worry
about him. He probably just went to play poker with the computer gremlins. You know how leprechauns are."

I didn't, but I nodded anyway.

She smiled at me. "Well, you've already met my ex-assistant,
Clover Bloomsbottle. Did he tell you that I'm here to grant you
three wishes?"

My mouth hung open for a moment. "Me? Why?"

Another smile. I noticed she had perfect teeth. "Fairies
have a long and rich history of helping deserving maidens.
And besides, I needed an extra-credit project." She put her
hands together. "Now that I'm officially your Fair Godmother
you can call me Chrissy. Chrysanthemum Everstar is much too
long, don't you think?"

"Fair Godmother? Don't you mean Fairy Godmother?"

She tossed her hair off one shoulder. "No, actually I'm just
a Fair Godmother."

"What does that mean?" I asked.

Her wings fluttered, but she looked at her fingernails instead of me. "It means that in Fairy Godmother School my grades weren't great, or even good. They were just, you know, fair."

"Oh," I said.

Her glance shot over to me. "Hey, the exams are hard. You turn one pumpkin into an angry, bloated walrus and they never let you live it down."

I sat down on the bed. "Um, you're not going to try and turn *me* into anything, are you?"

"I don't have to," she said, her voice sounding offended. "That all depends on what you wish for, doesn't it?"

"What *can* I wish for?" I asked.

Chrissy pulled a sparklerlike wand from her handbag. "That's what I like about today's teenagers. They're all business. None of that 'Oh, thank you, Fair Godmother, for rescuing me from my pathetic life.' Or 'I'm unworthy of having such gifts bestowed on me.' Or even 'Tell me from whence thou came, Fair Godmother.' It's all 'What will you give me?' "

"I didn't mean it like that," I said. "I'm not ungrateful. I'm just not sure what to wish for."

She put her wand back in her purse, walked to my bed, and sank down onto it with a sigh. "All right then, let's hear it. Tell me all about your pathetic life."

Which wasn't what I'd meant. I'd meant that I wanted to know what the rules were before I flung wishes around, but since she asked, I told her about Hunter and Jane, including the most recent chapter in swimsuit humiliation.

Chrissy shook her head slowly when I'd finished. "That's so sad. I can totally relate to the whole prom thing." She gave a tinkling little laugh as though mentally correcting herself. "Well, actually, I've always gone to prom with buff elf guys, but I mean, I can understand how horrible it would be not to go." She sat up straighter. "So do you want me to change this Hunter guy into a frog?"

"No," I answered, aghast. "You can't go around turning people into frogs."

"Yes, I can." She held her wand up. "Do you want to see?"

"No, no. I meant that wouldn't solve anything."

"Then what do you want?" She laid her wand across her knees. "Oh, that reminds me, you need to sign this before I grant your wishes." She opened her purse, pulled out a scroll, and handed it to me. I didn't see how it had fit in her small purse, and supposed fairy magic must have been involved. She pulled out a quill as well and handed it to me. "The contract," she told me. "Sign at the bottom *X* where it reads: Damsel in distress."

I unrolled the scroll, which, besides being quite long, was written in a "thee, thou, and thine" sort of language.

"What does all of this say?" I asked.

"That you get three wishes and only three wishes, that all of them must pertain directly to you—like, you can't wish for world peace. You can't wish for more wishes either—everybody tries that, and your wishes must somehow be tangible. Meaning you can't wish to be lucky or popular or some vague sort of happy. Your wish has to be specific enough that I can actually wave my wand and make it happen.

"Also, side effects may include dizziness, nausea, lethargy, and an intense desire to eat woodland creatures if, during your magical journey, you happen to be turned into a bear. Contact your doctor if symptoms don't subside after a week, blah, blah, blah. We never had to do all this paperwork in the old days. I tell you, everything changes once lawyers get involved." She smiled at me and her wings spread out like a butterfly's. "And one more thing. Since you're my extra-credit assignment, you didn't earn your godmother the usual way—by helping poor strangers you met during a quest—so you'll need to be completely honest until your wishes are finished."

I shrugged. "Okay, but why?"

She let out a grunt like she couldn't believe I was asking. "Haven't you ever read any fairy tales? In the classic stories, maidens who come in contact with fairies and tell lies end up having a nasty enchantment. Reptiles and amphibians drop out of their mouths. It isn't pleasant. I'm just mentioning it because you don't want to get on the wrong side of magic."

"Oh." I put my hand to my mouth. "Thanks for the warning."

Chrissy picked up her wand and a new wave of sparks shot out the end. "All right then, as soon as you're done signing you can tell me your first wish."

I unrolled the scroll on my desk and signed my name across the bottom. Then Chrissy picked up the scroll, tugged at the end, and it rolled itself up as though it were a window shade. She put it back in her purse and turned to me with a satisfied smile. "All right, what's your heart's desire?"

"Well . . ." Now that she asked, I wasn't quite sure what to say. What did I want? My first thought had been to ask for Hunter to break up with Jane and fall in love with me again. But as soon as I opened my mouth, I couldn't bring myself to say the words. It wouldn't make me happy to have him back if he only cared about me because of a magic spell. I wanted someone who liked the real me, even if I was occasionally late and disorganized, and okay, I admit it—I don't always take school seriously.

So what did that leave as my heart's desire?

I guess when it came down to it, I wanted to be someplace different. I didn't know where, just someplace where no one would judge me against Jane-like standards, and where I hadn't proved to half the school that I was incompetent when it came to difficult tasks like identifying the right dressing room. But I didn't know where that place was.

I sat down on my bed, suddenly miserable. I wasn't happy and couldn't even think of a way to change my life so I would be.

Chrissy looked at me, her wings fluttering and the wand grasped in one hand. She checked her watch. "Is this going to take a long time? I hate to rush you, but I have a shopping trip planned with some mall pixies."

I fingered my pillow sham, thinking. "I just wish that somehow my life could be like a fairy tale. You know, with a handsome prince waiting for me at the ball, and that somehow when I meet him, everything will work out happily ever after."

Chrissy checked her wristwatch again, hardly paying attention to me. "Okay, great. One Cinderella coming up."

Before I could say another word—and I had planned to say, "Wait, that wasn't my wish!"—white sparks surrounded me. The next moment I found myself in a cold, dark room.

Chapter 4

After the flash from Chrissy's magic wand subsided and I could see again, I turned in a slow circle around the room. Rough-hewn stones made up the floor and walls. A limp and dirty mattress with straw sticking out of each side lay at my feet, and a wooden chest sat underneath a narrow, glassless window. Nothing else occupied the room.

"Oh no," I said, and then louder, "That wasn't what I meant!" I turned around the room, looking for a telltale sparkler of light that would let me know she was here. I saw nothing. I called her name—even her full name—but Chrissy didn't materialize.

Finally I pushed open a heavy wooden door and stepped out into a kitchen. Oddly enough, I could see the room in as much detail as if I were wearing my contacts. Perhaps since Cinderella had good eyesight, I did too.

A huge fireplace occupied one wall, with a pot hanging on a hook over the fire. Whatever was inside crackled and steamed, making the room smell good. A rickety cupboard pressed up against another wall. I could see dishes and pots stacked unevenly on its shelves. A plump woman pounded a lump of bread dough on a wooden table in the center of the kitchen. Her hair, assuming she had any, was hidden under a dirty kerchief.

I walked into the room cautiously, my bare feet hardly making a sound against the cold stone floor. I had no idea what to say.

The woman looked at me. Her face had so many wrinkles and jowl lines that it gave the impression her face was melting off her body. She turned her attention back to the bread dough, smacking it into the table. "You're up late. And a poor day you chose for it too. The mistress is in a foul mood."

I realized, with a mixture of relief and disappointment, that the woman knew me, or at least knew the person she thought I was: Cinderella.

I tried to guess who the woman at the table was. She was too old and shabbily dressed to be an ugly stepsister, and yet she wasn't the mistress either. Perhaps this was one of those pumpkin-into-bloated-walrus mistakes and Chrissy had transported me into an entirely wrong fairy tale?

"Don't stand there dawdling, child. Are you waiting for the cow to come calling on you? Get the bucket and go."

Apparently I needed to milk a cow. It would have been helpful to know certain things, like how to milk a cow and where the bucket was. You'd think that Chrissy might have helped me out with a few of those details before she sent me off to the Middle Ages. But no.

"Um, there's been a mistake," I said. "I'm not really supposed to be here doing this—"

"I know, I know. 'Twas your father's mistake in marrying

that she-wolf, but there's no time now for regretting what the dead have done. If our lady doesn't have milk with her breakfast we'll both see her fangs."

Okay, so probably this was the right fairy tale since my father had married a wicked stepmother—oh wait, Snow White also had a wicked stepmother and so did Hansel and Gretel. Come to think of it, fairy tales just brimmed with the wreckage of men who'd chosen the wrong women. Which went to show you that men hadn't changed over the centuries. Hunter. *Humph.*

Still, I needed to know what I was up against. When I met this stepmother was she going to work me to the bone or try to kill me?

I noticed a bucket hanging on a peg by a door and walked over to it. "Um . . . would you mind answering a couple questions for me? Do I happen to have a brother named Hansel?"

The woman looked at me blankly. Her bushy eyebrows knit together.

Which probably meant no. I took the bucket from the peg. "Or does anyone—particularly any enchanted mirrors—consider me to be the fairest in the land?"

Now she laughed. I caught sight of several blackened teeth. "What a notion, Ella. You, the fairest of the land. Yes, in between the suds and the cinders the bards line up to sing your praises. Off with you, and don't come back for your breakfast until the swine and the chickens are fed."

So I was in the right fairy tale, but none of the versions I'd read mentioned any other servants. How long was I going to be here before Chrissy checked on me? I mean, sooner or later she was going to have to come back and grant me my other two wishes. I walked outside, shivering as I left the warmth of the kitchen. I didn't have any shoes and the way to the barn was littered with animal droppings. I dodged around those like a dancer doing some odd hopping routine.

The cook may have thought I looked like Cinderella, but the cow clearly knew I was a stranger. Every time I set the stool and the bucket down beside her, she decided to take three steps forward. I would move the stool and bucket over, sit down, and she'd walk off again. For fifteen minutes I scooted around the barn in a slow cow chase.

An old man with a matted gray beard came into the barn carrying a bundle of hay. I didn't see him at first because I was busy giving a lecture to the cow on hamburger. He watched me for a moment then took a rope from the wall, looped it around the cow's neck and attached it to a peg on the wall. "You feeling all right today, Ella?" he asked me.

"Not really, well, you see . . ." Any excuse I could come up with—and actually I couldn't come up with any—would be a lie. I'd told Chrissy I wouldn't lie but I was only a few minutes into this fairy tale and already in danger of having reptiles drop from my mouth. I looked at the man, bit my lip, and then let out a sigh of defeat. "I don't know how to milk a cow. Could you show me?"

He did. He also showed me where to get the feed for the chickens and the pigs. He clearly thought I'd lost my mind, and kept eyeing me over like a shopper eyes defective merchandise. As he helped me with the last of the chores I said, "Thanks. You probably think it's strange that I've forgotten how to do all of this, don't you?"

He shook his scraggly head. "Not my place to say nothing about the master's daughter. God rest his soul."

I took the milk back to the kitchen and held the bucket out to the cook. She cut slices of meat onto a platter and glared at me as though I ought to know better. "Pour it in the pitcher and take it to the table. It's a miracle the mistress isn't already down and screeching at your sloth."

I found a pitcher in the cupboard, then walked out the

door, wandering around the manor house until I found the dining room. Two girls who looked to be my age sat at a long wooden table. I was expecting them to be hideous—I mean, so far I'd met two people in this fairy tale and neither had been attractive. For the girls to be known as the "ugly stepsisters" clearly indicated some sort of horrible deformity. But besides looking as though they hadn't showered in, well, ever, they both seemed like normal, attractive teenagers. One was a bit tall and had dirty blond hair—in this case the term "dirty blond" being a description of cleanliness, not hair color—but her features were even and proportioned. The shorter of the two was a bit on the plump side, but not overly so. It made her look healthy. When one overlooked her greasy brown hair, there was nothing wrong with her looks.

The surprise made me speak out loud. "You're both so pretty. I don't know why anyone would call you . . ."

It was at this point that both girls smiled at me. Between the two of them I saw only a dozen teeth.

"Oh," I said. "Never mind."

"Do go on, Ella," the taller one said. "You were telling me how well I look in your dresses. I think so too."

"Speaking of dresses," the shorter one said. "What have you got on? Did you trade clothes with a plow hand?"

"I've never seen leggings so loose," the tall one said. "He must have been a fat plow hand. I should tell Mamá that we're overfeeding them."

The short one giggled. "Perhaps Ella has just lost weight. I shall save you some scraps from my breakfast, Ella, unless I'm very hungry."

"You are always very hungry," the tall one said.

"True," her sister said. "Poor Ella will just have to find skinnier peasants to trade clothes with."

Yeah, that whole "ugly" part of their name just became

much clearer. I set the pitcher down on the table so hard that some of the milk sloshed over the edges.

It was then that the WSM—wicked stepmother—swept into the room. I could tell it was her, both by her dress and her air of authority. Her light brown hair had streaks of gray, and her skin had begun to loosen around her jawline, but she was still a handsome woman. She walked to the table, dabbed a finger into the spilled milk, and sat down. "You stupid, clumsy girl. If you can't do your duties inside I will send you outside with the field hands. Do you understand?"

I stared at her for a moment. Normally I wouldn't have put up with people treating me this way. I mean, it did occur to me that if there were field hands around, some might know how to wield pitchforks, and it was entirely likely I could get them to side with me and turn against these encroachers. But that wasn't how the fairy tale went, and I didn't dare mess it up. If I wasn't inside to hear about the prince's ball, I wouldn't get to the point where my Fair Godmother—aka Chrissy—stopped by to make my dreams come true. And when she stopped by, I was getting out of the wish.

I bowed my head in my WSM's direction. "Sorry."

"Sorry, what?" she repeated.

"Sorry I spilled the milk," I said.

She pounded her fist against the table, making the silverware jump. "No, you stupid, ignorant girl. You're to say, 'Sorry, m'lady.'"

"Oh. Sorry, m'lady."

She pointed to the door, her eyes sharp and glinting. "Back to the kitchen with you and make haste serving us. I've plenty of chores for you today."

This, by the way, was not an exaggeration. Along with a couple of scullery maids and a kitchen boy, I washed dishes, swept floors, laundered clothes, set them out to dry, helped prepare lunch, washed more dishes, ironed clothes, and churned butter. I also shoveled ashes out of the fireplaces and did my best to clean the chimney. That was my job alone, and by the time I was done with it, my hands, arms, face, and hair were smeared with greasy soot. The stepsisters breezed into the manor while I did that job to watch me and comment on my appearance.

"I rather like her hair black," the tall one said. "It matches her complexion quite well."

The plump one gave me a simpering smile. "Fine ladies always powder their faces. Ella uses cinders—that's why she's our *cinder*-ella."

I mostly ignored them whenever they were around. During the day, they did nothing as far as I could tell, except steal some candles from the cupboard, light them, and then take them out behind the barn, where they played guess-whose-straw-will-burn-quickest. I'm serious. Then they moved on to twigs, pine-cones, and beetles. They spent most of the afternoon igniting things. This apparently is what hoodlum teenagers did back before street corners were invented.

While I worked I sent whispered pleading messages to Chrissy and worried that my parents were panicked about my disappearance. She never answered.

The second day was worse. Not only did I have the same chores, but I also had to clean the garderobes, which is a fancy way of saying outhouses. I couldn't bathe—and trust me, I needed to after cleaning the garderobes—because unfortunately no one had had the sense to invent indoor plumbing yet. All I had was a bowl of water, a rag, and a hard, scratchy, foul-smelling block of something that they told me was soap, but it didn't resemble any soap I'd ever seen. They gave me a threadbare dress to wear and a pair of flimsy leather boots that didn't fit and smelled as though their last owner had died while wearing them.

I learned that I lived in a land called Pampovilla and that my stepsisters were named Matilda and Hildegard. When they weren't burning things they spent most of their time ordering me around. I hoped that one of the king's footmen would show up with the announcement of a ball. I counted on it, but no one visited.

Day three went about the same. The cook yelled at me as much as, if not more than, my stepfamily did—something, I might add, which has totally been overlooked in Grimm's version of the fairy tale. It should have been a story about the wicked stepmother, ugly pyromaniac stepsisters, and a trollish-looking, short-tempered cook.

Day four was only made interesting by the fact that Matilda—the brunette one—accidentally set her hair on fire. It involved a great deal of screaming on Matilda's part, and it could have led to serious injury if I hadn't been nearby with a bucket of pig slop. I threw it over her head to douse the flames. As usual, she didn't appreciate my efforts on her behalf. I spent the night in my room without supper.

More days came and went by in a blur of chores. My back and arms ached from the workload. Where they weren't blistered, my hands became dry and chapped. I wanted to cry every morning when I woke up, stiff and itchy from my straw mattress.

By the third week, I missed my home, my parents, and my friends so intently that it felt like a thick stone had wedged itself in my chest. I longed for a hot bath. Electricity. American food. I even missed little things that I'd taken for granted before. Carpet. Clear drinking water. Cold milk. My tennis shoes.

As I worked, I kept my mind on all the things my life had been in Virgina, trying to hold onto them. Even Hunter seemed almost like a dream now. And when he didn't—when I was washing clothes and the lines of his face suddenly forced their way into my mind—I tried to scrub them away along with the dirt and the grime. He didn't deserve a place in my memory. I refused to think of Jane or him at all, refused to wonder if either one of them missed me.

Where was my fairy? When was that stupid ball?

I had tried to ask about the ball in roundabout ways before, but no one seemed to know anything about it. One day as I was in my stepsisters' room braiding Hildegard's hair, I asked if she wouldn't like to visit the palace for a dance. Hildegard just sighed wistfully and said, "I do hope Prince Edmond throws one now that he's done putting down that peasant rebellion."

"Peasant rebellion?" I repeated.

Matilda said, "The peasants are always asking for too much. If it's not lower taxes from their lords, it's the right to leave their manors. As though they should be able to leave when there's work to be done." She sat across the room supposedly doing needlework, but I had yet to see her take a stitch. Mostly she was cleaning her fingernails with the needle.

I stopped braiding Hildegard's hair. "What exactly do you mean when you say he put down a peasant rebellion?"

"It wasn't a real rebellion," Hildegard said, as though proud of this fact. "Prince Edmond hung a few of them and the rest scattered. What are a few peasants against the knights of the royal army? They should have learned their place by now."

My hands gripped the brush harder. "The prince killed peasants? My prince?"

Hildegard's nose wrinkled in disdain. "Your prince? As though the likes of you had any claim to him."

Matilda tilted her head, which lost some of the dramatic effect since half her hair was missing. "You'd better watch your tongue or he'll hang you up with the rest of them. And why do you keep muttering the word 'Chrissy' under your breath? What is a Chrissy?"

That was the first I heard of Prince Edmond, but it certainly wasn't the last. Three days later a royal procession visited the estate.

Chapter 5

They sent notice they were coming, but only one day's notice, which was something the servants complained quite a bit about when the WSM wasn't around. It meant we all had to scurry around like panicked rodents trying to prepare the manor for royalty. Not that they were staying long. They were just resting here for the night, using us like a hotel stop on their journey to see some important noble in the south.

Since we not only had to provide food and quarters for the royals but for their knights, groomsmen, horses, and servants, the kitchen buzzed with activity all day long. When I wasn't working to the point of exhaustion, I admit I was curious about Edmond, the blind date—er, life—Chrissy was trying to set me up on. Surely my stepsisters were wrong about him. He couldn't be some tyrant who hanged people unnecessarily. Chrissy was supposed to find some wonderful, charming guy for me. The question was, could he be so wonderful that he'd make living in the Middle Ages, make everything I'd gone through, worth it?

I am obviously a hopeless romantic.

Late in the afternoon, Prince Edmond, his younger brother, Prince Hugh, and his sister, Princess Margaret, arrived in a procession of knights and carriages. The other servants and I crowded around one of the windows in a top room to watch them. When the royals descended from a gilded carriage, my stepfamily did a lot of bowing and fawning. Their colorful skirts swished and swayed as they moved. I had only soot-stained rags to wear, and I was embarrassed that Edmond would see me this way.

WSM ushered the guests into the manor and all of the servants went downstairs, ready to answer any whim or fancy of our visitors.

I recognized Edmond right away. He stood at least six feet tall—perhaps even a couple of inches more—a whole head taller than a lot of the men I'd met in the Middle Ages. He had sleek brown hair, a square jaw, and perfect teeth. Every time he looked in Hildegard's direction she giggled. Matilda wore a covering over her head to hide her missing hair and kept tugging on it nervously as she watched him.

Prince Edmond's younger brother, Prince Hugh, was no less handsome. Although he was not as tall and had a curl to his brown hair, he had the same flawless features and square jaw. The two of them walked, talked, and looked about the room with an air of haughtiness that only those doubly blessed with looks and fortune could pull off and still be considered charming.

Their younger sister, Princess Margaret, looked to be about my age. She had the same conceited expression as her brothers, and their good looks as well. Her blond hair was piled on her head with blue ribbons that exactly matched her velvet dress.

She glanced around the manor and let out a sigh. "I suppose it will do for the night."

If her brothers noticed her rudeness, they didn't say anything. They divided their time between talking to the WSM and ordering their groomsmen around.

Edmond, my Prince Charming, didn't look at me. Not even once.

A dozen tables had been set up in the great room and the meal started as soon as the royals dressed for dinner. We, the servants, hauled in a never-ending supply of food for our guests. Roasted pig. Roasted lamb. Roasted swan. We also carried in breads, cheeses, pies, and a sugary gelatin-like statue that had been molded into the shape of a castle in their honor. The WSM had hired musicians to play and I tried to hear her orders over the music. She sat on the left-hand side of Prince Edmond, a fact that seemed to elevate her importance in her own eyes, and she gave orders with extra disdain thrown in.

Once while I walked past the table with a pitcher of mead, Prince Edmond held up his goblet and said, "Serving wench, my glass is empty."

When I didn't move fast enough he snapped his fingers at me.

Real charming. I filled his glass and he turned away from me without giving me any more notice.

On his right side, Prince Hugh lifted his goblet to me as well. "Be quick about it, wench."

I bit my tongue and filled his glass too. Then I turned my gaze back to Edmond, who, for all of his impatience a moment before, hadn't taken a drink yet. Really, I was so unimpressed.

Hildegard walked up beside me. She had apparently come to talk to her mother, or to flirt with Prince Edmond, but since she was watching him and not me, she bumped into me as I turned to leave.

The mead in my pitcher sloshed over the edges, spilling mostly on the floor but also splattering both of our dresses.

As I steadied the pitcher, trying not to spill anything more, she reached out and slapped me.

"Oaf!" she yelled. "Look what you've done to my dress!"

The WSM turned to me, her gaze all spikes and daggers. "Ella, your clumsiness will not be tolerated." The next moment she looked over at the prince and her voice smoothed over with honey. "I'm so sorry, your highness. Did any spill on you? I promise the girl will not go unpunished."

Edmond wiped at his embroidered tunic, though I doubt anything had splattered there. "Very good. I find that servants are like dogs. Left undisciplined, they become worthless."

The WSM turned back to me, her lips set in a tight smile. "Well, Ella, what do you have to say?"

I knew she expected me to beg for lenience, to apologize over and over again. But I'd had enough of these people, this life, and everything to do with it. "I *am* clumsy," I said. "Constantly spilling things. In fact—oops!" I held out the pitcher and emptied its contents over my stepmother's head.

She gasped, sputtered, then shrieked as the mead flowed from her hair down her face, and then soaked her dress. A group of the knights at the next table over laughed uproariously at the sight of my WSM wiping strands of hair out of her face and jiggling in her seat, as though this would stop the liquid from running down her back. But the only sound from the royal table was Edmond, who said, with a tone between smugness and reproach, "Undisciplined and worthless."

I didn't wait around to hear further critiques. I dropped the pitcher on the ground, hiked up my skirt, and ran. My WSM shouted, "Stop her! Stop her at once!"

Neither Hildegard nor any of the servants did though. Whether out of fear of me or admiration, they stood openmouthed while I rushed by.

I sped out of the manor, past the barn, and into the forest. I had nowhere to go and no way to live, but anger pushed me instead of fear.

How, even for a moment, could a fairy think someone could wish for this sort of life? And why wasn't she answering me when I called?

I wasn't exactly sure where fairies lived, but I had the vague idea that it was inside mushrooms. So I walked around stomping on every one I saw. When that didn't do anything I kicked the trees. Since my boots had never been sturdy to begin with, this probably hurt my feet more than it hurt the trees.

"You're supposed to be granting me wishes!" I called. "You can't just leave me here!"

And then I heard Chrissy's voice behind me. "You know, Cinderella is supposed to have a sweet disposition. I turn my back on you and you're drenching your elders and kicking poor defenseless trees. Is that really keeping in character?"

I spun around. She wore the same tank top and miniskirt I'd seen her in before, with her sunglasses in place even though it was dusk.

I clenched my hands into fists. "Where have you been? I've been calling you for three weeks straight."

"I told you I was going shopping. I'm still not done and I get, like, forty messages from you on my godmother cell phone. Has anyone ever told you that you need to develop a little patience?"

I glared at her.

"No? Well, let me be the first then. Get some patience—it will help you out in life."

Yeah, I could put that on the list right behind my milking skills, which were also woefully undeveloped. "Who goes shopping for three weeks?" I asked. "Exactly what kind of sale is that?"

Chrissy slipped her sunglasses onto the top of her head and gave me a condescending look. "Time isn't the same here as it is in your world. You obviously don't read fantasy books or you'd already know that sort of thing."

"How much time has elapsed back home?" I asked.

"Well, ideally with these wishes you could live here for years and only seconds would have passed back in your world. Then when you wanted to, you'd come home physically unchanged." She examined her nails instead of looking at me.

"But . . . ," I prompted.

"Well, that was one of those areas that I didn't do so well on in school. I never could get time to stop spinning, just to slow down. For every week that passes here, an hour passes back in your world. That's not really so bad. Your parents are still downstairs at your house watching TV. They won't miss you until tomorrow morning, and the way you sleep in and then hole up in your room, well, that should give you months here. Then you can decide whether—"

"I don't want to stay here for months," I said. "All I've done here is work like a dog. No, I take that back. Dogs don't have to clean out the toilets. I've worked like . . . like . . ."

"Cinderella?" she asked.

"Yes, but with no ball in sight and a prince who is an arrogant jerk."

She shrugged. "The ball is in about eight months. It wouldn't be the full Cinderella experience if you only worked a few days and then got to go to the ball. Anyone can do that. It takes no long-term suffering at all."

I held out my rough and calloused hands toward her. "And who said I wanted to be long-suffering? I don't remember wishing for that."

"If the prince is going to rescue you from your dreary life," she continued, "it has to be dreary in the first place, doesn't it?"

Her logic made me sputter. She actually thought she'd done me a favor by turning me into some sort of serf. "My life was plenty dreary as it was, and besides, I didn't wish to be Cinderella in the first place. You never let me finish telling you what I wanted."

Her eyebrows arched up. "Well, excuse me for having other things to do with my time besides listen to your love-life woes— I told you I needed to go shopping." She tossed her hair off her shoulder and pulled first one, then two more shopping bags from her purse. At last she pulled out the scroll and opened it. "You said, and this is a quote, 'I just wish my life could be like a fairy tale with a handsome prince waiting for me at the ball, and that somehow when I met him, everything would work out happily ever after.'"

She pulled on the end of the scroll and it spun shut. "You asked for a fairy tale. One of us here is an expert on fairy tales, and the only tale with a handsome prince waiting at the ball is Cinderella, which I duly granted." Another toss of her hair. "If you had a different fairy tale in mind—well, I'm sorry you're so ill read that you got mixed up and wished for the wrong one."

"But I didn't actually think that . . ." I stopped. It wouldn't do any good to point out I hadn't meant those words as a wish at all. I'd just been speaking in generalities. Apparently fairies didn't do generalities. I tried to make my case in another way. "What about the prince? He's supposed to be wonderful so I can live happily ever after. That part of my wish wasn't granted."

She rolled her eyes like I was the one being unreasonable. "You only asked for a handsome prince. He is. I suppose charming is implied in the wish—trust me, he'll be very charming at the ball."

My mouth dropped open and a little squeak of disbelief popped out. "But besides that he's an arrogant tyrant? How am I supposed to live happily ever after with someone like that?"

"I already told you I couldn't grant vague statements like happily ever after. I grant specifics. Happy is entirely up to you and always has been." Her wings fluttered in agitation. "Besides, since when did you become so concerned with personality? You never worried about Hunter's personality, did you?" She picked up a shopping bag and pushed it, somehow, back into her purse. "You know, just out of curiosity, I checked in with him before my shopping trip. Do you know what he was doing? Talking with Jane over the phone about the benefits and drawbacks of testing out of freshman English. There's a thrill ride for you. Most people can make those kinds of decisions without talking it over extensively with their girlfriends."

Okay, granted, sometimes Hunter cared way too much about school, but he'd always worn such an endearingly earnest expression while he'd gone on about that sort of thing that I'd never minded. "This isn't about Hunter—," I said.

She held up one hand to stop me. "I know. It's about getting back at Hunter. I totally understand how dating works between humans. You want a boyfriend who's handsome *and* popular. Well, Prince Edmond is the epitome of that. You'll be the envy of the kingdom. That's what you really wished for, wasn't it, to be envied?"

It sounded so superficial when she said it that way that it took me aback. I had to stop and think about it for a moment. "It's not that I have to be envied by an entire kingdom . . ."

Chrissy wedged her last bag back into her purse. "Oh, that's right. You just want to be envied by Jane and Hunter. I can arrange that then. I can bring them here. They could be poor peasants in your stepmother's manor." She pulled the wand from somewhere beneath all the shopping bags and looked ready to wave it in my direction.

"No, wait, I don't want that." Even though I hadn't forgiven them, I wouldn't wish the type of life I'd just been living on either of them.

Chrissy put the wand down at her side. "Well, what do you want then? You called me here away from my shopping trip and I haven't even made it to the shoe section yet."

I tried to think of how to form my next wish. For almost a month I'd just wanted to leave, but now with Chrissy standing in front of me, tapping one foot while she waited for me to speak, I didn't want to waste a wish on just going home. I should wish for something new, something spectacular, for a situation where I could be truly happy.

"Well..." I didn't know how to phrase my wish or even how to articulate what I wanted, what I longed for. Ironically, it struck me that Jane would know the right way to say it. Jane could write a thousand-word essay on how she felt at any given time. But Jane didn't need wishes. Jane had Hunter.

Chrissy checked her watch. "I can come back later when you've had time to think about it—"

"No," I said, because if she left now who knew how many days I'd be stuck here, and after my scene inside, the WSM would undoubtedly throw me in a dungeon or something. "I just...um...I want to feel beautiful and loved, and although I like the idea of having a prince, he has to be more than just handsome and rich. He has to be nice, and kind..." I paused, trying to think of the next quality I wanted to add to the list.

That's when I learned a very important lesson about dealing with fairies. Don't pause when you're wishing for things.

Chrissy slipped her sunglasses back over her face. "One Snow White coming up!"

Chapter 6

Bright lights like hundreds of fireflies spun around me, and then I found myself in a completely different forest. The trees grew together so close and tall that I couldn't see the sky. Only slivers of light penetrated the canopy here and there, testifying that it was still day. What time of day, I wasn't sure.

"I didn't mean that I wanted to be Snow White!" I called out.

Only the sound of birds and tree branches rustling answered back.

"Chrissy?" I called. "Chrissy?" It had suddenly become very clear to me why she was only a *fair* godmother.

I called her name for a few more minutes, then wandered through the forest, frustrated and wondering if there was any way to get out of this. I did not like the idea of biting into a poisoned apple and lying unconscious until a prince showed up. How long would that take? Days? Years? I mean, yes, I sleep in but if I was lying around in the Middle Ages for years, my parents would notice I was missing.

Fairies really ought to give you some directions before they plop you down into the middle of a forest and take off to go shoe shopping. The only thing Chrissy had given me was new clothes. I now wore a simple crimson dress.

As I wondered which way to go, a little man with a long gray beard and a brown cap on his head burst through the trees.

His eyes zoomed in on me, anxiety etched into the wrinkles on his face. "Snow White," he said, "are you all right?"

"Yes."

He knew who I was, which meant I must have come into the fairy tale after Snow White had found the seven dwarfs' house. I had no idea which of the dwarfs this was, and come to think of it, I wasn't sure I could recall all of their names. There was, um . . . Happy, Sleepy, Bashful, Boring—no wait, Boring wasn't actually a dwarf. I was getting the dwarfs confused with my schoolteachers.

"Are you hurt?" The dwarf asked, still worried. "Why are you out in the forest?"

I knew I wasn't supposed to lie, but I couldn't very well tell him that I'd mistakenly been sent here from the twenty-first century.

"I, um, was out walking," I said. Which was true, if not vague.

"What?" he said indignantly. "You went wandering about when you know full well Queen Neferia is out to kill you?"

"I . . . guess."

He broke into a language I didn't understand but figured was dwarf cursing. He crossed over to me, took my hand, and none too gently towed me along beside him as he pushed his way back through the trees. "Have you not a lick of sense anywhere in your body? Did the good Lord spend so much time crafting your pretty head that he forgot to put anything inside? Do you not listen to anything we ever say?"

For someone so small he had a tight grip and moved incredibly fast. I tried not to stumble on rocks and tree roots as he pulled me along. "Let me guess—you're Grumpy?"

He let out a *humph*. "And you would be too, if you'd just spent the last hour searching the forest for your wayward charge." He walked even faster. "We tell you to stay inside, we tell you not to talk to strangers. But oh no, you must be out singing to the animals as if the birds didn't do a fine enough job of it. And this after Queen Neferia has already tried to kill you thrice."

"Thrice?" I repeated.

"Three times," he said as though I didn't know what *thrice* meant. Which I didn't, but still—in the movie there was only the time with the woodcutter and the poisoned apple.

"We already explained to you that the old lady peddler was Queen Neferia in disguise," he said slowly. "She tried to kill you with the poisoned comb and with the belt. Which is why you are not to go shopping anymore, no matter how pretty the wares, remember?"

"Oh, right." Now that he mentioned it, I vaguely remembered that in the Grimm version of Snow White, the queen had come twice before her trip with the apple and nearly killed Snow White with other deadly items.

And when you looked at it that way, Snow White had to be pretty idiotic to keep falling for the same trick.

I took a few steps in silence and realized what this meant. In this wish, apparently I was stupid. Or at least the dwarfs thought I was. I was going to have to set them straight about that right off.

We came to a clearing in the woods where not only one

house stood but an entire village, complete with a church, a mill, stables, and a well.

"Go into the house," the dwarf told me. "I'll ring the church bell to let the others know you're safe." He let go of my arm and headed toward the church. I stood there staring at a row of cottages and wondering which one was the dwarfs' home.

He turned back to check on me and when he noticed I hadn't moved, he said, "Well?"

"Which one is our house?" Okay, so this wasn't the best way to impress him with my intelligence, but what else could I do? He rolled his eyes, let out a sigh, and took me by the hand again.

"This way," he said and led me toward a large cottage in the middle of the street.

Oh. I should have guessed it was the biggest one since it had seven men living in it.

He might have said more, but just then two more dwarfs appeared out of different cottages as though going on a door-to-door search. One wore a gray cap, the other a black one, but both had long gray beards and wore the same baggy brown clothes that the first dwarf had on. They hadn't seen us yet, so the dwarf beside me waved at them. "I found her! She's fine."

The one in the black cap let out a relieved sigh. "I'll go ring the church bell to let the others know." He turned and trotted off toward the church. The one in the gray cap walked toward me, smiling.

I tried to guess his name. "Happy?"

"Of course we are," he said. "We were worried that the queen had taken you someplace." He took hold of my other hand and the three of us went into our cottage.

The dwarf in the brown cap took on the frustrated tone of a parent as he spoke to me. "You're far too trusting, Snow White. You'd like to help every stranger and animal that comes your

way—and that's admirable—but there are things to fear in the
forest: bears, and thieves, and your stepmother. So you mustn't
go walking there by yourself again, agreed?"

Instead of answering him I looked around at the cottage. A
rough-hewn table and benches sat before me, nothing like the
intricately carved furniture in the Cinderella manor. Large
beams spread across a low ceiling. If I stood on tiptoes I'd probably bang my head. Everything seemed narrow and cramped.
How could I promise them to stay inside all the time? Stairs in
the corner of the room must lead to the bedrooms. I wondered if
I had my own room. Even as Cinderella I had my own room.
Okay, it was a hovel off the kitchen with a straw mattress, but at
least I didn't have privacy issues.

"Agreed?" the dwarf prompted.

I couldn't answer him for fear that lizards would drop out
of my mouth. Instead I said, "Can we talk later? I'm a little
hungry right now."

"Yes," the first dwarf said. "It's past time for our supper.
We'll wash up while you see to the porridge."

"Oh." I'd forgotten that in this fairy tale, Snow White did all
the cooking and cleaning for the dwarfs. Great. Just great.
More chores.

I walked out of the main room and into the kitchen. Off in
the distance, I heard the church bell ring. To me it sounded
like a scolding parent. *Ring! Ring!* Our beautiful but idiotic
charge has been found wandering around the forest for no
apparent reason! *Ring!*

In the kitchen I found a pot of split-pea soup already hanging in a kettle over the fire. I'd learned from my stint as Cinderella that the cook never took the soup off the fire. They
didn't have refrigerators to store it, so they just left it there
cooking day after day and kept adding more beans and vegetables to it. Of course my WSM and stepsisters never ate the

soup. It was just for the servants. The nobility ate meat, wheat bread, and all sorts of pies that, trust me, after three weeks of eating porridge and rye bread, smelled fabulous.

Apparently here at the dwarfs' home we all ate like servants. A lump of bread dough sat rising on a board. I slid it into a dome-shaped oven that was built into the side of the hearth.

Then I picked vegetables from a basket on the floor, cut them up, and added them into the pot. *Pease porridge hot, pease porridge cold, pease porridge in the pot, nine days old.* I used to think that was just a nursery rhyme, not a way of life.

From the kitchen, I heard them discussing me as they came into the main room from outside. "One of us will just have to stay at the cottage and keep an eye on her. That's all there is to it."

"You know we can't do that. The mine takes all of our time."

"Let's see if Widow Hazel wouldn't take her in during the day, maybe teach her something useful—"

"No, remember when she learned how to knit? Now we're stuck wearing these dreadful hats."

"Not so loud! She'll hear you."

In a lower voice, one of the dwarfs said, "H. A. T. S."

Apparently Snow White didn't know how to knit *or* how to spell. I left the soup and stood by the doorway so I could hear them better.

"Besides," another dwarf said, "we can't pawn her off on our neighbor forever. We need to find her a proper husband."

"You've tasted her soup. What kind of man would be willing to take her for a wife?"

There was a long pause, then one of the dwarfs said, "One who's wealthy enough to have a cook. After all, Snow White's a beauty and from a royal line. And you couldn't find a more caring lass."

remember exactly what I'd told Chrissy I wanted in a guy. I'd said I wanted him to be more than just handsome and rich. He had to be nice and kind. And apparently Prince Hubert was kind. Kind of crazy.

Honestly, was she *trying* to get my wishes wrong and stick me with horrible guys?

I waved my hands over the bread in an attempt to cool it down. Perhaps I'd taken it out before it was completely ruined. It's hard to tell with rye bread since it's dark brown to start with. I hoped it was salvageable because I really didn't want to look incompetent right now. I had to present myself to the dwarfs as an intelligent, capable person so they wouldn't try to marry me off to some half-wit prince before Chrissy showed up again.

My hand waving wasn't very effective in cooling off the bread so I decided to flip it off the board, sort of like the way my dad flips pancakes when he makes them. And that's what I was doing when the dwarfs came into the kitchen to check on dinner.

Seven faces peered at me from the doorway. They wore seven different colored caps, and now that I saw them all together, I could tell how uneven and poorly knitted they were.

The one in the brown cap gave me a questioning smile. "What are you doing?"

"I'm cooling down the bread."

"Thank goodness," a dwarf in a red cap whispered. "For a moment I thought she was trying to teach it to fly."

The one in brown elbowed the one in red, then turned back to me. "Why don't you put it on the windowsill? That's always worked in the past."

I put the bread on the windowsill, feeling their gazes still on me. Then I thought of the perfect way to learn the dwarfs' names. I'd just call out a name and see which dwarf answered me. It would be easy. Ha—and they thought I wasn't smart.

A general murmuring of consensus floated around
room and some even threw out names in suggestion, until
of the dwarfs said, "None of those men would have her—
when her head's as empty as her dowry."

Another murmuring of consensus rose from the room
which I resented. My head was not empty.

"Aye, we're doomed. We'll be eating burned bread for the
rest of our lives."

"And chasing after her every time she wanders off into the
forest."

"And worrying that the queen will try to poison her again."

There was silence for a moment.

"I think Prince Hubert would do nicely for her."

"Prince Hubert? Who's he?"

"In the kingdom to the north—he's the fourth son. Not
really in line for the crown, but a decent chap. I hear he's kind
to animals."

Someone let out a low laugh. "I hear he talks to goats and
sheep—in their own language. They don't talk back, mind you,
but he keeps trying. He tells people that one day he'll make a
breakthrough and discover the secrets of animal speech."

More silence, then someone said, "Well, Snow White sings
to the animals. The two of them will never be short of friends."

"We should send a message to him."

"He doesn't read."

"Is that smoke coming from the kitchen?"

"I'll go north and read the message to him myself."

I didn't hear any more of their conversation because I had to
run to check on the bread, which was indeed burning. In my
defense, the cook from the last fairy tale always baked the bread.
Plus, did they really expect me to pay attention to the food while
they were discussing my future with Prince Hubert?

As I pulled the smoldering loaf out of the oven, I tried to

"Dopey?" I asked.

"Of course you're not," the one in the brown cap said. "You're just not used to cooking yet." He went to the cupboard, took out a stack of bowls and spoons, and handed them out.

A dwarf in a blue cap went to the soup pot and stirred it. He kept poking the spoon through it as though searching for something, then sighed, disappointed. "Well, bring over your bowls and we'll say grace."

The gray-capped dwarf looked into the pot. "Aye, it needs praying."

"Sleepy?" I called out.

"I am now," the gray-capped dwarf said. "Think I'll turn in for the night instead of eating."

I tried one more time, searching the dwarfs' faces. "Doc?"

"Don't be a pessimist," The brown-capped dwarf said and handed me a bowl. "No one's gotten sick from eating your food for days now."

Why was this not working? Should I just come right out and ask them their names? We all took our bowls out to the dining room where a long table with short benches waited for us. One of the dwarfs took the bread from the kitchen windowsill, another brought a cellar of salt. When I sat down, I bumped my knees against the table because it was so low.

The blue-capped dwarf said grace and then they passed around the loaf of rye bread. The custom was to tear off a piece of bread and then pass the loaf to the next person. This is what we'd done at the servants' table when I was Cinderella. But that was when the cook made the bread. As Snow White I'd cooked the loaf so long it had turned into a rye brick, and each dwarf struggled to break a piece off. Finally they took to smacking it against the edge of table in order to get a portion.

The brown-capped dwarf next to me smacked off a piece

for himself and then one for me. "Don't worry," he said. "It will soften right up once it's soaked in porridge."

"Thank you." I dipped my bread into the porridge, blew on it, then put it in my mouth. Only a sense of manners kept me from spitting it back out. I've never been a fan of rye bread to begin with, but burned rye bread in bad porridge is worse. I made myself swallow, then took a long drink of water. It was really the only decent thing on the table.

The dwarf in the yellow cap coughed into his napkin, a clear sign that he was spitting his food out instead of eating it. "Are you all right?" I asked him.

"Me? Oh yeah. You know me, I'm just sneezing again."

"You're Sneezy?" I asked, glad to at least have one name figured out.

"It's almost as though I'm allergic to dinnertime," he said, coughing into his napkin again.

It wasn't a compliment, but hey, at least I'd learned one name. Of course I still didn't know the other six names and none of my efforts had helped reveal them. I fiddled with my spoon for a moment, then decided to come right out and ask them. After all, they couldn't think me any more stupid than they already did.

"Um . . . which one of you is Dopey?"

From across the table, the black-capped dwarf took a sip of his soup, made a face, and muttered, "That would be Reginald for putting you in charge of cooking."

The green-capped dwarf sitting next to him, elbowed him sharply. "Stop it or you'll make her cry."

"Reginald?" I asked. "Who's Reginald?"

The brown-capped dwarf beside me let out a sigh of patience. "I am. And sitting beside me is Percival. Next to him is Cedric, then Edgar, Cuthbert, and Ethelred. Edwin already went up to bed." He patted my hand. "Don't worry, you'll learn our names soon enough." Another pat, this one decidedly forced. "Or if you don't, you can continue to call us whatever adjective suits your fancy at the moment."

"You're not really Happy, Sleepy . . ." I let my sentence drift off. Why did they have different names than in the story? Then it hit me. I remembered what my English teacher kept telling us about different kinds of narrators in books, specifically unreliable ones. The story of Snow White was told from her point of view, and unfortunately she was a raging idiot.

Still, I tried one more time. "No one here is Bashful?"

"Oh, I was plenty bashful when you walked in on me while I was taking a bath," Cedric's voice took on a parental tone. "But you'll remember now that you must knock before you walk into the kitchen on bathing day, won't you?"

My face burned with embarrassment. This is what I got for asking Chrissy to make me beautiful and loved and not throwing in things like respected or well thought of. I could barely bring myself to say anything else during dinner because every time I said something, the dwarfs spoke to me as though I were six years old.

I couldn't even prove to them that I was a reasonably intelligent person because I knew nothing about them, mining, or the Middle Ages. Which was really too bad since we studied the Middle Ages in World History. Yeah, who would have ever thought *that* would come in handy?

Finally dinner ended and I cleaned up. As I washed the dishes I analyzed my situation. The only advantage I had was that I knew what the evil queen would do next. She'd come peddling apples, and although Snow White might have been foolish enough to fall for that trick, I wouldn't be. Even if I was incredibly hungry and an apple sounded really good.

If I didn't eat the apple, I wouldn't fall into that coma or trance, or whatever it was that happened to Snow White, and half-wit Prince Hubert wouldn't have to awaken me with a kiss. I would just wait things out until Chrissy showed up. And while I waited I'd think of the perfect way to phrase my real wish so that Chrissy couldn't possibly mess it up next time.

When it grew dark we went upstairs to the bedrooms. Thankfully I had my own. It was cramped and dark, but I had a feather mattress instead of a straw one, and a warm fur blanket. All in all, a step up from being Cinderella. Although I still didn't like being treated as though I were an idiot. Because I was smart. Even if I had nothing to show for it, like knowledge.

Chapter 7

The next morning I decided I would prove to the dwarfs I was useful. I may not know how to cook, but I do know how to do hair. As we ate breakfast (more bread and porridge) I told the dwarfs I was an excellent hairdresser and wanted to give them all haircuts.

Well, you have never seen people bolt down their food and run out the door so quickly.

"Wait," I called to Reginald, because he was farthest away from the door and thus last to leave. "I'm good at it, really."

He turned back to face me, hands out in an apologetic manner. "You with scissors near our heads? It's just not a good idea, Snow White. Trust me on this." He pulled his cap down tighter over his ears as though to discourage me further and added, "Remember, don't let anyone in unless they're from the village—no matter what. And if anyone comes poking around, you run right over to Widow Hazel's home and tell her about it. She'll send someone to ring the bell and then the townsfolk will gather to help you."

"Which house is Widow Hazel's?" I asked.

He stared at me with a hopeless expression, and I thought he might break down and cry. "It's the one right next door." He pointed in that direction. "Right there. You've been there half a dozen times already."

"Oh. Right. Widow Hazel's. I won't forget again."

He let out a sigh as though he would have liked to believe me but didn't, then hurried after the others.

I cleaned up the breakfast dishes, then went behind the cottage and did the laundry. This involved hauling water from the well, pouring it in a barrel with soap, putting clothes in, and pounding them with a wooden stick. I was hanging their little tunics and leggings up on a line to dry when I saw her.

She wore a dark brown dress, a white wimple that covered most of her graying hair, and carried a basket under one arm. Her face was wrinkled, but she didn't look frail or even that elderly. She smiled in my direction and I noticed that, like many of the occupants of the Middle Ages, she was missing several teeth.

I dropped a tunic on the ground and didn't bother to pick it up. The queen had come for me already.

She walked slowly toward me. "There you are. Working hard and just as pretty as a robin."

I shook my head. "I'm not who you think I am. I'm not Snow White."

She laughed as though I'd been joking, then reached into her basket and pulled out a perfect red apple. "I've brought you a gift. Would you like something to eat, my dear?"

I took a step back from her, wishing I had some sort of weapon. "I'm not really the fairest in the land. I'm just the only one who has all of my teeth, that's all." Then I saw the laundry paddle. I picked it up and held it up like a baseball bat. "Get away from me."

She took a step back, her brows wrinkling. "Snow White, what's come over you? Is that any way for a proper young lady to act? Put down that stick at once."

I suppose it was bound to happen. You just can't put a modern, self-empowered girl into medieval times and not expect her to snap. I'd already had to bite my tongue and let myself be ordered around by Cinderella's stepfamily. I was not about to stand by and let myself be poisoned.

"You want to see what I can do with this stick?" I yelled. "I can make applesauce! Take a step closer and I'll show you how!"

She did not step closer; in fact, she ran in the other direction. Which is when I realized I couldn't let her get away. In the fairy tale, she poisoned Snow White and that was the end of her plotting, but in my version of the story, what would the evil queen do when she failed in that attempt? She'd try something else and I had no idea what—maybe send a dragon or an army or who knew what to destroy me. I couldn't let her. I couldn't let her return to the castle.

I ran around the side of the cottage after her. For an old woman, she was surprisingly fast, but I sped after her, stick in hand.

We reached the road that ran between the cottages. The old woman kept running, right toward the center of the village. Which would prove to be her final mistake.

"Help me!" I yelled at the doorways we passed. "Come out and help me!"

We reached the well and the old woman ran around it, putting it between the two of us. We both caught our breath, panting as villagers came out of their homes to see what the noise was about.

They jogged over to us, making a circle around the well. As

soon as they got within earshot, the old woman clutched the basket to her chest and pointed a finger in my direction. "Snow White has gone mad!"

"Don't tell them your lies," I said back. "I know who you are."

"Of course you know who I am," the woman said. "I'm your neighbor."

My next few breaths came especially hard. I lowered my stick and squinted at her as though this would somehow change what she'd just said. "You're . . . you're what?"

"I'm Widow Hazel. I live right next to you."

There was a murmur of consensus among the crowd and all of their gazes turned to me.

I pointed accusingly at her basket. "Well, if you're really Widow Hazel, why did you try to give me one of those?"

She took out an apple and held it in her hand. "This?"

"Yes."

"Because I thought you might want to eat something besides burned porridge."

The crowd all laughed, and one of the men came and took me by the arm. "Here then, Snow White, why don't I walk you back to your cottage and you can rest until the dwarfs get home."

"I'm sorry," I said in Widow Hazel's direction. "I . . . I thought you were the queen."

I know she heard me because the women standing around her all said things like, "Well, of course, who hasn't mistaken Hazel for the queen? I do it frequently myself."

"It's all of them jewels you wear, Hazel. I keep telling you that if you wear your tiara around, things like this are bound to happen."

Then there was a lot of laughing.

I went home red faced, and not because I'd just run down the street.

When I got back to the cottage, I sat in the dining room for a long time calling Chrissy's name.

Nothing.

And nothing again.

It could be days before she found enough shoes to match all her outfits.

Stupid mall. She was a fairy, for crying out loud. She flew places. What did it matter what shoes she wore? And why in the world did she keep sending me into these medieval fairy tales, anyway? Did she not realize that no modern girl in her right mind would choose to live in a place where no one took showers?

Finally, after calling Chrissy's name over and over again like it was a mantra, I went to the kitchen and dumped out the old porridge. I was not about to eat it again tonight and it was impossible to repair bad food. I had to start from scratch. Let me say right now that it's harder to cook with a cauldron and a fire than you might think.

As I cut up vegetables I thought about my situation. I was stuck here and I just had to make the best of it, but I didn't have to try and bluff my way through things and look like an idiot. It was time to tell the dwarfs the truth.

• • •

The truth, it turned out, would have sounded much more convincing if I'd been able to come up with some proof. When I told them who I was that night at dinner, the dwarfs sat around the table looking at me like I was not only stupid but insane as well. And this after I'd come up with an unburned dinner for them.

"No, really," I said, "I'm from the future. I just got here yesterday. That's why I don't know how to do very much or who anyone is."

Percival rubbed his chin with one hand. "Er, and what was your excuse for not knowing anything before yesterday?"

"I suppose before yesterday, Snow White had servants at the castle do everything for her so she didn't have to know how to cook or sew or remember people's names..." It suddenly occurred to me that both Snow White and Cinderella had been actual people, and I wondered where they were while I was being them.

Edwin looked at me suspiciously from underneath his bushy eyebrows. "So you're saying you've been bewitched?"

"Be-*fairy*-ed, technically. I mean, this was obviously a mistake." And then because they all still stared at me blankly, I added, "She's only a *fair* godmother, not a good one."

The dwarfs bent their heads together, talking with each other in murmured voices. The ones that had been sitting on my side of the table moved around to the other side to be included in the discussion. I sat there watching and wondering what conclusion they'd come to. They spoke in such hushed voices that I only caught snatches of their conversations.

Someone said, "She *can't* be bewitched. Bewitched people never know they are; that's part of the bewitchment."

"She's sick then."

"What sort of sickness makes you think you've seen fairies?"

More murmuring. Then Reginald's head popped up from the group and he looked over at me with a forced smile. "While you were lost in the forest you didn't perchance eat any of those mushrooms we warned you about, did you?"

I folded my arms. "No, I didn't eat any hallucinogenic mushrooms."

More murmuring from the dwarfs. "Maybe she's telling the truth. She just used a six-syllable word."

"Of course I'm telling the truth," I called over to them. "You can tell because there are no snakes falling out of my mouth."

Perhaps it wasn't the best thing to say. The dwarfs lowered their voices and murmured faster. I heard the words "doctor" and "medicine" thrown around.

Finally they stopped discussing my condition and Reginald stepped over to me. He took my hand, pulled me from the table, and walked with me toward the stairs. "We all think that a rest would do you good. Let's go to your room and you can lie down."

I went with him—what else was there to do? The rest of the dwarfs followed us up the stairs, eyeing me carefully like I might make a break for it. I protested all the way up. "I don't need to rest. I'm telling you the truth. I'm from the future. Look, I'll prove it to you. I'm taking geometry in school. Just ask me, I can find the perimeter of a triangle—or the area. Well, actually I'm not that good at the area and sometimes I mess up on the perimeter too—but I can do the angles for you. Could Snow White do that?"

He led me to my room like I was a little girl and this was all just some bedtime story I'd concocted. "And why do people in the future need to know how to find the area of a triangle? Is that a big problem in your day? Unidentified triangles?"

"Well . . . um . . . I don't know. It's just something they teach at school."

"Sounds like a lovely place. You go ahead and rest now."

He shut the door and then I heard scraping noises on the outside of the wood. I tried the door handle and confirmed my suspicions. It didn't budge. I pounded on the door to get their attention. "Hey! You can't lock me in here!"

"It won't be for long," someone yelled. "Just until we can find some leeches."

"Leeches!" I called back. Suddenly I remembered something from my history class. One little fact that had managed to stay lodged in my brain long after most of the teacher's lectures had rolled away. And that was that medieval doc-tors' favorite treatment was bleeding patients. It went without saying that this sort of medicine killed more people than it helped.

"Aye, Edgar—er, Doc—will have that bad blood out of you in no time and you'll be back to your normal self."

I heard the sound of footsteps going down the hallway and then down the stairs.

My first thought was one of disbelief. I was being held pris-oner by a bunch of dwarfs. Then my next thought was one of fear. Leeches. That so totally sucked.

I heard the front door shut and ran to the window in the room. The shutters were already open and the window didn't have glass. I leaned out and watched all seven dwarfs heading outside. They walked a few feet and then Edwin turned, looked back, and saw me. "We'll be back in a bit," he called to me. "Don't do anything stupid while we're gone."

This caused a rumble of laughter to move through the group, which I didn't appreciate.

Reginald also turned around to address me. "Don't try to leave the house. We've left Cuthbert there to stand guard."

I tapped my fingers against the windowsill. First of all, I knew which one was Cuthbert, and I could see him traipsing along with the rest of them. Second, I knew they had all left. Did they not think I could count to seven?

As they walked away from me, Cedric split away from the rest of the group. I could just make out the words he said to the others. "It's high time I went north and spoke with Prince Hubert."

Reginald nodded. "The sooner the better."

A few minutes later they all disappeared down the forest trail.

I went to the door and tried the handle again. I knew it was bolted on the outside and so I jiggled it, hoping I could somehow knock the bolt loose. Nothing happened. I looked at the hinges, fingering them. The door's construction had to be simple. After all, it had probably been made with only a handsaw and a mallet. Surely I could take it apart, find a weakness, something.

Or not.

You know, instead of teaching us completely pointless things like how to figure out the angles of a triangle, school ought to teach us something we could actually use in life, like how to escape from a room after you've been locked in by a bunch of dwarfs.

If I had a rope, I could secure one end to the doorknob and climb out the window. I searched the room for something I could use as a makeshift ladder, but all I had was that furry animal skin on my bed. I never asked what animal, because frankly I didn't want to know. I couldn't very well tie it to anything to use as a rope. This is why, apparently, Rapunzel had to throw down her hair. The Middle Ages were lacking in good ladder material.

I leaned out the window again and tried to judge the distance to the ground. The house wasn't smooth like the ones from the twenty-first century. It had been made from stones and mortar, which jutted out at all sorts of angles. A little like a rock-climbing wall. I'd done those before. Of course, I'd always done them with a harness and a rope tied around me, but this time I didn't have a choice.

I heaved myself out the window and carefully gripped onto the rocks. I inched downward, at every moment expecting the rock to give way under my feet or for my hands to slip, but neither happened. Slowly, I made my way down the wall.

At last I was able to jump to the ground. Without looking back, I ran into the forest, making sure to head in a different direction than the dwarves had gone.

I'd only made it a little way when I saw Chrissy leaning up against a tree, her hands folded across her chest. She shook her head solemnly at me.

"That was the most pathetic princess display I've ever seen." She craned her neck to see past me into the village. "You attacked an old woman, then convinced a group of dwarfs you were insane. One more day and the whole fairy tale would have to be rewritten to include a chapter where the villagers go to the castle, beg the queen for a poisoned apple, and administer it themselves just so they can have some peace and quiet."

It was hard to speak, hard to get out everything I wanted to say. I ended up just pointing at her and then waving my hand wildly. "This wasn't my fault. You made me stupid!"

Chrissy's wings fluttered, for a moment buzzing like a hummingbird. "Oh, excuse me, but you're the one who made yourself stupid. I was only working with what you gave me."

"I'm not stupid," I said.

Her expression turned patronizingly tolerant. "You only wanted to be loved and beautiful. Don't blame me if it didn't make you happy."

"I never asked you for a half-wit prince."

She looked up at the sky for a moment like it was a point hardly worth defending. "Well, what kind of guys do you think half-wit girls get in life? Do you think intelligent guys want to hang out with stupid girls for very long? I would have thought you'd already learned that lesson with the whole Hunter and Jane thing." She shrugged and smiled in my direction. "Don't worry, though, because Prince Hubert is very handsome and kind. That's all you wanted in a boyfriend, wasn't it?"

"No," I said.

She raised an eyebrow. "It must be. If you had admired any other qualities you would have developed them in yourself, wouldn't you?"

Which was really too much. I put my hands on my hips. "Aren't fairy godmothers supposed to be nice and make you feel better about yourself?"

She rolled her eyes. "No, you're confusing fairy godmothers with sales clerks." She stepped away from me, but continued to watch me carefully. As though she were talking to, well, Snow White, she said, "You'd think you would have learned something from your last wish. I didn't send you into Cinderella's life at the climax of that story; why would I do it this time? If you had paid attention to the weather or the trees in the village, you would have known that apples are in season right now. Why would the evil queen think you could be tempted to take one from a stranger when you could get them anywhere else? The queen doesn't show up until winter, when all the fresh fruit is gone and a fresh apple is a delicacy worth taking a risk for."

Okay, when she put it like that, it did make sense. But still, how was I supposed to know that? I lived in the land of supermarkets where you could get fresh fruit all year round. Besides, I wanted to go home, not to analyze whose fault it was that Snow White was stupid.

"Look," I said slowly. "I want to make a wish and I want you to listen very carefully to all of it so that you make sure you get it right this time. Can you do that before you rush back to the mall?"

Her wings fluttered in agitation and she folded her arms, but she nodded. "You have my full attention."

"I don't want to be in some medieval fairy tale. I want to live back home with my family. When I said I wanted a prince, I didn't mean somebody from history or the pages of a storybook. I meant that I wanted that type of guy, but I want him from my own day and age. I want a boyfriend who is nice, kind—and handsome too, but that's not the most important thing.

"As I've thought about Jane and Hunter during my time

here, I realize the problem was he never really liked *me*, he just liked what I looked like. He always wanted someone who was more like Jane and when they met, well, it was just bound to turn out that way. So I want someone who is loyal and has integrity—but most important I want a guy who likes me for me, who likes my personality." It was hard to say that part after Chrissy had just accused me of being stupid, so I added, "And okay, I admit that in the past I haven't applied myself in school like I should have, but I'm turning over a new leaf, so I want a guy who is smart too. And I want this guy to go to prom with me."

She stared at me for another moment, then finally said, "That's it? You're done and won't accuse me of not listening to the whole thing?"

"Right. I'm done." I held out one hand to her. "You heard the part where I said I wanted all of this to happen back home in my day and age, right?"

"Yes. I heard that part."

"Good, because I *so* want to take a—" Before I'd even said the words "hot shower," the two of us were standing back in my bedroom.

Chapter 8

I looked around, blinking at the things that seemed familiar and yet so new. Relief engulfed me, and then surprise. "Hey, everything's still in focus and I'm not wearing my contacts."

Chrissy shrugged. "Yes, well, that's one of those side effects of magic that I warned you about. After people live through a couple of wishes they almost always see things more clearly."

I went over to my bed, ran my hand across the soft comforter, and sat down. Now that I was safely back home all the questions that I'd thought of over the last few weeks rose to the surface of my mind. "Where were the real Cinderella and Snow White while I was being them? And how come everyone thought I was them even though I still looked like me whenever I saw myself in a mirror?"

Chrissy took her sunglasses from her purse and slid them over her eyes again. "I gave the real Cinderella and Snow White lovely vacations in Costa Rica, and everyone thought you were them because the magic made it seem that it was your face that had always been the face of Cinderella or the face of Snow White." She took the wand from her purse and said, "As much as I'd like to stay around chatting about the intricacies of magic, I've got to go find your prom date." She glanced down at her watch, "And get ready for a party." Glittering lights sparkled up and down her length, then the next moment she'd disappeared altogether and I was alone in my room.

I sat on my bed for a moment longer. The clock on my dresser read 10:00, but it felt like I'd been gone for years. I wanted to find my parents—and even Jane—throw my arms around them, and tell them I'd missed them.

Of course I couldn't do it, especially not looking like I did. I took off my Snow White dress, grabbed some clothes from my dresser, and darted into the bathroom. The beautiful, marvelous, completely modern bathroom.

I must have stood in the shower letting the warm water run over me for a good twenty minutes before I even picked up the shampoo bottle. And then I nearly cried when I did. Shampoo instead of that hard, bad-smelling soap. It made bubbles in my hair. Could anything be more wonderful?

As it turned out, I discovered many things that were. I put creamy, soothing hand lotion on my hands that were still chapped and blistered from my days as Cinderella. I found my parents just as they were about to turn in for the night and gave them both big hugs. My mother smelled of a mixture of her perfume and hairspray. I'd missed that smell.

My dad's embrace felt so secure. This more than anything convinced me I was really home. No memories of wicked stepmothers in all their evil glory could bother me while my dad was around. With that one hug they vanished back into the pages of fiction.

Jane was talking on the phone with Hunter, so I didn't say anything to her, and she averted her eyes when she saw me. I flipped the lights on and off in the kitchen just because I could. Ditto for the water in the sink. My reunion with the refrigerator was especially touching.

I stood in front of it staring at the many contents and felt tears press against my eyes. Cold milk and leftover pizza. Yogurt, jam, oranges, lunchmeat, and little prepackaged slices of American cheese. I didn't know what to eat first.

Jane walked into the kitchen to return the phone to its cradle and saw me crying in front of the fridge. "What's wrong?" she asked in a tentative voice, like she was afraid of the answer.

"Nothing." I emptied the fridge of several items, putting it all on the table. I caught sight of a loaf of bread and picked it up, cradling it in my hands like it was a baby. "Can you believe how light and soft this is?" I asked Jane. "There's no gritty little hard pieces in it."

She didn't answer, just watched as I grabbed the ice cream from the freezer. I kissed the carton, set it down on the table, and grabbed a bowl. I served myself two large scoops, which I ate in between nibbling on everything else.

Jane looked at me then said, "I see," in this prim sort of way like she was psychoanalyzing me, but I didn't even care.

•　•　•

The next morning while I poured myself a bowl of cereal, my mom walked by and caught sight of my hands. She took hold of my wrist and her eyebrows drew together in concern. "What happened? How did your hands get like this?"

"Um ..." I'd hoped no one would notice them until after they'd healed. I stuttered for another moment then said, "I guess I forgot to wear gloves a few times while I weeded the backyard."

As soon as I said it, I felt something cold and slippery filling my mouth. How could this be? I thought the whole no-lying rule was only for the Middle Ages, but something was definitely squirming on my tongue and Mom was just not going to understand if I upchucked a snake on the kitchen floor.

I sprinted past her to the guest bathroom, slammed the door shut, leaned over the countertop, and spit out a toad. There is nothing as repulsive as having a live toad sitting in your mouth. I've heard they're not really as slimy as they look, but tell that to my tongue. I spent the next few minutes spitting into the sink and trying to wash the amphibian taste out of my mouth. The toad hopped around the counter and repeatedly tried to jump through the mirror.

My mom knocked softly on the door. "Are you all right?"

"Yeah, I'm fine."

From the kitchen I heard Jane say, "Well, what did she expect after she ate all of that junk last night? No one can fill up on pastrami and ice cream and not have it take its toll."

Thank you for those words of advice, Jane.

I cupped the toad in my hands—and even this was gross—rushed past my mother to the back door, and then before she could follow me to see what I was doing, I dropped it on the lawn.

It sat there blinking up at me. I hurried back inside and went into the bathroom to wash my hands. While I did this, Mom and Jane peered in through the doorway at me.

"Why did you just run outside?" Jane asked.

I didn't answer her question.

"Are you sure you're all right?" Mom asked.

"Yeah." I wiped my hands on a towel. "I'm just going to go upstairs and brush my teeth." Multiple times.

My mother let the subject drop, but Jane kept sending me sharp glances like she thought I was plotting some sort of revenge.

To tell you the truth, though, I wasn't thinking about the

whole Jane and Hunter drama even though she was with me again—a constant reminder of her betrayal. It seemed like I'd dated Hunter so long ago. When my mind turned from the wonder and comforts of my world—and I was seeing everything around me like I'd never seen it before—it was only to think about the fact that magic still existed here too. I'd proved that when I'd spit up a toad.

The fairy spell was still on me and would be until Chrissy fulfilled her part of the bargain and got some princely guy to ask me to prom. In between working on my homework, I daydreamed about this mystery guy.

Maybe tomorrow as I walked to school some sleek Trans Am would pull up and the studly young driver would ask me for directions to the high school because he was going to start school there.

At 4:30 Emily called me. "Did you hear about Tristan?"

Tristan. I hadn't thought about him or the swimsuit incident in so long. It was odd to think that in this world it had just happened yesterday. "No. What's up with Tristan?"

"He disappeared last night. He was in his room and when his parents went to tell him to turn off the light he was gone. Vanished. Just like that—from his own house."

"Disappeared?" A sick, horrible feeling gnawed at my stomach.

"His parents have called all his friends and no one knows what happened to him. Tristan's room is on the second floor and his parents were downstairs in their living room the whole time with the doors locked. So the police say he must have climbed out the window on his own—I guess it would have been hard for a kidnapper to scale the wall and carry him off that way, but still—can you imagine Tristan running away?"

No, Tristan wasn't the type to run away. I'd never heard that he didn't get along with his family. In fact, they came to every track meet to cheer him on. And Tristan was so responsible. He cared about his grades. Did a person who'd put that much effort into school just take off without explanation?

It didn't make sense.

Then I remembered that Chrissy had volunteered to turn Hunter into a frog. She hadn't said the same about Tristan, had she? Had I even told her about Tristan and the swimsuit thing? I couldn't remember.

After I hung up with Emily, I stood in the middle of my room and hissed out, "Chrissy!" several times. I was afraid that she wouldn't come for days and by that time Tristan could have been eaten by—well, whatever unfortunate creature in the food chain was designated to eat frogs.

Nothing happened. I kept calling Chrissy's name, all the while hoping that Emily would call me back and tell me Tristan had come home, it was all a mistake, he hadn't been missing at all. That didn't happen either, but after a few minutes a fountain of sparkles erupted in my room, and then there she was, decked out in a black cocktail dress complete with spiky black heels and a sequined handbag.

She put one hand on her hip and eyed me over in a disappointed fashion. "You really need to develop some patience. Do you think princes just appear spontaneously every time you make a wish? These things take time, you know."

"I didn't call you here to talk about princes."

"Good, because frankly I was getting tired of all that whining." She smoothed down the front of her dress. "What do you think of my new outfit? It's to die for, isn't it—and you'll never believe the bargain I got on these shoes. They were such a good price I had to buy some in yellow too, and I don't even own a yellow dress. Well, not yet anyway."

"Look, do you know anything about Tristan Hawkins disappearing? Because I distinctly remember telling you that I didn't want you to turn anybody into a frog."

"Oh, that." She flipped her hair off her shoulder in an unconcerned manner. "Of course I didn't turn him into a *frog*. He was much too nice for that."

The way she said it confirmed my fears. I grasped hold of the front of my shirt in an attempt to keep my heart from pounding its way out of my chest. "But you turned him into something else?"

"Not yet; I'm still in the process."

"In the process?"

"Of turning him into a prince."

"What?"

She straightened her purse strap on her shoulder as though she were about to leave. "You gave me a long list of things you wanted in a guy and he fit them all, except for the fact that he's a commoner. So I sent him back to the Middle Ages with the instructions that I would bring him back after he became a prince. Your orders." She gave me a bemused shrug of her shoulders. "I don't understand it. He's been there for months and he's not even a knight yet. I really expected more of him."

"He's been there for months?" I gasped out.

She let out a sigh. "I've explained the time thing to you before. One hour here equals a week back—"

"Yes, I understand the concept. What I meant was that you've got to bring him back right now. You can't just zap people from their bedrooms and drop them into the Middle Ages."

"I can if you ask me to," she said with a smile.

I shook my head. It felt like the room was closing in on me. "I never asked you to do that."

She opened her purse, pulled out the scroll and unrolled it.

"You said you wanted a prince type of guy. That leaves emperors, czars, and dictators. I thought it would be easiest just to turn him into a prince."

"That's not what I meant!"

She lowered the scroll from her face. "Then I guess you need to learn to articulate better."

I let out several deep breaths and tried to think about this logically. Which was very hard to do since I could feel myself sliding into a full-blown panic. Tristan was missing. He'd been in the Middle Ages for months and it was my fault. "Okay, if my wish sent him there, then how about I just wish that you bring him back?"

She rolled the scroll up and placed it back in her purse. "You've already used up all of your wishes. First you wished to be Cinderella, then Snow White, and lastly you wished to send Tristan to the Middle Ages to become your prince."

I clenched my hands into fists. "No, that was the same wish that you just messed up a bunch of times!"

"Hopefully he'll accomplish the whole prince thing by this prom," she said as if she hadn't heard me at all. "But if not, don't worry. You didn't specify which prom and there are a lot of other guys I could send to medieval times to make their fortune. Eventually one of them is bound to become a prince, right?"

"No," I said. "You can't do that. You have to bring—," but she didn't listen to the rest of my sentence.

With a flash of light, she disappeared.

Chapter 9

I stood there for several more moments, just gasping at the empty space in my room. I called her name. I demanded she come back. I even stomped my foot, but she didn't return. And every minute I stood here, Tristan was back in the Middle Ages experiencing—how much time exactly? Every ten minutes that went by here was more than a day there. Four hours was a month. I didn't have any time to spare, and yet I had no idea how to bring him back.

I paced the room for probably a complete day in Tristan's time, and then decided that if I couldn't talk to Chrissy, I could at least try to talk to the leprechaun. Maybe as an ex-assistant he had some leverage on Chrissy and could make her undo the last wish.

I looked around the house in places I thought a leprechaun might be—under the beds, in drawers, hiding in the kitchen cabinets. I remembered Chrissy had said something about him playing poker with the computer gremlins so I did a thorough check of all the computers. Then I walked around the backyard, looking behind trees and pushing away branches of bushes so I could see inside them. "Hey, Mr. Bloomsbottle," I kept whispering. "I need to talk to you. It's urgent." I checked another bush. "Clover? Where are you?"

I peered around a tree and saw Jane standing there, eyeing me suspiciously. "What are you looking for?"

"Uh, nothing."

Oh no. That was a lie. And there was the consequence, already growing between my teeth. I rushed to the nearest large bush so Jane couldn't see what came out of my mouth. The whole time I ran I was afraid that if I didn't make it in time, whatever it was squirming around in my mouth would try to crawl down my throat. When I got to the bush, I leaned over and spit up a gecko. And yes, I knew it was a gecko because I recognized it from the TV commercials.

As I stood there gagging, Jane walked over. "So this is your new method of making me feel guilty? You're pretending to be bulimic?"

"I am not pretending to be bulimic."

"Oh. You just throw up every time I'm around, then? That's a real subtle message."

Even though Jane was being unnecessarily snotty, I decided to tell her everything. First of all, it would save me from spitting up more geckos every time I talked to her. Plus she was smart enough to possibly find a solution to this problem.

So I did. Right there in the backyard I told her about Clover and how I needed to find him because he knew my fairy godmother and I needed advice about undoing wishes.

The whole time I spoke she folded her arms and gave me this humorless stare. When I finished she just nodded and said, "Okay, don't tell me what you're looking for. I don't care." Then she turned on her heel and went back inside.

I sighed and looked around the lawn again, trying to fend off the overpowering feeling of helplessness. How did one contact a leprechaun? They made a point of staying hidden, and it's not likely he'd walk into a trap—that is, unless I made it an especially tempting trap.

I went to the store and bought a package of Ding Dongs and some Barbie doll furniture. Then I went back home, took my dad's gopher traps out of the garage, and hauled them inside. I set up furniture in all the traps complete with Ding Dong slices and little cups of milk. Just for good measure I threw a flash drive into each of the traps. If a few computer gremlins were lured into the traps along with the leprechaun, all the better.

I put one trap by the computer in my room, one by the computer in Jane's room, and the other in the family room where my parents' computer sat. Maybe he'd come by for another poker game soon. If he was still around at all.

I checked the traps after dinner. Nothing. I went back to the computer in my bedroom and looked up information about leprechauns and fairies. After almost an hour of sifting through sites of artwork, craft projects, party ideas, and historic origins of mystical creatures, I heard the doorbell ring. Jane answered it and I heard Hunter's voice.

I tried to tune out Jane and him and concentrate on Web sites. Somewhere among the thousands of references, there had to be someone who'd dealt with magical creatures. Surely someone out there could help me.

I heard Jane and Hunter walk into the family room and realized I should have told my family not to mess with the traps I'd set up. I hurried toward the family room but Jane and Hunter were already there.

They stared at the Barbie furniture I'd set up in the trap and spoke in low voices to each other. Hunter shook his head. When they heard me walking toward them they fell silent.

I lowered my voice as well. "Stop looking at me like I'm crazy because I'm not—and don't stand so close to that. You'll scare off the leprechaun."

Which perhaps was not the best method of proving my sanity, but there was no point in defending myself. I'd either keep looking like an idiot or I'd start covering the carpet in reptiles. I turned and left the room.

I went back to my computer to look up more Internet sites. And there in the middle of the trap eating a Ding Dong was Clover T. Bloomsbottle.

He wasn't the sole occupant of the trap. Behind him, two creatures that looked like two-inch pale gray bats had pulled my flash drive apart. They sat beside each other grunting and chewing on the contents.

As I approached, Clover looked up at me—first with agitation, then with complacent disregard. "Oh, it's just you." He waved a finger in my direction. "You can't have me gold, so don't even ask." He shoved another piece of Ding Dong into his mouth, getting cream filling all over his beard, then shook his head happily. "These are much better than those dried-out crackers and boxes of cereal you have around." He took another bite. "Which reminds me, that Cap'n Crunch fellow cheats at cards. As for the Pillsbury Doughboy—aye, there's a sop for you. You really could do with a higher class of magical folk in the kitchen."

I was so happy to see him I didn't know where to begin or what to say first. I ended up saying, "I didn't realize we had magical tenants living in the cupboards."

He took another bite. "And I don't care what you Yanks say, cheese should not whiz."

The gremlins looked up and said something too, but it all sounded like clicks to me.

"What did they just say?" I asked Clover.

"Ah, don't mind them. The only ones that can understand them is magical folk and computer programmers. They're just complaining that your flash drive is stale. They like the newer versions. More of a challenge for them." He leaned back in his chair. "Now, are you going to let me out of this trap or are you foolish enough to try for me gold?"

I bent over to be on his eye level. "I don't need your gold, just your help."

"My help, eh? You already got three wishes from a fairy. What else could you need help with?"

"The wishes from the fairy. See, she sent a friend of mine back to the Middle Ages and won't bring him back."

Clover wiped Ding Dong filling off his beard and didn't look at me. "Why in the world did you wish for something you didn't want?"

I told him a condensed version of the story. I wasn't sure he paid attention, though. He kept shoving Ding Dong pieces in his mouth and making "Mmmmm" noises while I spoke.

"So is there anything you can do to help me?" I asked.

"You can't have me gold so don't . . ." He didn't finish his sentence. He was too busy eating again.

"Are you even listening to me? You know, I have you trapped in there. Doesn't that mean you have to help me?"

Now he waved a finger at me. "You mortals are all the same. We bestow favors upon you but it's never enough. You always want more, more, more."

"Oh, right. This is all my fault. I've been cooking and cleaning in the Middle Ages for nearly a month, and now I have lizards springing out of my mouth. Do you have any idea what that's like? How am I ever going to make it through a job interview, or . . . or meeting my in-laws, or—what am I thinking?—

high school tomorrow? A person just can't do those things without telling a few white lies. And on top of all that, my sister now thinks I'm insane."

Clover broke off another piece of Ding Dong. "Well, that will keep her on her toes then, won't it? She'll think twice before pilfering the next lad from you."

"The point is, I don't want magical help with my life anymore. I just want to bring Tristan home." I bent even closer to him. "You understand magic. There's got to be something you can do to help me. Please?"

He shook his head and looked away from me. "Oh, don't turn that pretty-lass expression on me. I'm a leprechaun, not a unicorn. We're unmoved by that type of thing."

Which let me know he wasn't. "Please?" I said again. "I really need your help."

He finished off the last bite of Ding Dong and wiped his hands together, brushing away the crumbs. "It's not my way to get involved in the problems of mortals. They have so very many. They multiply faster than mice, they do." He rubbed his beard, seeming to consider my situation. "But I might be able to help you if you'd help me in return."

"And how would I help you in return?" One thing that I'd learned when I was on the Internet was that leprechauns have a reputation for being wily creatures, so I was immediately cautious.

"I want to go back to Ireland, back to me beloved Lisdoonvarna. You see to it that I do."

Well, this was a problem. It's not like I could buy an airplane ticket for a man who was five inches tall.

He must have taken my hesitance for reluctance because he waved another finger at me. "Ah, see, your kind are all the same. Always wanting something from the magical folk, but let us ask

a favor and all we'll receive back is blank stares. Your greed and selfishness will be the downfall of your kind, it will."

The Internet said nothing at all about leprechauns being so touchy, which is just one more reason you can't always trust what you read there. "It's not that I don't want to help you," I said. "I just don't know how to send you there. I can't just put you in a box and drop you off at the post office."

"Why not?"

"Well, because it takes a few days to get there and don't you need things like air, and food, and water?"

He patted his stomach, which did indeed seem bigger than the first time I'd seen him. "Just pack me away with a few of those Ding Dongs and I'll be fine."

Which is how Clover T. Bloomsbottle and I came upon our agreement.

Once we'd worked out the details, I let him out of the trap. I made the computer gremlins stay for the time being, because I didn't want them anywhere near my computer.

Clover made me promise that I would in no way ever try to trick, manipulate, sway, maneuver, or influence him for magical reward and that at no time would I ever touch, steal, take, borrow, embezzle, or abscond with any of his gold. Seriously, he made me put it in writing and sign it. Right after I wrote down in our contract that I would send him and his personal effects to Lisdoonvarna, Ireland. Personally, I didn't think I needed to sign anything. He knew I was telling the truth because nothing slimy dropped out of my mouth while I spoke to him.

My stipulations were that he would help me get Tristan back and that he would take the computer gremlins with him. I went downstairs and came back with several Ding Dongs and a medium-size box.

Clover saw it and shook his head. "That will never do. The box needs to be bigger, and much sturdier."

I brought up two more boxes but Clover vetoed them both. Finally I brought him one of my parents' sturdy green Rubbermaid containers. "We can just tape it shut and put the label on top," I said. "And look, it has handles for carrying."

He nodded and said, "That should do for me gold."

"Your gold?"

"Aye, you didn't think I'd be leaving it here, did you?"

"I didn't think you had it with you."

From on top of my dresser he stomped one foot and glared at me as though I'd insulted him. "What kind of leprechaun do you think I am?"

A bad-tempered one. Only I didn't say that out loud. Instead I said, "Sorry. I guess I should have known you'd be sending your gold home, too. Is there a lot of it?"

His glare increased.

"I'm not trying to take any. I only asked because of the postage. Gold is heavy, you know."

I realized I'd said the wrong thing again because he folded his arms tightly. "Gold is twenty times denser than water. If you had a gold bar the size of a bread loaf, you'd never be able to lift it. Are there any other gold facts you'd like to know?"

"Yeah," I said. "How heavy is this package going to be when I take it to the post office?"

"About seventy pounds."

"Seventy pounds?" My mouth dropped open. "That's going to cost me a fortune to send to Ireland."

"Aye, well you should read and understand contracts thoroughly before you sign them."

I let out a sigh and tried not to be too upset. After all, even if I had known the bargain included sending his gold back, I still would have agreed. What other choice did I have?

"Okay, fine," I said, "I'll come up with the money somehow to pay for postage. Now, can you please tell me how to get Tristan back home?"

"Read and understand contracts thoroughly," he said.

I waited for him to say more. He didn't. Instead he jumped down into the box and walked around, examining it.

"I did read our contract thoroughly," I said through gritted teeth. "And you promised to help me get Tristan back."

"Not *our* contract," he said with exasperation. "The *fairy* contract. The one you signed with Chrysanthemum Everstar. Now hand over another of those Ding Dongs. I need to keep my strength up to make the trip."

That was it? It would end up costing me hundreds of dollars to mail him back to Ireland and all the help he was going to be was to tell me to read my contract? "Where am I even going to get a copy of that contract?" I asked. "Chrissy didn't give me one."

"Of course she did. That's part of the agreement. Check your magic files under *C* for contracts."

"I don't have any magic files."

He actually rolled his eyes at me. Even standing less than half a foot tall I could see him do it. He pointed over to the computer sitting on my desk. "And what do you call that?"

"A Macintosh."

More eye rolling. "Run a search for magic," he said, "and then check *C* for contract. Really, you don't think those things were built without the help of magic, did you?"

Actually, I thought they were built with the help of technology, but perhaps those things were closer together than I'd realized.

I sat down at my desk and turned on my computer. And the weird thing was that sure enough, when I ran a search under the keyword "magic" a file came up. I hit the Print button and the contract emerged from my laser printer in the same long parchment form it had been in when I'd signed it for Chrissy. I read it while Clover dragged Ding Dongs around the Rubbermaid box, effectively turning them into Hostess furniture.

After searching halfway through the contract and not finding anything of use for getting Tristan back, I glanced over and saw a black pot—about the width of a cereal bowl but with much higher sides—had been added to the box. It was filled to the brim with golden coins. Clover must have put it in the box through magic, as there was no way he could have lifted it. I let out a sigh. It was too bad he couldn't just use magic to return it to Ireland. Postage rates being what they are and all.

I kept reading the contract. I read about the First Party, hereafter known as Chrysanthemum Everstar, who was, as directed in Provision Five Article B, obligated to fulfill three of my wishes. I read about the limitation on the wishes—there were a lot of those—including that I couldn't wish for something that would violate any of the already stated, or hereafter stated, provisions and articles.

Really, the sentence lengths alone were enough to give me a headache.

The part that made my stomach sink—about four feet down the parchment roll, near the end—was the statement that all wishes were considered permanent and binding, their consequences real and lasting. That meant I couldn't undo wishes.

I laid the contract on my lap and looked down at Clover, who had stolen a pair of my socks and seemed to be using them as a beanbag chair. "How does this help? It says wishes are permanent."

"Aye, but didn't you read the part that says you're allowed to oversee all efforts made on your behalf to fulfill your wishes?

That means if you ask, Chrissy is required to let you go to the Middle Ages and oversee Tristan's progress."

"And how exactly would that be a good thing?"

Clover held out his hand in my direction. "Lass, it's as clear as the ink it's written with. You have to go back and help him become a prince so he can come home again."

Chapter 10

I pressed the contract against my chest, wrinkling the paper. "But I . . . I hated the Middle Ages. It was smelly and cold, and they didn't have plumbing. Isn't there an easier way?"

Clover leaned back into my socks and shook his head. "Mortals. You're a terminally lazy bunch. You can't walk anywhere so you've got to invent cars. You can't do your own work so you've got to invent dishwashers and washing machines. You can't even walk up the bloomin' stairs. You've got to invent elevators."

I didn't point out that I thought all of those inventions were actually a good thing. I just said, "How can I help him become a prince? I thought the only way you became a prince was if your father was a king. Tristan's dad is a dentist."

"Aye, well that's the fly in the ointment, isn't it? Still, I've done me part to help you. Could you throw in a few Froot Loops for the trip? I've become fond of those."

I went downstairs, grabbed the box of Fruit Loops and the duct tape, and then stomped back upstairs.

"Okay," I told him after I'd sprinkled a layer of Froot Loops into the box. "Once I dump the computer gremlins in there with you, I'm going to tape this thing up tight. Any last bits of advice?"

"Aye. If someone tells you that you're worth your weight in gold, they're either ignorant or an insincere flatterer. Right now gold is worth upward of $9,000 a pound. And a lass like you"— he surveyed me for a moment—"must weigh at least $1,203,660." He squinted and nodded a bit. "Maybe even $1,299,950."

"Okay, thank you very much for that assessment on my weight."

As I carried the trap over to the box, the computer gremlins clicked away in my direction.

Clover said, "The gremlins wanted you to let the rest of their mates know they can't make that soccer tournament/data-eating party they throw in your computer every year. But don't worry, I'll just have the lads e-mail that information to your computer when we reach Ireland."

Okay, there are some things it is just better not to know about, especially if you can't think about updating your computer protection because you've got to plan a trip to the Middle Ages. And that's what I was doing. I slid the computer gremlins into the box and slammed the lid on tight, but my mind kept going over the things I'd need to bring. Soap. Shampoo. Deodorant.

I cut off pieces of duct tape and secured the sides of the box. "You'll go out in the mail tomorrow," I said loud enough for him to hear me. Which immediately presented a problem. I couldn't wait until tomorrow after the post office opened to go back to the Middle Ages. It was nearly 6:30 now. Every hour I delayed going back to the other world would be another week gone by in Tristan's life.

I mulled this over while I wrote out and taped an address label to the top of the box. Then I checked the computer for postal rates. According to the USPS Web site, it cost about

$250 to mail a seventy-pound package to Ireland. After my prom dress purchase, I had about $35 to my name.

The only thing I could do was return the prom dress to the store, get my money back, and use it for postage. I took the dress out of my closet—a pale cream vision of lace and beading—and stared at it for a moment. Even though I didn't have a date, even though my ex-boyfriend was somewhere in my house right now with my sister, it was depressing to take it back. It was like admitting defeat, like saying no one would ever again think that I was special enough to wear it.

I cradled it in my arms so it wouldn't drag on the floor and left my room.

Jane and Hunter sat on the couch in the family room with their schoolwork spread out in front of them on the coffee table. They stared at me as I walked down the stairs. I realized Jane would ask less questions about mailing the package than my parents so I walked over to her. "Hey, I need someone to mail a package for me first thing in the morning. Can you do it before school?"

She looked at the dress and then at me, uncertainly. "Okay."

"I'll leave you some money for postage. It's going to cost about two hundred and fifty dollars since I'm mailing it to Ireland."

"Two hundred and fifty dollars?" Hunter spit out. "What are you mailing?"

I laid my dress on the back of our ottoman while I grabbed my purse from the coat closet. "It would probably be better if I didn't tell you."

"You have to tell me," Jane said. "The post office clerks ask about the contents of international packages for customs' paperwork."

"Oh." I sifted through the contents of my purse looking for the dress receipt. "In that case you'll need to lie." Which was a bonus reason for having Jane mail it for me. She could lie without creating reptile buddies to keep her company.

"It's nothing dangerous, is it?" Hunter asked.

I had to think before answering that question. Were leprechauns dangerous? Would the lie police send my mouth a special little gift if I answered the wrong way? Slowly, carefully, I said, "Nooo."

Apparently my hesitation wasn't reassuring. Jane let out a grunt and folded her arms. "This is another one of your revenge things, isn't it? You're probably sending firearms to the IRA, and you'll have a good laugh when the police arrest me in the post office."

"It's not firearms," I said.

"Then what? Explosives? Illegal drugs? I'm not sending it until you tell me."

I located my receipt in my purse and walked back over to pick up the dress. "Fine, if you have to know, it's a leprechaun, two computer gremlins, and a pot of gold."

She threw up her hand in exasperation. "That, of course, was my next guess."

I slung the dress over my shoulder while I got the car keys out of my purse. "I've got to head off to the dress shop. The package is up in my room. I'll leave the money on top of it."

They didn't say anything else, which was good. As long as she agreed to mail the package, I didn't care what they thought.

· · ·

After I returned my dress I went to a thrift shop. I figured I would need to barter for a lot of things once I got back to the Middle Ages, and costume jewelry would be a great thing to barter with. Perhaps I could even buy a piece of land that Tristan could preside over as prince. It was pure luck that I noticed they had a costume rack, and one of the costumes was a medieval princess dress. Ten dollars for the dress, fifty dollars for a whole bag of rings, necklaces, and earrings. That's all it cost me. I nearly skipped out of the store.

When I got home, Jane and Hunter were still sitting in the family room. I tried to ignore them as I ran around the house packing things I'd need. My parents were in their bedroom watching TV, which was a good thing since I'd dragged my dad's camping backpack out of the garage to use for my supplies and was now dumping things into it. It was just better to avoid telling them why.

I took some of my mom's spices from the kitchen cupboards. Spices were a big-ticket item in the Middle Ages that I could use for bartering. I also packed a flashlight, silverware, my Snow White dress, a couple of water bottles, a first-aid kit, granola bars, and—I couldn't help myself—a bag of chocolate chips.

I walked through the kitchen and bathroom shoving more things into the backpack pockets. Matches, hand cream, toothpaste, and an extra toothbrush for Tristan. After I'd packed all the supplies that could possibly fit into Dad's pack, I changed into the medieval dress. It was polyester and had a zipper, two things which I'd never seen the natives wear, but I would still look like a lady.

Finally I was ready to go. All that was left to do was to tell Jane, so that if I wasn't back by morning, my family would know what had happened to me.

It was 8:30 here, which meant Tristan had been gone between twenty-one and twenty-two hours. Converting that into medieval days was . . . um, math . . . so it was going to take me a moment to figure out. I walked toward the family room calculating it. Twenty-two divided by four weeks in a month—nearly six months had passed. Which is when I realized I had not thought this through as clearly as I should have.

Jane and Hunter saw me walking toward them. Jane let out a sigh and under her breath said, "I guess this is the next lap of her nervous breakdown. She's joined the Renaissance club."

If it had been almost six months since I'd been there, it would be winter there now. I wasn't dressed for winter. I walked to the coat closet and pulled on my long coat. Then I put on my gloves, hat, and scarf. I stepped out of my tennis shoes, slipped them into my coat pockets, and put on my snow boots. When I turned back to Hunter and Jane they were watching me with disbelieving expressions.

"Air conditioning set too low for you?" Jane asked.

"Listen, I don't have time for a lot of lengthy explanations that you won't believe anyway. So I'm just going to tell you and be done with it: I'm asking my fairy godmother to send me to the Middle Ages. Time is slower there than it is here, so hopefully I'll be back before Mom and Dad notice I'm missing, but if I'm not, please cover for me."

"Cover for you while you're in the Middle Ages?"

"Right."

She sent me a humorless smile. "Your secret is safe with us."

"Great. And don't forget to mail that package. I left the money for postage sitting on top of it." I turned, then remembered one last thing. "Oh, and be gentle with the package when you're moving it. According to some of the Internet sites, leprechauns can curse you."

"Sure thing," she said.

I knew she wasn't taking me seriously, but I didn't have time to press the point. I needed to call Chrissy.

Fully dressed and with my backpack leaning up against my bed, I stood in my room and called her name. Nothing happened. I should have expected as much. When had she ever come the first time I'd called? I paced around my room, calling for her every few minutes. Still nothing.

Eventually the front door to my house opened and closed. Hunter must have gone home. I heard footsteps come up the stairs and then the noises of Jane brushing her teeth in the bathroom. I called Chrissy again, emphasizing that I needed to talk to her about our contract immediately. I watched the numbers on my digital clock creep higher and higher. In my mind I could feel the sun rising and setting in Tristan's world multiple times.

Finally I decided that I could at least make good use of the time by reading my history book. Maybe I'd learn something about the Middle Ages that would come in handy. I sat down on my bed, still fully dressed, and opened the book. I should have known it was a mistake. Somewhere in the middle of an explanation of iconoclasm, I drifted off to sleep.

• • •

I woke up to pale sunlight drifting in through my blinds and Jane poking her head into my room. In an overly cheerful voice, she said, "Oh. I see you're back from the Middle Ages. I guess I won't have to cover for you after all. I'm going to school now."

After she left, I groaned, blinked, and looked at the clock. It read 7:12. I groaned again. Not only was I not in the Middle Ages, now I'd be late for school. There was no way I could go in a medieval dress and carrying a hiking backpack, which totally messed up my plans. Plus, I hadn't finished my homework. Mr. Morgan, my geometry teacher, was not going to buy my I-was-distracted-by-time-travel excuse. I rolled over and hit the side of my bed with my fist. "Chrissy, where are you?"

She came that time. My room lit up with a flash and then she stood before me in a tight red cocktail dress and spiky red heels to match. Her hair had turned platinum, and instead of a star, a bright red heart glowed on the end of her wand. Her sunglasses, also shaped like two dark hearts, perched on the end of her nose.

"Sorry it took me so long to answer you. I was busy playing cupid at a dance."

"You do that for people too?"

She put the sunglasses on top of her head and gazed at me like it was a silly question. "Not for people. For me. There were some totally buff fairy guys there."

I stumbled off the bed and reached for my backpack. "You know how my contract says I can oversee all wishes made on my behalf?" I swung the backpack onto my shoulders. "Well, I want to go wherever it is that you sent Tristan."

Her eyebrows rose in surprise. "I thought you hated the Middle Ages."

"I do, but I can't just leave Tristan there and not help him."

She stared at me for a moment, her lips twitching in disapproval. "You know, people who don't know what they want in life really shouldn't make wishes. It's a waste of perfectly good magic. But fine, whatever. You can stay with him in the Middle Ages until the terms of the contract are met."

The next moment I stood on a hill overlooking a village. Beyond the village off in the distance I saw an imposing castle surrounded by high gray walls. A thick wall of trees crowded behind me.

It would have been nice for Chrissy to drop me off a little bit closer to the village, seeing as my backpack must have weighed forty pounds. But then, perhaps it was for the best. Maybe villagers didn't take well to people flashing into existence in the middle of the town square.

I set off in that direction, peeling off my winter clothes as I went. A slight chill hung in the air but nothing that required a hat, gloves, or a scarf. By my calculations, it was now probably May and, judging by the angle of the sun—I'd gotten quite good at that during my last trip to the Middle Ages—it was midmorning. I walked down the hill, too nervous to enjoy the scenery of lush trees, grass, and wildflowers. When I got close to the village the sounds became more distinct. The thud of horse hooves on the street. The twang of a black-smith's hammer. The occasional call of wares. I'd apparently come on market day. That worked out nicely, since I had things to sell.

I came to the outskirts of town. Rundown shacks, put together with mostly straw and mud, stood by the path. Animals and children ran around while the children's mothers tended to the cooking fires. Some of them whispered and pointed at me, probably pointing out to one another all of the ways I was odd and different—which pretty much described junior high for me, so I didn't let it rattle me.

Next I noticed the smells. It's funny how you can smell manure from so far away. Well, not really funny, more like horrible, actually. I had definitely returned.

I walked down the cobblestone street—no sidewalks—and kept checking to make sure I didn't step on any animal droppings. Other than that, I looked around, trying to catch sight of Tristan's blond hair. I saw a few blond men, their hair darkened by dirt and grime, but not Tristan.

I found an inn—at least the sign read The Cat's Paw Inn—but once I stepped inside it seemed more like a tavern. Benches and tables lined the room with a fair amount of people already eating their noon meal. A scruffy dog wandered from table to table begging for scraps.

A woman with a ruddy complexion walked up to me. Her gaze traveled over me, clearly not knowing what to make of me. "Can I help you, miss?"

"I hope so. I'm looking for a friend of mine. Tristan Hawkins. Do you know where I can find him?"

"Ah, I should have guessed as much." She nodded, wiping her hands on her apron. "A foreigner. Are you from the land of Herndon too?"

"Yes." She knew who Tristan was. I was close. I could feel it. "Where can I find him?"

She shrugged. "Probably up in the hills. That's where he goes most days."

"The hills?" I let out a sigh, and the energy immediately drained from me. I'd just come from the hills. He'd probably been within earshot. I'd been so quick to assume Chrissy had meant to send me to the village, I hadn't even called out his name.

"He'll be back," the woman said, in response to my disappointment. "He hasn't missed dinner once."

"He's staying here?"

"Ever since he set out to slay the ogre." She crossed herself after saying the name. "Filthy beast. We'll all sleep better once it's gone. Bad enough that we have to worry about robbers on the road and the dragon in the sky." She eyed me over again, her gaze stopping on the many rings I wore on my fingers.

"Do you have a place to stay, m'lady?"

"I suppose I'll need one." I looked toward the stairs, and the rooms that must be on the second level. "I brought some things from my land to trade with." I took out a sterling silver ring with three stones—probably glass, although they might have been cubic zirconia. I didn't feel bad either way. Even glass was valuable in medieval times. "Will this be enough to pay for my food and lodging until I leave?"

She gasped and grabbed the ring from my hand. "I'll have one of the girls make a room right up."

She also volunteered lodging for my servants and the stable for my horses, but didn't seem surprised when I told her I had neither, or offended when I told her I'd rather not talk about how I arrived. Wealth apparently brings you unquestioned acceptance.

I ate a dinner of bread and boiled eggs while Scuppers the inn dog sat and watched every movement of my hand. He had such a pathetic expression that I had to feed him. After that I settled into my room. It was small with a tiny window that only let a slice of sunlight into the room. A narrow bed stood in the corner, next to a washbasin perched on top of a rickety table. Still, it was private. I had passed by rows of beds in the main room where less wealthy patrons were staying.

Next I went to the market and traded some spices for money and a satchel to carry it in. Then I went to the shoemaker so I could be fitted for some proper lace-up boots, and to the tailor to be fitted for a dress. I also bought a funky-looking hat I'd seen other medieval women wear. This apparently was their answer to a bad-hair century.

All in all, it was the best day I'd spent in the Middle Ages. I went back to the inn and unpacked some more. I was sitting on the floor trying to decide where to put the shampoo and conditioner I'd brought when the door flung open and Tristan walked in.

Chapter 11

I recognized him even though he wore a tunic and leggings like the other medieval men. His hair had grown to his shoulders, shoulders which had become much more muscular over the last eight months. He looked taller, tanner, and somehow so indefinably handsome that I could only stare at him. The medieval look worked for him.

He stared back at me, not especially happy to see me. "You," he said, and he glared at me for so long I wasn't sure if he planned on saying more.

"Hi, Tristan."

He pointed a finger in my direction. "You sent me here."

I stood up and the bottle of shampoo slipped from my fingers to the ground. "No, I didn't. It was all an accident, really."

His eyes didn't leave my face. I'd never noticed what an intense blue they were, although maybe they were just intense because he was using them to burn holes into me. He took slow steps across the room toward me. "Your fairy godmother told me that you asked her to send me here."

I shook my head. "It wasn't like that."

He took more steps and held up both hands for emphasis. "I know I announced to the entire track team that your bikini top came off, but most girls would just get over that, not call upon magical forces to toss somebody back into the Middle Ages."

I took a step backward, and then another. "I didn't tell Chrissy to send you here. And I came to help you as soon as I heard you were missing."

His eyes narrowed. "It's been over eight months, Savannah. It took you eight months to notice I was gone?"

"No. Time is different here. One week in this place is only an hour back home. In Virginia it's still the Monday morning after you left. School hasn't even started yet."

For the first time his shoulders relaxed, and he let out a deep breath. "How are my parents? Are they really worried?"

I shrugged. "I'm sure they are. I didn't see them before I left."

His expression grew intense again. "You didn't tell them where I was?"

"Sure, Tristan. I marched right over to your house and told them my fairy godmother sent you back in time." I held out a hand to him, trying to make him see my point. "They wouldn't have believed me."

He shut his eyes. When he opened them he looked at the ceiling and not at me. "I've been here too long. Magic doesn't seem peculiar anymore." He dragged his gaze away from the ceiling and looked back at me. "So is your fairy godmother going to set everything right?"

I twisted the material of my skirt around my fingers just to give them something to do. "Um, actually no. Technically you still have to become a prince before she brings you back."

He folded his arms. "Then exactly how are you going to help me?"

"Well, I brought things from home." I let go of my skirt, waved my fingers to show him my rings, then went and knelt by my backpack. "Besides all the jewelry, I also have spices, perfume . . . I took a bunch of my mom's sterling silverware—the women here are all about the silverware—but I also brought things they'll think are magical. Flashlights. Matches. I figure with all this stuff we can just buy some land and call you a prince. Voila, you can come home."

His arms remained folded. "Even if I buy land, it's still land in someone else's kingdom. They go by the feudal system here and every blade of grass on the continent already has a lord, baron, and king reigning over it. What's your second plan?"

I didn't say anything. Really, I'd never thought of Tristan as an intimidating person before, but he seemed to have aged so thoroughly in the time he'd spent here. He wasn't shy Tristan from the track club; he was a competent and assertive adult.

He raised an eyebrow. "You did have a backup plan, didn't you?"

When I still didn't answer, he grunted and looked at the ceiling again.

"I'm sorry," I said. "I've just never been very . . . smart."

Instead of looking apologetic for insulting me, or at least sympathetic, his gaze shot back to me with exasperation. "Don't give me that. I've known you long enough to know how smart you are." Then, as if to prove his point, he pointed to the backpack. "You knew what to pack to bring to the Middle Ages."

"That's because I lived here for several memorable, if not enjoyable, weeks." As soon as I said this, I remembered something that might help. I reached into one of the side pockets and handed Tristan my contract with Chrissy. I told him about it, adding that I'd brought it along to study for possible loopholes—or if worse came to worst, to use for kindling. Tristan might find something I'd overlooked.

He sat down on the corner of the bed and read it. After a couple of minutes he stopped reading and held the paper down to look at me. "You wanted to be Cinderella? You actually wished for that?"

"No. That was another matter of misinterpretation." I stood up and held out my hand for the contract. "You know, maybe it's not such a good idea to have you read that after all . . ."

He ignored my request. The contract went back up, then in another moment it came back down. "You wanted to be Snow White too?" He shook his head. "I take back everything I said about you being smart."

I grabbed for the paper but he held me away with one arm. He was strong. I looked down at his arm and noticed not only his muscles, but some bruises and pale scars crisscrossing over his arm. Those hadn't been there before, had they?

Still reading he said, "And I suppose this is where I come in. You wanted a princely guy from your own day."

"I'm sorry." My words came out sounding more defiant than apologetic, but he wasn't listening to me anyway.

"I have to take you to prom too? Oh, this just keeps getting better all the time."

I tried to grab the paper away from him again, but he held me away effortlessly. "You couldn't have wished for something normal like money or fame. You wanted," and here his voice took on a particularly disdainful tone, "a *prince*?"

"Well, if you have a prince then money and fame naturally follow, don't they?" I said, just because I didn't like the way he was speaking to me. "It's killing two birds with one stone."

Tristan slapped the contract down on the bed and looked at me scornfully. "Women."

"Well, hey, when your girlfriend dumps you for your brother you can tell me what you'd wish for."

His eyes softened and the room fell silent for a moment. "Oh yeah, Hunter and Jane. I'd completely forgotten about them." His attention returned to me. "I guess it wasn't that long ago for you though, was it?"

I didn't answer, but he didn't seem to expect me to. Instead he handed the contract back to me. "I don't see any way out of this except the way I was already working on." He stood up, hefted my backpack onto the bed like it weighed nothing, and unzipped the largest pocket. "I don't suppose you brought anything suitable for capturing cyclopses or killing dragons?"

Probably not. "Why do you need to do that?"

He told his story while he took everything out of the backpack for inspection. His voice was casual, with just enough cynicism to let me know he didn't think any of it was casual at all. "Your fairy godmother showed up in my bedroom one night, dropped me into this lovely village, and told me I had to become a prince in order to come back home. There's not a lot of chance of that happening, by the way, if you don't have an army at your command.

"I told people I'd come from a distant land to earn my fortune. Which, coincidentally, there was also not a lot of chance of happening. Even if I'd had a specialized skill—which I didn't—everything here is controlled by guilds. You can't just set up shop somewhere. I only kept from starving by working as a jongleur." He must have seen the blank expression on my face because he added, "That's a storyteller. I had plenty of stories." Here he gave me a crooked smile. "And Mom always told me that watching TV was a waste of my time. I tell you what, the people here are big *Battlestar Galactica* fans."

He picked up the first-aid kit from the backpack and smiled. I was glad that at least I'd brought something that made him happy. But he didn't comment on it, just set it aside from the other things. "I even told stories for the royal court—for King Roderick up on the hill. He liked me enough to let me become a page. Mostly because I'm a fast runner. When the king sends a message to someone in the palace or out in the courtyard he wants it done quickly. That was the only reason I even heard about the quest." He found my package of chocolate chips and held it in front of him reverently. A nearly silent "ohhh" escaped his lips.

"You can have some," I said.

He ripped open the package, popped a few in his mouth, and shut his eyes.

"Have as many as you want," I said.

He closed the bag and shook his head. "I've been living on pottage and bread for so long that if I eat too many it will make me sick."

"So what is this quest thing all about?"

He let out a sigh. "Maybe just a few more." Then he opened the bag and put another small handful in his mouth.

"The quest?" I prompted.

"Right. His highness, King Roderick, has been troubled with three things: a dragon that comes around on a monthly basis to fly off with cattle or unfortunate village folk; a cave cyclops that goes marauding at night, stealing goods and killing anyone who gets in his way; and the Black Knight." Tristan put the chocolate chips down and surveyed my supplies again. He picked up a knife I'd taken from my kitchen and gingerly felt the blade. I couldn't tell whether he was happy with it or not. He simply set it down and unzipped the backpack's side pockets.

"Who is the Black Knight?"

"No one knows. That's part of the problem. The only thing we know about him is that he wears black armor, carries no

colors on his shield, and he's immensely good. He keeps challenging Prince Edmond, the heir to the throne, to send his best
knight or come out and fight the Black Knight himself—"

The name caught me by surprise and I interrupted Tristan.
"Prince Edmond? The Prince Edmond who has a younger
brother Hugh and a younger sister Margaret?"

Tristan looked at me in surprise. "You've heard of him?"

I nodded. "I met his family when I was Cinderella."

Tristan's voice took on a mocking tone. "Ahh. A prom date
rival. Did you go to a ball with him?"

"No, he stopped by our manor and I decided he was not so
charming."

"Well, that's true enough. Anyway, our mutual friend Prince
Edmond is running out of champions. Even the most accomplished knights in court have lost their purses to the Black
Knight. No one else in the country will joust or sword fight
with him, not when the Black Knight has obviously got some
sort of magic working for him. He's disgraced the entire court,
and so King Roderick has issued the quest to all able-bodied
men." Tristan let a handful of silverware jangle onto the bed.
"Anyone who can kill the dragon or the cyclops—they refer to
him as the ogre—will be granted knighthood, and anyone who
can kill them both will get a sizable purse to use to challenge
the Black Knight. Whoever can defeat the Black Knight will be
made a prince."

"Which is why you're trying to kill the cyclops."

He pulled out my makeup kit and held it up between one
finger and a thumb as though it might be contagious. "Makeup?
Out of all the things you could have packed, you wasted space
bringing makeup with you?"

I grabbed it out of his hand and held it to my chest defen-
sively. "I like to look my best."

He wrinkled his nose at me. "Have you actually seen the women here? All you need to do to look better than the rest of them is occasionally wash your hair."

"Which is why I also brought shampoo. It's no use trying to use that stuff they call soap."

He pulled out my flashlight and flipped it on with such evident happiness that I knew the whole makeup issue had been forgotten. "It works. How new are the batteries?"

"New, plus I brought extra batteries."

"Perfect." He turned it off, examined the handle, then held the flashlight to his hip. "I'll have to figure out some way to strap it to my body."

"Why?"

"The cyclops only has one eye, but he can see in the dark. That's why he lives deep inside caves and only comes out at night. He's got an advantage then. Anyone who fights him—and there haven't been a lot who've tried—had to fight while holding a torch. Unfortunately the cyclops is fast, has claws as sharp as swords, and is at least seven feet tall.

"I tried setting a trap for him using a fishing net, but he cut right through it. Next I dug a pit. He used his claws to crawl up the sides. Both times I barely escaped with my life."

I stared at Tristan, once again noticing the pale scars on his forearms. I hadn't realized just how dangerous this wish was for him. Without thinking about it, I reached over and touched one of the scars on his arms. "Is that how you got these?"

His gaze landed on my fingers and suddenly I felt awkward for touching him. I let my hand drop away.

"I got those scars from sword practice. Once I joined the quest, I practiced with the other knights. As you can tell, they're much better than I am."

"You use real swords to practice?"

"No, I wouldn't have any arms left if we used real swords. Knights practice from childhood, for hours a day."

None of this was comforting news. "Then how are you going to defeat a cyclops, a dragon, and the Black Knight?"

Tristan picked up my supplies and one by one put them back in the backpack. "I'm pretty good with a javelin—the modern-day equivalent of the spear. Now that I'll actually be able to see the cyclops, I think I should be able to hit him before he reaches me." He took a couple of my spice bottles and slipped them into the bag he wore around his hips. "I'll go up to the castle armory and buy some spears tomorrow."

"All right. What do you want me to do to help?"

He stopped repacking long enough to glance at me. "You want to help?"

"That's why I came." A thought came to my mind and an automatic "oh" popped out of my mouth. "I could talk to the Black Knight. He doesn't know who I am, and I could try and find out the secret of his magic."

Tristan's face stayed free of emotion but his eyes glinted. "You mean use your beauty and wiles to cause his downfall?"

"Well, it sounds *bad* when you put it that way."

He shook his head. "No, the Black Knight is dangerous and you're to stay away from him."

"Knights are supposed to honor ladies, so if I—"

"No," Tristan said firmly. "That's an order."

I folded my arms. "Well, I suppose an order would mean something if we were both in the marines, but since we're not—"

Tristan walked over until he stood right in front of me. He folded his arms, matching my stance, except that he made far more of an imposing figure doing it. "You're right. We're not in the marines. We're in the Middle Ages, where, as you might recall from world history class, men own women. You're considered property like horses, saddles, and land. Since you sent me here, I can only assume you want me to obey the laws of this society. So while we're here, you will listen to me, and I'm telling you to stay far away from the Black Knight."

"I am not your property," I said.

He made no acknowledgment that I'd spoken. "If you want to be helpful, you can come with me to the castle and see if you can get an audience with Princess Margaret. I think she knows more about the Black Knight then she lets on."

"Why?" I asked, too curious to press the issue of property rights further.

"Everyone else in the court is either speculating about his identity or predicting what sort of havoc he'll raise when he finally forces Edmond into a fight. But not her. She sits by, content as a cat."

"Maybe she's just not a worrier?"

"It's her family that's being challenged. If they're driven from the throne, her life is in peril too."

I noticed the space, or lack of it, between us, but I didn't step away from Tristan. "Do you think they have a romantic relationship, then?"

Tristan shook his head, but without much conviction. "If the Black Knight wanted her hand in marriage, he would have gone about things differently. A knight that powerful would have been useful to the kingdom. King Roderick would have gladly given his daughter to him if it would have made the knight an ally."

"Then why do you think she's so unconcerned about the knight?" I asked.

Tristan shrugged and smiled at me. "A page could never ask those sorts of questions of a princess. But perhaps a visiting lady could find some answers."

Chapter 12

We didn't leave that night, which frustrated me since it seemed that once we had a plan, we should get started right away. But things worked slowly in the Middle Ages. We couldn't jump into a car, drive the eight miles to the castle, and then throw the spears in the trunk. We needed horses.

No self-respecting lady would walk the distance to the castle. And besides, no one ever defeated a dragon on foot. So Tristan went off to buy horses and saddles, which cost me three necklaces and two rings, and also diminished our spice supply quite a bit.

After dinner, everyone sat around the fire and listened to Tristan tell stories from the Chronicles of Narnia. One man requested he tell the story of the enchantress Savannah, who toyed with men's affections and then banished them to strange lands.

I stared at Tristan and said, "Oh, definitely—I want to hear that story."

But Tristan just blushed and said it was time to turn in for the night. Before we went to bed—and people in the Middle Ages pretty much went to sleep when the sun went down—the innkeeper filled a tub with hot water for baths. The people didn't change water in between baths, so I was doubly grateful that I got to use the bathwater first. It totally paid to be rich in the Middle Ages. And despite Tristan's snide remarks about the luxury items I'd brought with me, he didn't turn me down when I offered to let him use my soap and shampoo.

We woke up the next morning at sunrise—everyone did. Tristan had bought me a tawny brown mare with a pale, flowing mane. He gave me instructions on how to use the reins, instructions that apparently no one had given the horse, because she did whatever she pleased. She went as fast or as slow as she wanted, sometimes dawdling to sample grass along the path and other times running to catch up with Tristan's chestnut brown stallion. Tristan kept yelling really useful hints to me like "show her you mean business" and "she won't listen to you unless you're firm with her."

I tried being firm, but apparently the horse had already figured out that she was much bigger than I was, and basically ignored me altogether.

For part of the trip, the path took us through a forest. Tristan pulled out his sword then, and rode with it grasped in his hand. His gaze swung between the trees, and he told me in a hushed voice that he was watching for thieves who sometimes waylaid travelers on this road. I never saw anything out of the ordinary, though, and we passed through the forest with only the birds and a grazing doe taking note of us.

Eventually we came to the castle walls. The guards let us in without question. They knew who Tristan was and he told them I was a lady from his land who wanted to pay her respects to Princess Margaret.

We brought our horses to the stables and Tristan gave a boy some coins to tend to them. Then Tristan walked to the armory to buy spears and order armor, a task that would take a good part of the afternoon since he had to be measured for it. I made my way toward the castle.

I had expected the grounds to be mostly empty, but it looked like a miniature version of a city within the walls. Several shops lined the castle perimeter. Chickens ran free, pecking at the grounds one moment and then scurrying out of the way of pedestrians the next. Washerwomen set linens out to dry. Others pulled buckets of water from the well.

Some men unloaded large barrels from a wagon and I heard them discussing the banquet that would be held in three days' time. It was the twenty-fifth anniversary of the inauguration of King Roderick, and they were expecting guests from all over the kingdom.

I walked slowly toward the main entrance, trying to think of what to say to Princess Margaret and how I could get information about the Black Knight. Right now, I only knew what little Tristan had told me yesterday and a few more facts he'd mentioned on the ride up.

According to Tristan, the Black Knight had first ridden to the castle gates several months ago, challenging the knights of the court. Now that no one would accept his challenges, he only came every couple of weeks. He'd sit atop his black warhorse just beyond the drawbridge and shout, "Are there no knights who support the heir of the throne? Is not Prince Edmond capable of defending his title?"

This was the sort of thing that basically angered and embarrassed the court. Once, while the Black Knight was shouting all of this, Prince Edmond had sent six guards to knock him off his horse, drag him inside, and make his identity known. But the Black Knight had defeated all of them. Their swords had simply bounced off him like they'd been nothing more than twigs. That's why everyone thought he was enchanted.

After that incident, the Black Knight vowed that one day soon he would come back and take revenge for such treatment. If anyone found the courage to fight him in the meantime, they could ring the tower bell three times to signal a competition to be fought just outside the castle walls.

It would be normal enough for me, a visitor to this land, to ask Princess Margaret questions about the Black Knight. It wouldn't be normal, however, if a visitor started spitting up snakes during the conversation. I hadn't told Tristan about that little habit of mine.

I also worried that Princess Margaret would recognize me as Cinderella. True, it had been eight months ago and I'd been dressed in rags and smeared with soot when I met her, but what if she was one of those people who never forgot a face— especially if it was a face that had dumped a pitcher of mead over a noblewoman's head? Would the princess assume I was an impostor?

I was thinking about these things so intently that I almost didn't notice the man. I only saw him because all the children had stopped playing and stood in an eager line to watch him come out of the castle.

"It's Lord Pergis," they whispered to one another. "Perchance he'll do some magic for us."

I stopped walking and looked at the man. He had a full gray beard, eyebrows sprouting in disarray over deep-set eyes, and a cap that looked more like it belonged on a peasant than anyone of importance. He wore an embroidered maroon robe that nearly swept the ground, and the circles and stars on the fabric shimmered as he strode out of the castle and walked toward a wagon.

A young man, perhaps a few years older than myself,

followed after him, hauling a pack on his back that was even bigger and looked considerably heavier than the one I'd brought with me. My gaze automatically stopped on him, the way it does whenever a good-looking guy comes into view. He had thick dark hair and brown eyes that reminded me for a moment of Hunter. His maroon robe—just as long as the wizard's but without any embroidery—hid most of his build, but his shoulders were broad, and I could tell by the ease with which he hauled the pack around that he was muscular.

The two men walked over to a wagon that waited in the courtyard. One of the bigger children pushed a little boy forward. "Ask him. Ask the wizard to do a trick for us."

"Not I," said the little one. "He might turn me into a rabbit."

I didn't blame him for being scared. The wizard had a scowl on his face and muttered things under his breath as he and his apprentice unloaded his pack into the wagon.

I walked over to him anyway. Wizards knew magic. Perhaps they knew how to undo fairy spells put on people through signing foolish contracts.

He didn't look at me as I approached, just kept unloading flasks, dried plants, and several objects I couldn't identify. I heard him mumbling angrily, and as I approached the wagon I could make out his words. "Queen Neferia didn't find me worthless. She's been happy enough with my wares. Twice she's bought my disguise potion. And a magic mirror. Paid me well, too. But now I'm worthless because I've nothing to defeat the Black Knight. As if I could break the laws of magic. The royals know nothing of the ways of enchantments. Nothing. Aye, there's a lesson for you to mark, Simon." He turned to his apprentice and waved a bundle of something to emphasize the point. "When royalty is too important to learn the ways of magic and too impatient to listen to the instructions of wizards, it will be their downfall."

I waited to catch his eye and when I didn't, I said, "Excuse me—"

Without looking up he said, "I'm all out of love charms, and even if I wasn't, I only sell to royalty or them that have magic to trade." He glanced up, squinted in my direction, and then added, "Bah, you don't need love charms anyway. What are you wasting my time for?" He waved a dismissive hand at me, then continued to unpack. "Just swoon a bit for your gentleman and that should do the trick. Off with you now."

I didn't move, and neither did Simon. He'd stopped unpacking and was blatantly appraising me until the wizard nudged him. Then Simon went back to sorting things in the wagon, but I took a step closer to the wizard. "I'm not looking for a love charm."

The wizard took a pair of small wooden boxes from his apprentice and stacked them in the wagon. "It matters not. I see no crown on your head, and I only sell to royals. They like it that way, so unless you've magic to trade with me, I've nothing more to say."

Muttering to himself again he added, "I've stayed in these parts too long."

"I have some things you might like." I walked over to his side. "I have instant fire on little sticks. Here, I'll show you." I had some of the valuables I'd brought from home in a satchel tied around my hip. I took out the box of matches and struck one. "See how easy it is?"

He grunted, unimpressed. "Any wizard's apprentice can make fire out of naught. What else do you have?"

I pulled out a spoon from my pouch. "A place setting of silverware that never needs to be polished."

He took the spoon from my hand and turned it over in his palm. "Nicely made, but my clients have servants to polish their silver. What else do you have?"

"Tylenol." I took a medium-size bottle out of my satchel. "One or two pills will kill pain and bring down fevers."

"Fever cure. Now that's useful magic." He took the bottle from my hand and tapped the side. "I see the bottle is enchanted too."

"It's plastic; that means it keeps water out and it won't break if you drop it. Here, this is how you open it." I lined up the arrows and flipped the lid off, showed it to him, then snapped it back on.

His eyes widened and he nodded happily. "Ahh, it's fine magic. What do you ask for it?"

"Do you have anything to break spells?"

He humphed at me as though I ought to know better than to ask such a question. "Breaking spells is a complicated business. I couldn't do it for all the wealth the royal family is promising, and I can't do it for you. Is it the Black Knight's armor that is enchanted? His sword? Himself? Where came his magic from? I'll never be able to get close enough to tell so I can give no counterspells."

"I didn't mean the Black Knight's spell. I was thinking of a spell a fairy put on a friend."

Before I could explain what had happened, the wizard shook his head. "There are as many fairy spells as there are flowers. It's near impossible to know the recipe for undoing a specific one. Casting a spell is like throwing mice into your neighbor's barn. Easy enough to do, but near impossible to undo." He turned the Tylenol bottle in his hand, clearly displeased to have to give it back.

"Is there anything I could do to make a spell better, to modify it somehow?"

"Not unless you know someone with a better enchantment who's willing to switch."

"To switch?" I repeated.

A grimace crossed the wizard's face. "I should have thought

of it when I was talking to the prince." His grip tightened on the bottle. "I do have some switching potion. It's an obscure bit of magic. Takes years to make a single batch. He can't fault me for not remembering. How often are two enchanted people in the same place?" The wizard looked at the castle as though debating whether or not to go back inside.

"I want to buy it," I said. Because even though it wouldn't break Tristan's enchantment, it suddenly occurred to me I could still help him defeat the Black Knight. I could switch enchantments with the knight and then he would no longer be invincible.

Simon, who'd been busy placing things into the wagon, stopped his work. His hands froze somewhere among the bottles and boxes, and he turned a pair of startled eyes in my direction. I knew he wanted to say something, but the wizard didn't give him time.

"You want to buy it?" The wizard's voice changed so quickly—suddenly all business—that I wondered if his speech about selling it to King Roderick was just for my benefit. He pulled at his beard thoughtfully. "Such an important commodity is expensive. It will cost you the pills, the fire sticks, and the silverware."

I fingered the spoon, suddenly unsure. This could be either a very good decision or a great financial loss. I glanced at Simon, but he was no longer looking at me. He'd gone back to putting things into the wagon with a grimace set fiercely on his face.

"How does it work?" I asked.

The wizard dug through things in his wagon, sending some of them spilling in a noisy clatter as he retrieved a small mirror. Before I could question what it was, he took my hand in his bony grasp and held it under the mirror. Almost as quickly, he released my hand and held the mirror up to study. His eyes squinted and his eyebrows drew together like two furry caterpillars. "Ahh," he said. "So you *are* under an enchantment. Certainly not the worst I've encountered. Still, I can understand why you'd want to switch with someone."

I took the mirror from his hand to see what he was looking at. On its face, and fading as I watched, were the words: *When said occupant tells a lie, a reptile or amphibian will appear on his or her tongue.*

The wizard took the mirror from me and tucked it back into the wagon. He sorted through several more items and finally pulled out a blue clay jar no taller than his thumb. He wiped off the dust with the sleeve of his tunic until the bottle shone like a robin's egg. "This is the potion you need, m'lady, and this is how it works. As you know, a kiss can be powerful magic—"

He must have seen my blank look because he added impatiently, "A kiss can awaken a princess from an enchanted sleep. It can break the spell that keeps a prince in the form of a frog."

I nodded, at last remembering my fairy-tale lore. "Right. A kiss. Powerful magic."

He swirled the bottle, mixing the contents, and looked firmly into my eyes. "But once you drink of this potion your kiss will lose that power. For seven days, anyone who you kiss or who kisses you—anyone who carries an enchantment—will take yours from you and leave you theirs." His eyes grew stern, as though I needed to be told the next part. "Therefore, you mustn't tell anyone of your state or the way the enchantments pass. If you do, you risk all sorts of folks with bad enchantments trying to give you theirs.

"And don't think you can simply kiss the offender back. Once two enchantments switch, they won't switch back no matter how many times you kiss." For a moment he didn't seem like a man making a business deal, but like my father warning me about something he thought I'd probably do anyway. "So don't be rash or impulsive. Magic is a downfall to those who don't think it through. Make certain you want another's enchantment before you kiss them."

But I was already certain. After all, if the Black Knight wasn't enchanted, then kissing him wouldn't change me at all. And if he was enchanted, well, then I knew what the enchantment was, and I wouldn't mind having it. Invincibility. I reached into my purse, took out the matchbox and the silverware, and handed them to him. "Can I buy the mirror too?"

He shook his head as he tucked the things I'd given him into his wagon. "What is a wizard without his divining tools? Besides, it most likely wouldn't do you any good. They that have favorable enchantments usually wear gloves for just that reason."

The wizard pulled the cork from the switching potion and handed it to me. "Drink up, m'lady."

I took the bottle from him, but hesitated. Simon had caught my attention again, and was looking at me with agitation, one hand clenched far too tightly on the edge of the wagon. Perhaps the wizard wasn't telling me everything, or perhaps this was just a bad idea.

Magic *was* dangerous. That had been my problem since the beginning. I'd tried to use fairy magic to solve problems that were best left alone. I'd gotten Tristan into a terrible predicament and now I owed it to him to help him however I could. If that meant taking some risks, well, it had to be done.

I put the bottle to my lips, tilted it upward, and let the bitter liquid burn its way down my throat. The taste made me cringe and shiver.

The wizard grinned at my reaction and took the bottle back from my hand. "A word to the wise: don't let any animals lick you for a week—it's as good as a kiss, and any skin of yours is vulnerable to the switch. You won't know if they're enchanted folk until it's too late and you're mewing for your supper."

He dismissed me with a nod of his head, then tucked the empty bottle back into the wagon. His attention turned to Simon and his voice grew gruff. "Finish loading things, but mind you, don't break anything or you'll be finishing your apprenticeship as a goat."

Then the wizard walked to the front of the wagon, muttering things I couldn't understand. Simon's gaze stayed on me, the agitation still in his eyes. I knew he thought I'd acted foolishly and I turned away from him.

I headed for the castle, but I'd only taken a few steps when I felt a tug on my sleeve. Simon had followed me. He held a finger to his lips, then glanced over his shoulder to check and see if the wizard was watching us. He wasn't. The wizard had settled into the wagon's seat with his hat pulled down over his eyes as though about to take a nap.

With soft steps, Simon led me to the back of the wagon until we were out of sight from the wizard. He whispered, "Do you mean to switch enchantments with the Black Knight?"

I didn't answer. It seemed like such a lofty goal to say out loud.

His expression grew urgent. "Do you?"

I nodded.

"It's a dangerous thing to do, but I have a potion that will help you." He put a small red jar into my hand and closed my fingers around it. It felt warm, as though it had been sitting in the sun. "Drink it right when you meet the Black Knight. He'll straightway fall in love with you and do whatever you ask of him. All you need to do is ask for a kiss."

"What are you charging for it?" I asked.

For a moment he said nothing, then his gaze fell on my hands. "A ring. That one." He pointed to one that had been mine all along, a ring with three golden hibiscus flowers that my dad had bought me during a trip to Hawaii.

I hated to give that one up, but I pulled it from my finger anyway and held it out to him. "This is a very nice ring. It will cost you the potion and the use of the divining mirror for the week as well."

He clenched his jaw but nodded. He turned back to the wagon, and his fingers sifted through the contents quickly.

From the front of the wagon the wizard called out, "Simon, haven't you finished yet?"

"I'm almost done with my work, Master." Simon extracted the mirror from the wagon's contents and slipped it into my palm. "Be very careful with it or we'll both pay a price."

I nodded. "How will I return it to you?"

"It's magic. It will come back to the wizard of its own accord." Simon checked over his shoulder again, and when he deemed it was still safe to talk to me, he added, "Don't forget to drink the potion." Without another word he turned and walked back to the wagon calling, "I'm done, Master Pergis."

Almost immediately the wagon began to move. Simon only had time to pick up the empty pack, throw it into the back of the wagon, and get on himself.

I put the mirror in my satchel, but decided to put the potion someplace easier to reach. I slipped it into my pocket. Then I turned away from the castle entrance and walked toward the bell tower, because I didn't need to talk to Princess Margaret anymore. I had everything I needed to switch enchantments with the Black Knight. Now all that was left to do was to call him.

Chapter 13

The watchman rang the bell for me three times. He didn't like doing it. He warned me it was dangerous to get mixed up with dark knights, and I was likely to find myself used as dragon bait. And didn't I have a father or brother who would be angry at my doings?

But when I gave him a few coins, he put his concerns aside.

After the bell rang I went and stood in the designated spot outside the castle, along with all of the children in the vicinity. They followed me out like I was the Pied Piper.

"You can't fight the Black Knight," one little boy told me. "He won't fight ladies."

"Let's hope not," I said. "I just want to speak to him."

Another boy crinkled his eyebrows at me. "He's not a real talkative one, the Black Knight. Mostly he just knocks people off their horses. Perhaps you should choose another gentle-man to talk to."

They continued to supply me with these types of helpful

details while I scanned the countryside, waiting. The land around the castle had been cleared of trees for quite a ways in every direction—probably to make sure any attacking armies didn't have cover—but beyond the clearing, the forest grew thick and wild. I wondered how close the Black Knight had to be in order to hear the bell and how soon he would arrive.

I also wondered when I should take the potion and how long the effects lasted. I couldn't believe I hadn't asked Simon these questions. And this after the wizard had given me the speech about how magic was a downfall to those who didn't think it through.

I mulled it over and decided it would be best to take it as soon as I saw his horse in the distance. When he came close, I would ask him to take off his helmet and kiss me. Or could I just ask him to fight Tristan and lose? How much of a sway did this potion carry?

Several people climbed the towers nearest to the castle gates to see who had challenged the knight. Some people laughed outright when they saw me, others yelled that I'd brought evil on myself.

As I waited, I thought of what I would say. I tried to string together phrases that sounded ladylike, but in my nervousness the words fell away from me like so many scattered beads.

I wondered when Tristan would be done with his business at the armory. He wasn't going to be happy that I was standing out here waiting for the Black Knight, but I'd explain it to him later.

In fact, after I kissed the Black Knight I could help Tristan on his quest by kissing him and giving him the invincibility enchantment, then nothing would keep him from becoming a prince.

Oh, wait—if I kissed Tristan he wouldn't need to become a prince, I would. And since that couldn't ever happen, I'd be stuck in the Middle Ages forever.

Another thought swept through my mind. If Tristan knew that all he had to do to get home was kiss me—would he do it?

I dismissed the thought. He wouldn't leave me stranded in the Middle Ages.

But then again, he'd already been here for eight months. He was risking his life to try and make it home—the cyclops had nearly killed him twice already. Kissing me would be so easy, such a quick and painless answer to his dilemma. In fact, he'd probably think it was fitting justice for me to be stuck in the Middle Ages among the princes I admired.

I couldn't tell him about this. Not until the week had passed.

After about an hour, quite a few adults sauntered out of the castle gate and stood milling around, forming a crowd. So apparently this was about how long it took for the Black Knight to show up once he'd been called. I twisted the strap of my satchel, winding it around my finger until it hurt. I hadn't planned on kissing the knight in front of an audience of washerwomen and stable hands.

I saw Tristan strolling through the crowd. He walked over to me, looking around as though searching for someone. "What are you doing out here? I thought you were trying to visit the princess."

"I'm waiting for the Black Knight," I said.

"Yeah, I can see that. Where's the knight that challenged him?"

I squeezed the bottle of love potion until its heat pulsed through my fingers. I couldn't explain to Tristan what I was doing and I really didn't want to get into a discussion of why I shouldn't be out here. I said, "Are you done with your business already?"

"Nope, but all the armorers wanted to come out and watch the fight." His eyebrows creased as he continued to scan the area. "So who challenged him?"

I didn't answer, just looked out at the grassy plains in front of us.

"That's really odd," he said. "Someone must have rung the bell but I don't see . . ."

His stance stiffened as his sentence drifted off. "Savannah, why are so many people staring at us?"

I still didn't answer.

Tristan took hold of my arm and pulled me to face him. In a low voice he said, "Tell me you didn't ring that bell."

"Tristan, you have to understand, I'm doing this for you."

He let go of my arm as though burned. "You rang it to have *me* challenge the Black Knight?"

I stepped toward him and whispered. "No, I rang it for me. I'm going to . . . talk with him."

Tristan took hold of my arm again. "I want you to go back inside the castle gates—"

I didn't see the Black Knight arrive, I only heard the gasp from the crowd and looked to see what had caught their attention. He hadn't come out of the forest in front of us like I'd supposed. He galloped around the side of the castle wall riding a massive black warhorse. The sight of his dark, gleaming armor momentarily chased all thought from my mind. I hadn't expected him to be so big or to bear down on us so quickly.

I tried to pull my arm away from Tristan so I could uncork the bottle, but Tristan not only didn't let me go, he pulled me a couple of steps toward the castle gate.

I dug my heels into the dirt. "Tristan, stop it. You don't understand."

"You're going inside," he hissed. "Right now."

I attempted to open the bottle with one hand, pushing at the cork with my thumbnail. It was going to be nearly impossible to drink it with Tristan yanking me through the crowd.

"Stop it!" I yelled and I tried again to wrench my arm out of

Tristan's hands. He pulled back with even more strength and the bottle tumbled from my fingers. It fell to the ground with a crack, and I watched as the liquid seeped out of the broken jar onto the ground.

"No," I said. It was only a gasp though, a cry of defeat.

The Black Knight slowed his horse to a stop. I heard the *swoosh* as he pulled his sword from its sheath and held it up. It glinted in his hand like a bolt of lightning. The armor muffled his voice, but he spoke loud enough for the entire crowd to hear. "Who summoned me here to fight?"

Half the crowd pointed to me and the children yelled, "She did! She did!" with such excitement that I wondered whose side they were on.

The Black Knight turned his head in my direction. I saw his hands tighten on the reins.

The next moment Tristan stood in front of me, shielding me. "It was a mistake," he said.

The knight said nothing, just surveyed us with a faceless stare that made me shiver. Still, I broke Tristan's grasp on my arm and stepped away from him. I had to at least try. "May a lady talk to a knight?" I asked and nearly managed to keep my voice from shaking. "The Black Knight obeys the laws of chivalry, does he not?"

The knight didn't answer. His horse took two steps toward me and looked at me with piercing eyes.

"What does the lady wish from me?" the knight called, and I couldn't tell if he was mocking me or not.

Tristan stepped in front of me again. "Nothing."

I moved away from Tristan. "I want to speak with you." And then, because I also had food in my satchel, I added, "I want you to dine with me."

The knight remained silent and I thought he might turn around and leave, but instead he urged the horse forward. I heard the thud of every hoofbeat as the horse picked up speed coming toward me. The crowd spilled away but I stood there transfixed, unsure of what was happening.

Tristan pushed me sideways. I knew he was trying to keep me out of the pathway of the horse, but it didn't have the desired effect. The Black Knight veered as well. Tristan and I now stood so far apart that there was no way to stop the Black Knight when he reached down and grabbed me by the waist.

The next moment I found myself sitting sidesaddle in front of the knight. The only thing that kept me from falling off the horse at every bump and jostle was the knight's arm, which held me pinned to his chest. His armor bit into my side, but I clung to it anyway. If I slipped I'd be trampled.

We raced across the grassy plains toward the forest, and I watched the castle grow smaller with every passing minute. "Where are you taking me?" I asked.

"To dine," he said and didn't say any more.

Finally we reached the edge of the forest and the horse plunged into the foliage. It wasn't until I looked down that I saw the horse was following a narrow path. The horse slowed his pace, but I still had to lean away from tree branches so they didn't slap across my face.

I told myself that everything would be all right. He had said we were going to dine; that's what I'd asked him to do.

But another part of me, a part that was squeezing my stomach into pieces, screamed that Tristan had been right, the Black Knight was dangerous and I'd been beyond stupid to summon him. This wasn't some picture book where knights always acted honorably. I'd been kidnapped and if I had any sense at all I'd take my chances, jump from the horse, and try to escape.

"It's not much farther," the knight said, and now his voice was soft and teasing.

Minutes went by with nothing but the sound of the horse's

hooves beating against the path and branches reaching out for me. Then abruptly the wall of trees gave way to a clearing with a small river. The horse sauntered up to it and lowered its head to drink, lapping the water in noisy gulps. The knight released his grip on me. "You can dismount now."

I breathed a sigh of relief at this. He wouldn't have let me off first if he was kidnapping me, would he?

I slid from the horse and waited for him to dismount, something that was considerably slower and more complicated for him in his heavy armor. I should have felt safer once he'd reached the ground. After all, a knight in armor off his horse was slow-moving and easy to escape from. Instead, I noticed how tall and broad-shouldered he was.

He turned to his saddlebag and took out a long thin strip of material. "Choose a place to dine, m'lady," he said, sweeping a hand in front of him.

I looked around and saw only decaying leaves, dirt, and vegetation. It all seemed damp and unsuitable but I finally pointed to a flat spot.

"Very well." He walked toward me, holding the material between his hands as though he were going to use it as a gag.

I stepped away from him. "What are you doing?"

"Blindfolding you, m'lady. You didn't think I would take off my helmet and eat in your view, did you?"

"I guess not." But I still took another step backward. The ground felt rocky and uncertain beneath my feet. I hoped I wasn't about to bump into a tree.

He kept holding the material taut between his hands. "You don't trust me." It was a statement, not a question, and I could hear the amusement in his voice.

"Should I?" I asked.

"You're the one who asked to dine with me. Do we eat or not?"

My legs shook but I walked the distance that separated us and held up my face. "We eat."

He tied the strip of cloth across my eyes. As he pulled it tight and knotted it, he whispered, "Do not attempt to take off your blindfold or you'll risk losing one of your hands to my sword. My identity will stay unknown." Then he slowly led me to the spot I'd chosen. I sat down and heard metal clanking. I didn't know if he'd sat down or whether it was the sound of him taking off his armor. I couldn't be sure and wasn't curious enough to move my blindfold to see for myself.

A few minutes passed, then I felt him untying the satchel from my waist. "As you cannot see, m'lady, it shall be my pleasure to feed you." His voice was unmuffled now and had a smooth, familiar sound to it. Silky, seductive.

"If you put the food in my hand, I can feed myself."

"I wouldn't have you dirty your hands. Here is some of the cheese you brought."

I opened my mouth and he set a slice on my tongue. I couldn't tell whether he was eating too. As soon as I'd finished it, I opened my mouth to ask him a question, but he put a piece of meat in my mouth. I finished that too, wondering how I was ever going to start up a conversation if every time I opened my mouth he put food into it.

I know how to flirt; I just can't do it blindfolded and chewing.

The third time I opened my mouth, he said, "Here is something to drink," and poured a liquid into my mouth. I didn't recognize the taste. It wasn't the water I'd brought, but instead had a bitter, tinny taste. Poison? Some sort of drug? Whatever it was, I knew something had just gone terribly, dangerously wrong.

Chapter 14

I spit the liquid out on the ground and reached up to pull the blindfold off. I didn't care about trying to switch enchantments anymore. I would run away from him and make my way back to the castle.

He caught hold of my hands and held them tight. "It won't do you any good." All the softness had dropped from his voice, and now he only sounded angry. "That was truth potion I gave you. Unless you speak the truth to me your tongue will burn out of your mouth and you'll never speak lies again. Do you think I don't recognize an enchantress when I see one? Your beauty is not of this world. What sort of trickery is Prince Edmond up to?"

And Tristan thought it was a mistake for me to bring my makeup along. I said, "I appreciate the compliment, because I'm not an enchantress. And Prince Edmond didn't send me." I opened my mouth so he could see my tongue. "See, it's still there. Will you let go of my hands now?"

He loosened his grip, but not much. His voice didn't sound as angry now, but still just as suspicious. "Beautiful women are always the bait in someone's trap and I will discover who my enemies are. Who sent you then?"

I tried not to shake. I tried not to think about what he would do if he found out the truth of my intentions. "No one. It was my own idea to ring the bell."

"And your kinsmen want to know the secret of how to defeat me? They plan my destruction?"

"No."

"Your husband?"

"I'm unmarried."

"Then who was the man who tried to protect you?"

"Just a friend who's afraid you're going to hurt me." I stretched my fingers, hoping he'd let go of my hands.

He didn't.

"You're not going to hurt me, are you? Honor is all-important to a knight, right?"

He laughed softly. "You're not well acquainted with many knights, are you?"

This was not a comforting answer. My breathing was beginning to go ragged with fear.

The Black Knight's voice grew stern and suspicious again. "You don't want my destruction?"

"No." Which was the truth. I didn't want his destruction; I only wanted Tristan to beat him in jousting or some sort of contest so that King Roderick would count it as defeat and make Tristan a prince.

I could hear the impatience in the knight's voice. "Then why did you want to dine with me?"

I didn't answer. His grip tightened around my wrists and he dragged me closer to him. "Why?"

"I wanted to find out more about you."

"And?"

I took several breaths. "I wanted . . . I was hoping that . . . you would kiss me."

A moment passed with nothing but the sound of my breath, coming too fast. Then I heard him chuckle and his grip loosened. My hands weren't free, but at least they no longer throbbed. When he spoke next his voice was amused. "Ah, yes. I'd forgotten that aspect of women. They find power so inexplicably attractive." He kept hold of my wrists with one of his hands while the other stroked a path across my jawline. His voice dropped to a whisper. "I might be old and ugly, you know."

"You're not."

"No, I'm not." The next moment I felt his lips against mine, at first soft, questioning, and then he wound his fingers through my hair and pulled me closer to him. His kiss grew more intent. Whoever the Black Knight was, he'd had plenty of practice at this. There, with his lips against mine and my heart beating so hard it lost all rhythm, I began to regret what I'd done.

Who was I to take away the Black Knight's enchantment? For all I knew he was a good man—a defender of the people, a king that would rival Arthur. I had no loyalty to King Roderick or Prince Edmond. Prince Edmond was not above oppressing peasants, and I had perhaps just undone the one man who could stop him. Why hadn't this occurred to me before?

Then again, perhaps the Black Knight was every bit as dark as his name suggested. Perhaps I'd done not only Tristan but the whole kingdom a favor. I had no way of knowing. I didn't even know if my kiss had actually affected his enchantment at all. The magic might have been on his armor or his sword or something I hadn't even guessed at.

When he lifted his head away from mine I trembled,

caught between reproach and hope. Reproach being the heavier of the two.

I didn't move, even though he had moved away from me. "I think we need to talk," I said.

"Talk?"

"I need to know more about you," I said. "I need to know—"

But he cut me off with an exasperated sigh. "You have kissed the Black Knight. Now you have a tale to tell to your maidens, but you mustn't ever try to see me again. Never ring the bell for me again. Do you understand?"

Yes, I understood. He was breaking up with me after our first kiss. And okay, I'd only wanted to kiss him to try and steal his power, but he didn't know that. What was it about me that made guys immediately want to dump me?

I nodded, stung.

He still had ahold of my wrists and I felt something wind around them. I tried to move them but he held onto them tighter.

"What are you doing?" I demanded.

"Tying your hands so you can't take off your blindfold until I'm gone."

"You're going to leave me here? Blindfolded with my hands tied?"

He laughed. I wasn't sure whether that was a yes or a no. In a moment he let go of my hands but I still couldn't move them.

"You can't leave me here like this," I said. "That isn't chivalrous."

I heard him stand, heard the armor clanking again. "Hatred and love are both dangers to a man; a woman is as dangerous as the blade. Don't pine for me though, m'lady. Eventually another will take hold of your heart."

Yeah, and that other could be a wolf or a bear if he left me here defenseless. I tugged at my hands, trying to loosen the bands. Nothing happened. I put them to my mouth and bit at them. They didn't budge.

"One more thing," he called to me above the clanking of his armor. "The truth potion will only work against you when you're talking to me, but as you don't know my identity, perhaps it's best if you're always truthful when talking to men—at least the young, handsome ones."

"Can I still insult you without consequence?"

He laughed and his footsteps clunked away from me. "Insult all you like—as long as you believe it to be the truth."

Before I could think of a proper medieval insult, he whistled and then I heard the horse trot over to him.

More clanking while I twisted pointlessly at my hands. For a minute everything was quiet and I wondered if he'd gone, but then I heard his horse walking toward me and his voice came from higher up. "Stand up and I'll cut off your bindings with my sword."

I stood up but didn't hold my hands out. "Won't you cut me if you try that?"

He let out a mocking sigh. "And I thought you'd heard of my fame. Don't you know I never cut amiss?"

Or at least he didn't when he'd still had that invincibility enchantment. I didn't know if he had that anymore, which meant that if he accidentally lopped off some of my fingers, I'd at least appreciate the irony of the situation.

Oh wait—if I had the invincibility enchantment, he wouldn't be able to chop off my fingers, would he? What exactly was involved in invincibility?

I still didn't hold out my hands. "If you wouldn't mind, I'd rather have you untie them."

Something knocked against my hands and then the next moment they were free. I stretched out my fingers. The feeling came back into them with pinpricks but nothing seemed to be cut. I heard the horse trotting away from me and tugged at the blindfold until I was free of it.

I stared at my hands, which were whole, uncut. So if neither of us were enchanted, he was an excellent swordsman. I looked over to the river and saw him atop his horse, walking at a leisurely pace along the bank and away from me.

At my feet, the contents of my satchel had been dumped out. Apparently he'd been looking for something incriminating. The mirror lay next to the cheese. He must not have recognized it as a wizard's mirror but thought it belonged to me—a vain, enamored maiden who'd brought it along because I'd wanted to make sure I looked my best when I met him.

I knelt down, picked up the mirror, and held it over my hand. When I turned it over, the breath went out of my lungs. Scrolled on the face of the mirror were the words: *No weapon shall hurt you, nor any man defeat you in battle.*

I repeated the words in my mind, staring at the disappearing writing, then I shoved the mirror into my satchel.

I shouldn't have been afraid that the knight would suddenly turn around and wonder what I was up to. I was invincible now. But perhaps it wasn't fear at all; perhaps it was shame.

The sound of a horse running made me look back over at the riverbank. It wasn't the Black Knight's horse but another rider on a horse running toward him. The Black Knight drew his sword and waited. He looked like a glossy black statue.

A young man with a lean, muscular build rode up to the knight. His shoulder-length blond hair had been mussed by the ride, making his profile even more handsome. He stared at the Black Knight with such fierceness that it took me several seconds before it registered that this was Tristan. He reined in the horse with one hand, and drew his sword with the other.

"What have you done with her?" Tristan yelled. "Where is she?"

The Black Knight didn't answer, just pointed his sword in my direction. Tristan glanced at me, then looked back at the knight. He still didn't lower his sword. "Did he hurt you?" he called to me.

"What would you do if I had, little page?" The Black Knight said. "Fight me without armor? You're no knight."

I gathered my skirts and got to my feet. "He didn't hurt me."

I knew Tristan heard me, but he didn't lower his sword. He prodded his horse toward me, keeping his gaze firmly on the knight as though waiting for an attack.

The Black Knight turned to Tristan. "Don't raise your sword to me again," he said, "unless you want it cut out of your hands." The knight sheathed his sword, probably using more force than he needed, then spurred his horse forward. In another moment he had vanished into the forest.

After he left, Tristan turned his attention to me. His gaze ran over me, examining me. A good deal of the anger dropped from his face as he put his sword away. "You're really all right?"

"Yes. Unless I lie to him, then apparently my tongue will burn out of my mouth. He made me drink truth potion." I put my hand to my tongue checking to see if I could feel any difference in it. Man, by the time I was through with these wishes I was going to be the most honest person alive.

Tristan gave me an I-told-you-not-to-mess-with-the-Black-Knight look, but he didn't say it. Instead he dismounted from his horse and helped me pick up the scattered things from my satchel. He brushed off a roll and handed it to me. Back home neither one of us would have kept dirty bread, but I put it back in my satchel.

"Is truth potion a usual commodity around here?" I asked

him. "Do people just carry a vial on them in case they meet up with any suspicious women?"

Tristan shook his head. "I've heard of truth potion, but I've never known anyone who had any. It's rare and expensive—but then I guess we already knew the Black Knight had access to a wizard."

What else did I know about him? "He asked me who you were, but then he called you a page, so he must have known that much about you. How many people knew you were a page?"

Tristan handed me a couple of now cracked hard-boiled eggs. "Anyone who's been to the castle in the last few months. I'm pretty well known because of my stories."

Well, that probably wasn't a clue that would be useful.

I picked up the last of the spilled things. The Black Knight hadn't touched the spices, the money, anything I'd brought from the future. All this wealth must have been tempting, but he hadn't taken it. Which must mean that he was honest and not greedy.

I stood up and brushed off my dress, unable to clean a couple of spots of mud that had found their way to my skirt. I tried to think of more clues to the Black Knight's identity, but my mind kept dwelling on our kiss, on the electric intensity I'd felt when his lips had touched mine. I glanced at Tristan, at his concerned blue eyes. If he kissed me would it be as passionate?

I blushed as though he could read my mind and looked away from him.

Tristan walked back over to the horse. "Was the Black Knight angry when he found out you were trying to help defeat him?"

"I'm not stupid. I didn't tell him that."

"How did you get around not telling him?"

I didn't want to talk about it. I tied the satchel around my waist and joined him next to the horse. "Tristan, what do you really know about the Black Knight? I mean, you're trying to defeat him and I just helped you, but what if it isn't the right thing? What if he's not supposed to be defeated?"

Tristan's eyebrows drew together like he had no idea what I was talking about. "You helped me? I told you to stay away from the Black Knight, but no, you wouldn't listen. So he carried you off, and I've spent the last hour out looking for you, worried sick that I'd find you somewhere in tiny pieces. When I did come across you—amazingly intact—the Black Knight threatened to cut off my hands if I ever lifted a sword to him again. So exactly which part of all of that was you helping me?"

I scanned the forest to make sure we were alone, then lowered my voice to a whisper. I couldn't tell him that I'd switched enchantments with the Black Knight, but I could tell Tristan part of the truth. "I took the Black Knight's enchantment from him. He's not invincible anymore."

Tristan gave me a look of frank disbelief, so I added, "Okay, granted he may still be an excellent swordsman. In fact, he cut the ties from my hand without giving me so much as a scratch. It was amazing."

Tristan took up the horse reins. "Yes, he's an amazing swordsman. I think that fact has already been established."

He turned his back on me and led the horse toward the river. I followed after him, hurrying until I was side by side with him. "The point is, he's not *invincible* anymore. You could beat him at something."

"Like a friendly game of poker, perhaps?"

"I'm being serious."

Tristan finally stopped and gave me his complete attention. "And just how did you take his enchantment away from him?"

I didn't answer. I couldn't.

"Not even the royal court, which has access to wizards, could break the Black Knight's enchantment. How could you do it?"

"The royal court may have access to wizards, but they aren't using them. I met a wizard coming out of the castle and he helped me do it."

Tristan tugged at the horse's reins and walked the rest of the distance to the river. The horse took a couple of steps into the water and lowered his head to drink. Tristan no longer seemed concerned with my story. In fact, he only seemed to be asking me questions to prove what an idiot I was. "And why would a wizard help you?"

"I paid him well enough. I gave him matches, some silverware, and a bottle of Tylenol."

Tristan's head swung around to face me. "You gave him all of that?"

"It was worth it. I mean, it was worth it if the Black Knight is really a villain—which suddenly I'm not sure about." I walked to Tristan with my hands held out. "What if he was supposed to be some sort of great hero like King Arthur or Hercules and I just betrayed him?"

Tristan shrugged, seeming more amused than worried. "Then I guess it would be doubly ironic, wouldn't it?"

When he saw I didn't know what he was talking about he added, "Hercules and King Arthur were both betrayed by women."

Hearing this felt like a bad omen. "They were?"

"Didn't you ever pay attention in school?"

"Okay, that's not the point. The point is I don't know if I've done a good thing or a horrible one."

Tristan folded his arms. "I doubt you've done anything but lost a few things and caused us both trouble. Enchantments are very hard to break, you know."

"I didn't break it, I took it." I remembered the mirror and opened up my satchel. "Here—I can prove it." I sifted through the contents. "The wizard's assistant let me take his magic mirror for the week. When you put it over your hand, it tells you what enchantments you carry." I kept sifting through the satchel but didn't find the mirror. I looked through the contents again, feeling Tristan's disbelieving gaze on me as I did. Finally I took items out, handing a few of them to Tristan. I knew I had put the mirror in the satchel, and yet even after I'd pulled almost everything out, I didn't find it.

"It isn't here," I said, my voice tinged with outrage. "He said I could have it for a week and now it's disappeared."

Tristan put the items he held back into the satchel. "Savannah, have you ever gone to a big city and seen the guys on the street corners selling Rolex watches for twenty dollars? Or the sleazy-looking guys who say they can get you a cut-rate deal on designer purses?"

"It was real magic."

"I'm sure it was. It was a mirror that told you whatever you wanted to hear and then disappeared along with a good chunk of your wealth. You can buy that sort of magic from a lot of wizards, so from now on let me do the bargaining, okay?"

The horse finished drinking and walked back over to Tristan, flicking its ears. Tristan patted his neck. "You ready to go, boy?"

I shoved the rest of the things back into the satchel, biting back my disappointment. I didn't want Tristan to be right, but suddenly I wondered if he was. Thus far my dealings with magic—fairies and leprechauns—had been less than successful. Perhaps wizards were the same.

The apprentice had told me I'd have the mirror for a week and it had disappeared in just hours. If he hadn't told the truth about that, what else had been lies?

I should have felt relieved at the idea that the Black Knight's future wasn't my responsibility, but I just felt cheated, unsure of myself, and small.

Tristan helped me up on the horse and then got up in front of me. I put my arms around him in order to hang on. It felt oddly intimate but at the same time comforting. When I'd ridden with the Black Knight I'd felt nothing but armor, heard nothing but my own frightened breaths. Now I could feel the warmth coming through Tristan's tattered wool tunic. It smelled of smoke, dirt, and sweat, but mostly smoke. With only fire for warmth, most people smelled of smoke. It was the pervading smell of the Middle Ages.

It suddenly struck me that the Black Knight hadn't smelled like smoke, or dirt, or anything.

I thought of this as the horse plodded along. I listened to Tristan breathing in a rhythm that almost matched the horse's hoofbeats and had to fight the impulse to lean forward and rest my head against his back.

What was wrong with me? How could I kiss one guy so passionately I started to have feelings for him and then only minutes later be fighting the desire to lean my head against another guy's back? And all of this when I still had feelings for Hunter.

Hunter. I thought of his name, pictured his face, and waited for emotion to clench around my heart. Only it didn't. Everything about Hunter seemed so far away, like someone I'd only dreamed about once. The modern world was beginning to fade away and everything here—the smell of grass and horse and smoke, the way the sun warmed the top of my head, the smudges of dirt on Tristan's hands—all of this felt much more real. It was hard to concentrate on Hunter and I found I simply didn't want to.

I wanted to lean into Tristan. I wanted him to put an arm

around me and say I didn't have to worry because everything would work out all right. I wanted him to tell me, like he had back in the inn, that I was smart. I wasn't sure he thought so anymore, though.

This thought, oddly enough, made my heart clench.

Chapter 15

Without saying much of anything to each other, Tristan and I rode back to the castle. After we entered the courtyard, several people came out to stare at me and to congratulate Tristan on rescuing me. They seemed genuinely impressed that Tristan was in one piece and I wasn't weeping.

They insisted that we stay for dinner at the castle so we could tell the tale of our escape. Tristan accepted, even though I was already shaking my head no. He twisted his head around to face me. "The horse needs to rest so we might as well stay. Don't worry, I'll tell the story."

He dismounted, ignoring my protests. "You'll never eat a better meal than at the king's table. It's an honor to be asked."

After I dismounted, he took the horse's reins in one hand, my arm in the other, and walked toward the stable. "Besides, I still need to finish up with the armory and you're coming with me this time. I'm not letting you out of my sight again."

I walked beside him feeling like an errant child. "I wasn't planning on trying to contact the Black Knight again."

"Good," he said with false cheerfulness. "I'm glad it only takes you one abduction to figure out who your enemies are."

I didn't argue the point. Instead I said, "I can't tell everyone at dinner what happened between the Black Knight and me. I can't let people know I tried to steal his enchantment. He'll find out and be angry about it."

Tristan only shrugged. "Well, I wasn't planning on telling the truth. There's not much of a good story to that, is there?"

"Then just leave me out of it all together."

He smirked at me, enjoying my discomfort. "That would be hard to do since you are the main point of the story, but don't worry, you can get up afterward and give a rebuttal. Tell them all how you saved me."

"I can't lie—," I started, but then realized if the enchantments had actually switched, I could.

Tristan shrugged again. "Everyone gives their own glorious account of their deeds at the king's table. This is like the TV of the Middle Ages. They don't care about it being true as much as they care about it being exciting—" Tristan looked at me, understanding filling his eyes. "Oh, you mean in case the Black Knight is there. Good point. For all we know he's one of the men in King Roderick's court."

I stopped walking and Tristan turned to see why. The horse swished his head impatiently but I couldn't take another step. I let out a nervous breath. "The sky is purple."

Tristan's gaze shot upward. He looked from one end of the sky to the other. "No, it's not."

I didn't feel anything. I touched my tongue. "Nothing happened."

Tristan tilted his head, examining me. "Savannah, you know *I'm* not the Black Knight. You saw us together."

I nearly told Tristan about my lying-equals-toads-and-other-gross-things-in-my-mouth enchantment, but stopped myself. That was as good as telling him I'd switched enchantments with the Black Knight and if he knew that, he might be able to learn how I'd done the rest. I couldn't let him know that if he kissed me he could go home.

"Right . . . ," I said, "I know you're not the Black Knight. I was just . . . well . . ." The horse had decided to find something to eat and he nuzzled my satchel. I pushed his head away. People were milling all around the courtyard so I stepped close to Tristan. On my tiptoes, I put my lips to his ear and whispered, "I did take the Black Knight's enchantment. He's not invincible. I am."

Tristan whispered back to me, but I could tell he was just humoring me. "Because the sky is purple?"

"If you don't believe me, I'll prove it to you."

Tristan folded his arms and regarded me with amused interest. "Okay."

"Try to hit me."

He rolled his eyes and pulled the horse forward toward the stables. "As tempting as that offer is, no."

I followed after him. "Why not? It won't hurt me, you'll see."

"Call me old-fashioned. I don't hit girls."

"I'm asking you to."

He shook his head and laughed. "You know, after what you've put me through during the last eight months, you really shouldn't push your luck."

Which was when I knew I was right not to tell him anything about switching enchantments.

· · ·

Our trip to the armory was noisy, boring, and cost most of the things I'd brought with me. I sat on a hard wooden bench by the door while Tristan stood, arms out like a scarecrow, having his measurements taken. The armorer walked around Tristan holding up a piece of string to different parts of his body, and then yelling out numbers to his assistant. In between the numbers, the armorer kept throwing out little compliments like, "You're nicely tall, just as a well-bred lad should be."

I fluttered my eyelashes at Tristan and mouthed the words "well bred." He rolled his eyes, then pretended he didn't see me.

When he'd finally finished with his measurements, we walked slowly across the castle grounds. Tristan didn't take my arm like he had before, and I found that I missed it. The space between us seemed too large somehow. My hands swung awkwardly at my sides.

They hadn't rung the bell for dinner yet but it wouldn't be long. The sun wasn't too far away from setting. "So what should we do until dinner, Monsieur Well Bred?"

He cast me the barest of glances. "You are *so* twenty-first century."

"And that's a good thing."

He didn't answer, which made me think he'd meant to insult me. I tilted my chin down. "Do you like that whole property-rights view of women? We should keep in our place and all that?"

"I didn't say that."

"What then? You think the peasant look is hot? After all, on their diet of porridge, they're naturally as skinny as supermodels."

He slid me an exasperated glance. "See, that is exactly what I mean. I never realized how sarcastic modern girls were until I came here. No one back home even tries to be ladylike or demure."

"I might if I knew what *demure* meant."

"No, you wouldn't."

How could I argue about it when I didn't know what the word meant? This is why it totally sucks to argue with smart people. You'd think after all my years of living with Jane I would have picked up a huge vocabulary, but no. I took several steps, prickled by this fact, and planned to come up with a really good comeback just as soon as I got hold of a dictionary.

Tristan headed to the orchards, and the noise of the castle yard slowly faded behind us as we walked through the trees. Layers of fallen white blossoms covered the ground so that they almost looked like snow.

I could have changed the subject. The setting was so relaxing that I didn't want to argue, but still, as we strolled among the trees I said, "Modern girls have their own benefits. We may be sarcastic but we're clean."

A smile picked up the corner of his lips. "Modern girls don't come with dowries."

I put my hand out, brushing my fingers against low-hanging branches that we passed. "Maybe, but modern girls have access to supermarkets for cooking. Besides, what are your chances of getting a girl with a decent dowry?"

Our conversation died because Princess Margaret and another young woman, probably a lady-in-waiting, came through the trees on the path heading toward us. The princess wore a different dress than I'd seen her in when I was Cinderella, but her elegant looks and her arrogance were still the same.

In the moment before she saw us, the princess's face flashed with anger. She looked at the woman walking beside her, but her voice, low and piercing, carried down the lane to us. "He can send all the gifts he likes, it is not his place to make me wait. I shan't wear it if he thinks so ill of me that he asks for a meeting and then doesn't come." She pulled a ring off her finger, gripped it in her palm, then looked up and saw us. Her eyes flew open in surprise and it took her several steps to compose her expression back into a hard mask of self-importance.

Tristan was right. I *was* too twenty-first century. I didn't even think about bowing until I saw Tristan do it. Then I gave a hurried curtsy and waited for her and her lady to pass by us.

But Princess Margaret didn't. She sashayed up to Tristan, her skirts swishing about her ankles. A smile slid across her lips. "Ahh, it's one of my would-be suitors."

She still held the ring tightly in one fist, but she put her other hand out in front of her. Tristan took her hand in his own, brought it to his lips, and murmured, "Your highness."

My mouth dropped open and I stared at them. Would-be suitor? Exactly what did she mean by that? Since when did a storytelling page court a princess? I didn't ask, which probably didn't matter since neither of them took any notice of me.

While the lady's maid eyed me suspiciously, Princess Margaret leaned closer to Tristan. "I hear you challenged the Black Knight and lived to tell of it."

He let go of her hand with a nod. "It shall be my pleasure to share the adventure with all of your father's household at dinner." As though just remembering me, he turned his hand in my direction. "May I present Lady Savannah to you? She came from my land to bring me the funds to buy armor and weapons."

Princess Margaret's gaze shifted to me like a cold breeze and she held out her hand to me. "How nice of you to come."

I couldn't kiss her. In fairy stories princes and princesses were the most frequent recipients of enchantments. If Princess Margaret was about to prick her finger on a spinning wheel and sleep for a hundred years, I did not want to volunteer to do it for her. But I couldn't explain my refusal without insult. I stared at her openmouthed, then shut my eyes, swooned, and hoped Tristan would catch me.

He didn't.

My head hit the ground with a thud that sent sparks through my darkened eyes. I wanted to cry out. Instead I lay motionless at everyone's feet.

The rustle of skirts came toward me. With more annoyance than concern in her voice, the lady-in-waiting said, "She's fainted."

I heard Tristan drop to his knees beside me. "Savannah?"

I didn't move.

He put his hand underneath my head and shook my shoulders in an attempt to wake me.

I let my eyelids flutter open.

Tristan's clear blue eyes searched my face, worry etched into his expression. "Are you all right?"

I nodded.

Princess Margaret took several steps so she could look directly down at me. "I've had peasants faint when meeting me, but never a noblewoman." A calculating smile cut across her face. "Are you sure you're not a peasant?"

A chill crept down my spine. Did she recognize me?

She let her gaze run over me, taking in my outfit, face, and hair. As though still talking to Tristan and with a large dose of disdain, she added, "Such a pretty maiden."

I sat up, acted as though I was too weak to stand, and lay back against Tristan's chest. "Perhaps I should lie down somewhere instead of trying to make it to dinner."

The worry left Tristan's voice, replaced by skepticism. "You want to miss dinner?"

If it meant kissing a bunch of people's hands, yes. "I don't think I'm up to it."

Into my ear Tristan whispered, "Would you be willing to swear to that in front of the Black Knight?"

I stiffened, but didn't answer. It was aggravating how easily he could see through me. "Is there somewhere in the castle that I could lay down?"

Princess Margaret turned to her lady-in-waiting. "Theodora, take our guest to my room and see that she's brought some broth and bread for dinner." A measure of smugness crept into her voice as though she enjoyed depriving me of real food. "I fear anything stronger would upset her stomach."

Tristan stood up, then held out his hand to help me to my feet. I didn't let go of his hand, even after I stood. "Perhaps we'd better just head back home."

"I'm sure you'll be fine," he said. "I'll check on you after dinner."

Lady Theodora had already curtsied a good-bye to Princess Margaret and was motioning me to follow her, but I hesitated. "You won't stay long?"

He let out a chuckle that told me I should know better. "The king's dinners can go on for a while."

Which meant there was no hope of leaving tonight. I dropped his hand from mine with a frustrated sigh.

Princess Margaret absentmindedly slipped the ring she'd been clutching back onto her finger, her anger at its bestower apparently forgotten. She held out her arm to Tristan. "That leaves you to escort me to dinner. I trust it isn't an imposition."

Without another look in my direction he took Princess Margaret's arm. "It would be a delight."

I would have felt snubbed by all of this, but I was too surprised to allow for any lesser emotions. I'd gotten a glimpse of Princess Margaret's ring as she held out her arm to Tristan. Three golden hibiscus flowers. It was the ring I'd given Simon.

Chapter 16

Lady Theodora walked briskly through the castle hallways. I followed after her several steps behind. I didn't care that she wasn't speaking to me or even pretending to be hospitable. My mind was back on the ring and how it had gotten from Simon to Princess Margaret's finger. Was that who she had been planning to meet? And if so, why? On the other hand, the wizard and his apprentice both sold their wares. It was possible someone had purchased the ring from Simon and given it to Princess Margaret.

I also thought of Princess Margaret's proclamation that Tristan was a would-be suitor and the way she'd taken hold of his arm with the self-satisfaction of a cat settling down on a favorite windowsill.

Lady Theodora reached the doorway of a tower. I could see the beginnings of a circular set of stairs. She turned to me with impatience and said, "This way, m'lady," then disappeared through the doorway without waiting to see if I followed.

I went after her, holding up my skirt with one hand and keeping the other on the rough stone wall. The stairs twisted upward, one steep and rugged stone after another. I didn't dare climb them as fast as Theodora. No banister curved along the wall and if I made one misstep, I'd tumble down the whole thing.

I heard another set of footsteps echoing down the stairs and then an angry voice. "Is my sister with you? I've been looking all over for her and that—"

"Your majesty," Theodora cut him off. "I'm taking a guest to Princess Margaret's room. The former page, Tristan, is escorting your sister to dinner." Her voice had an edge of contempt when she said Tristan's name. "He'll be telling of his adventure with the Black Knight tonight at dinner."

"Will he?" the prince said dryly. His voice sounded familiar but I couldn't tell whether it was the elder brother, Edmond, or his younger brother, Hugh.

The next moment I rounded the corner and caught up with the two. Prince Hugh looked down at me from several steps above. He seemed unchanged from the time I'd seen him eight months ago. The wavy brown hair, square jaw, confident stance. Your basic Prince Charming.

He gazed at me, one eyebrow slightly lifted as he took me in. "And you are?"

"Tired of climbing stairs." I leaned against the wall, ready to slump into a faint again if he held out his hand for me to kiss. I threw in a curtsy as an afterthought.

Theodora pointed a reluctant hand in my direction. "This is Lady Savannah. She came from Tristan's land to bring him funds for his quest."

The prince momentarily twisted his lips and a flash of disapproval crossed his face. "Is that so?"

I curtsied again even though I probably wasn't supposed to. "Yes, sire."

"You are his sister? His betrothed?"

"No, sire, just a friend."

"Certainly you must be more than that to travel such a long distance to bring him funds."

"No, sire."

"Then you are a very good friend indeed."

I blushed. No one would consider me a good friend if they knew I was the one who got Tristan sent here in the first place. "I'm trying to be," I said.

His gaze grew intense, his voice a little stiff. "And you are hoping that your friend will be able to defeat the Black Knight?"

The question stabbed me with remorse. I wasn't sure anymore, but whether it was Tristan who defeated him or the castle guard who dragged him inside for Edmond to kill, I would be the cause of the Black Knight's downfall. I swallowed hard, my gaze on the stairs.

"You don't have an answer?" Prince Hugh asked, and I blushed again. It was his brother who was being challenged, his family that was in danger. He wasn't likely to understand my sympathies or feelings of regret.

My gaze flickered over to his eyes. "I just want Tristan to come home safe and sound."

Prince Hugh let out a half-laugh and tilted his head. "Then I suppose you wish for your friend's defeat."

"Why do you say that?" I asked.

Prince Hugh shrugged as if it was obvious. "If Tristan is able to do all that my father asks, he'll win my sister's hand in marriage and live here in the castle."

My heartbeat stopped altogether. Tristan was trying to wed Princess Margaret?

With a growing sickness in my stomach, I chided myself for not figuring it out beforehand. What had I expected? That after Tristan had destroyed the cyclops, killed the dragon, and beaten the Black Knight, King Roderick would just hand over part of his kingdom for Tristan to rule? Tristan was going to be made a prince by marrying a princess. That's how all the fairy tales worked.

Prince Hugh's gaze turned concerned and he took a step toward me. "Are you well?"

"She's feeling ill," Theodora said. "That's why she's going to Princess Margaret's room to lie down."

"See to it before she topples down the stairs."

The prince pressed himself against the wall in order to let us pass, but I didn't move. I just stared at him. All of this was so that Tristan could marry Princess Margaret? I was helping Tristan to become Prince Edmond's brother-in-law? Ironic, since if I'd married Prince Edmond, I would have been his sister-in-law.

Prince Hugh took hold of my arm and half-pulled, half-led me the rest of the way up the stairs to the princess's room. He told me that he wished for my speedy recovery, but I hardly heard anything he said.

• • •

Princess Margaret's room was on the top floor of the tower. A tapestry depicting unicorns lay against one wall, a fireplace stood at the other. That's how you know you're royalty. You have your own fireplace in your room.

Her bed had an ornately carved frame, and linen hangings were tied back to the bedposts. Two less glamorous beds— pallets, they called them, lay in the room; I supposed for her attendants.

I laid down on one of the pallets while Lady Theodora busied herself with starting a fire. I didn't want to talk to Theodora about Tristan. I already knew her opinion of him, but as the fire began to catch hold of the larger logs in the fireplace, I asked, "Are Tristan and Princess Margaret . . . fond of each other?"

Lady Theodora turned to me with indifferent eyes. "It's not my place to talk about the princess." She stood up and brushed off her skirt. "I'll ask one of the kitchen girls to bring up bread and broth for you presently."

She swept out of the room and I was left to sit on the cold pallet and watch the light from the windows grow dimmer and dimmer until all I could see out of them were the pinpricks of stars. Eventually a young servant girl brought me a small loaf of bread and a bowl of broth. Both cold. I thanked her anyway and ate it. I'd had worse in the Middle Ages.

I didn't expect to fall asleep, but I did. I dreamed that, along with the entire high school, I was at Tristan's and Princess Margaret's wedding. They walked down the aisle and everyone clapped and threw rice while I stood there trying to catch his attention. I wanted to talk to him desperately, I wanted to tell him not to do it, but he never looked at me.

Then the Black Knight was behind me. I couldn't see him but I recognized his voice, smooth and silky, whispering into my ear, "It's all right." His hand ran down the length of my arm. "I'm the one you really came to the Middle Ages to find."

His fingers intertwined with mine and he held my hand tightly. "I'm what you've wanted all along."

I leaned against him, happy that he was there and that he wanted to hold my hand. I knew I could turn and see his face, learn his identity, but instead I just stared after Tristan and wondered why he wouldn't look at me.

I was awakened by the sound of the door scraping open. I blinked in the darkness, for a moment not remembering where I was.

Then I sat bolt upright, half expecting to see the Black Knight, but Tristan walked in the room, holding a torch. The shadows flickered across his face, making him look handsome one moment, sinister the next. "Are you awake?" he asked.

A chill had taken hold of the room. The fire had almost gone completely out. I pulled the blanket around my shoulders. "Yes."

After he attached the torch to a wall holder—where it did little to dismiss the darkness—he walked to the fireplace, threw a log on the embers, and nudged it with a poker until it crackled to life. Then he sat down on the pallet beside me and pulled something from his pocket. "Since you chickened out and hid in here instead of telling your side of the Black Knight story, I brought you some dinner."

He held out something to me, some sort of pastry, but I couldn't tell what it was. I thanked him and bit into it anyway. A meat pie. It tasted savory and rich and I kept it on my tongue just to enjoy the taste of it.

Tristan leaned back on his hands. "In case you're wondering how the story of Lady Savannah's rescue went, I found you in the forest by following your cries. You were horribly frightened— pathetic, really—and getting ready to flee for your life. The Black Knight and I raised swords, circling one another and yelling threats, but we didn't fight because you begged me not to duel while I didn't have armor on."

He tilted his chin down and smiled. "That, of course, took all of your maidenly persuasion because I am so immensely brave. But I gave you my word and now I fear I can never sword fight with the Black Knight lest I break my promise to you. When the time comes to challenge him, I will have to find some other method of defeating him. Which works out well for me, since I never wanted to cross swords with him in the first place."

I popped the last of the meat pie into my mouth and didn't say anything.

"The Black Knight, awed by my bravery, ran off. Then you clung to me all the way home, sobbing with gratitude and promising never to speak to knavish rogues again. It was beautiful. The crowd loved it."

I still didn't say anything, just gave him a considering stare. Behind us, the fire grew in strength and spit out sparks onto the mantle.

"What?" he asked.

"Oh, nothing. I was just thinking about how awkward it will be to go to prom with you, considering you'll be married at the time."

"Ah," he said. "Lady Theodora told you about the details of the king's reward for his quest."

I brushed the crumbs off my hands and kept my voice even. "What exactly were you planning on doing with your wife during our date?"

"I was planning that as soon as Princess Margaret and I married, I would be zapped back to the future and she could get an annulment."

I watched the way the light from the fire made Tristan's features glow and tried not to imagine Princess Margaret standing beside him in a wedding dress. "I should warn you that my fairy godmother is slow about getting back to people. So you could be married for weeks before she gets around to bringing you home."

Tristan sent me a rakish smile and shrugged. "Then I guess I'll have time to enjoy all of the wedding feasting."

Which irked me in ways I couldn't explain. "Are you saying you *want* to marry Princess Margaret?"

He looked upward as though contemplating it. "Well, she is

royalty . . . and you were just telling me how a crown makes a person totally hot and prom worthy."

"I never said that."

He leaned closer to me. "You might as well have. You thought it. That's why I'm here—because no one but a prince was good enough to take you out."

I stood up and walked away from him, glad that in the low light he couldn't see my face flush. "Fine, go ahead and marry her then. She's a conceited shrew but I'm sure you'll be very happy with her."

He shrugged, still relaxed. "Maybe not, but I'll be happy to see you bowing every time I go by."

"You won't have the chance because I won't come near you after you're married."

Tristan stood, walked to the door, and took the torch from the wall. "Oh, I know we'll see each other again, because we still have a prom date set up."

He left the room, taking a good portion of the light with him.

Princess Margaret and Lady Theodora came into the room about a half hour later. Even though I was still completely dressed, I pretended to be asleep so I wouldn't have to talk to them. I didn't sleep though. Not until long after the two of them were softly snoring in their respective corners of the room.

I lay there with my eyes pressed together tightly. I'd come back to the Middle Ages—back to a place that I hated—to help Tristan, but somehow that didn't matter to him. He was never going to forgive me for sending him here in the first place.

What's more, now that I had time to think about it—replaying it in my mind, perhaps more than was necessary—I was convinced that if I had turned around and looked at the Black Knight in my dream, I would have somehow found out his identity. But I hadn't turned around because I'd been so busy staring at Tristan, trying to tell him not to marry that horrible, awful woman.

He wouldn't mind the feasting. I bet. Men.

I tried to erase thoughts of Tristan. I thought of my dream again and wondered if the Black Knight's words were true. Was he what I'd been looking for all along?

Chapter 17

In the morning, before I'd even gotten off the pallet, Princess Margaret was up, dressed, and shaking her head at me. "I need not ask how you fare this morning. Your face is sickly and gaunt."

"I'm sure I'll be up to traveling."

She sent me a condescending smile. "Nay, you must rest this day. I insist."

I opened my mouth to argue, then shut it again. I'd already learned from my stint as Cinderella that when someone of greater rank gave you an order, you didn't have a choice. So I was stuck here for the time being even though I was pretty sure Princess Margaret was only declaring me sick in order to torment me.

Had she known I was faking it at first—perhaps Tristan even told her as much—and so now she thought this was fitting punishment? Or maybe she had feelings for Tristan and didn't like that I'd suddenly shown up and taken his attention away from her. Or maybe she just hated me because I was pretty.

"Will you tell Tristan I'd like to talk with him?"

She paused before leaving the room and smiled at me. "Of course."

Hours went by and he didn't come. I wasn't sure if this was because he was angry about the things we'd said last night or because Princess Margaret just hadn't told him I'd asked in the first place. I would have gone to try and find him, but Princess Margaret had left Lady Theodora to tend to my needs, and she seemed to think I shouldn't venture far out of bed at all.

She sat on a bench in the corner somehow transforming a formless pile of wool into thread, then spinning it around a wooden spool. Her fingers rubbed together, twisting and stretching the fibers, and never seemed to tire.

At midday a servant brought Lady Theodora a spread of meats and bread. I got more cold broth.

After I finished eating, I looked out the window several times in hopes that I would see Tristan somewhere down in the courtyard. Where was he? Even if Princess Margaret hadn't told him that I wanted to talk to him, you'd think he would have at least stopped by to see me.

On my third window check, Lady Theodora told me the draft would make me worse, and if I didn't stay in bed she would be required to call the physician to attend to me. So I went back to the pallet and pretended to sleep. I didn't want anyone coming near me with leeches, or worse yet, knives that had never been disinfected.

Finally the door opened, but it wasn't Tristan. Princess Margaret breezed back in to change clothes as her gown had grown too hot. She completely ignored me, but spoke with Theodora about a Sir William of Burglen. He'd sent word he was coming to the king's celebration early in order to challenge the Black Knight. He hoped that Princess Margaret would give him a token of hers to take with him into battle.

Theodora thought this was "exceedingly romantic," whereas Princess Margaret declared he was a hairy red bear and she would have nothing to do with him. "The Black Knight will give him tokens enough of his battle—bruises and scars, if he lives at all."

Her words sent shivers through me. I'd been so busy dwelling on my kiss with the Black Knight, I'd forgotten he was dangerous. Perhaps he was as brutal as Princess Margaret just suggested, and he had me in a bad situation. If I said the wrong thing at the wrong time, my tongue would burn out of my mouth. I shuddered as I thought about how that would feel.

Theodora rebraided Princess Margaret's hair, and I hoped she would say more about the Black Knight, but instead they went on to discussing Sir William's purse. Apparently, instead of betting any of his own wealth, he planned to slay the ogre first, and had asked King Roderick to give him a reward for such since he already held the title of knight.

He'd killed a different ogre in his own land and so felt confident he could dispatch this one as well.

I wondered if Tristan knew about this. And then a worse thought hit me—if he did, then he wouldn't have stayed here at the castle waiting for me to get better from my faked illness. He would have left as soon as possible to go try and kill the cyclops before Sir William arrived.

He wasn't going to come check on me at all—he was already gone.

Perhaps because they thought I would sleep for a while, or perhaps because Princess Margaret had found something more important for Theodora to do besides guard me, they left the room together.

I waited for a few minutes to give them time to reach wherever it was they were headed, then I slipped out of the room and went down the stairs myself. I barely cared that there wasn't a banister to hang on to now. I just needed to get away as quickly as possible.

I'd go out to the stables and ask them to get my horse ready, then ride back to the inn. Princess Margaret would be upset, no doubt, that I'd left without her permission, but hopefully she had enough people here at the castle to torment that she wouldn't think it was worth her while to find me.

Once I reached the main floor, I looked cautiously around. No sight of the princess or Theodora. I made my way toward the main doors. I walked by washerwomen with baskets of linens and a boy lugging buckets of water in each hand. Then, thankfully, happily, I was outside.

I paused before heading to the stables. Not far from the castle door was the wizard's wagon, and a man in maroon robes bent over the wares inside of it.

The wizard would know about truth potion. Perhaps he could sell me a cure, or wait—had that enchantment been switched to the Black Knight when he kissed me? Hopefully the wizard could tell me.

As I walked up to him, I said, "Pardon me, sir—"

The man turned around and I stopped short. It wasn't the wizard and it wasn't Simon either. A freckle-faced boy who couldn't have been more than fourteen faced me.

"Oh," I said, and then, "I thought you were the wizard."

"Not yet," he said with a nod. "I just was advanced from assistant to apprentice. The wizard is inside showing Prince Edmond his wares."

A goat that was tethered to the side of the wagon bleated and walked toward me. The rope around its neck had tangled around the bottom of the wagon wheel, and it bleated another noisy protest.

I suddenly wondered if this was a different wizard's wagon

altogether. Maybe they all had similar-looking wagons, like police departments had similar cars. I couldn't remember his name. "Was he here two days ago?" I asked.

"Aye, but he only talked to Prince Hugh then. Prince Edmond thought his brother dismissed my master too speedily, though, and called him back. A good thing too. Master Pergis was getting ready to pack up and leave the region altogether."

Pergis—then it was the same wizard. The goat pulled on the rope again. He gained a couple of steps, but bumped into the apprentice in the process. The boy absentmindedly pushed the goat away and returned his attention to me. "If you haven't got business with my master, I don't suggest you be about when he comes out. He's in a powerful foul mood." The boy's voice dropped to a whisper. "He sold his only switching potion and now is wishing he could offer it to the prince."

"Oh." It didn't seem like a good idea to volunteer the information that I'd been the one who'd bought it. Still, I wanted to find out about truth potion and I didn't know how else to do it. "Switching potion," I said, as though I found it an interesting subject. "When a person uses switching potion, do all of their enchantments switch or just one?"

"All of their magical enchantments." The boy tilted his head as though unsure why I was asking. "But as I said, the master has no more of it."

"Magical enchantments?" I asked. "Is there any other kind?"

The goat tried to butt the apprentice out of the way. The boy pushed him back angrily, and yelled, "Stop it!" Then he turned back to me. "Aye, there's all kinds of enchantments." As though reciting a lesson he rattled off: "There's the enchantment of wishing stars, and ancient wells, of droughts and potions, of a mother's love—"

"Potions?" I asked. "What about truth potion? Would that switch?"

He shook his head. "Truth potion changes a person's tongue. The only way to change it back is to take the antidote—blood of a politician."

I put my hand to my chest. "Blood?"

He laughed at my expression, clearly pleased to be the expert. "Only a few drops, and it's not like we have to kill them for it. They sell it quick enough. The problem is it won't keep longer than a day or two. It's something Master Pergis would have to make special for you." He cast a glance toward the castle doors. "I'm not sure how much longer he'll be, but if you want to wait, that's fine by me."

The goat pulled on the rope. His hoofed feet pushed at the ground, straining, but all he managed to do was knock into the boy again as he tried to get past him. The boy shoved the goat away. "Let off, Simon, or I'll give you to the next kitchen boy that passes by."

"Simon?" I repeated, and gave the goat my full attention. "Wasn't that the name of the wizard's last apprentice?"

The boy looked around, saw we were alone, and said, "Aye, he's one and the same. Master Pergis found out that Simon had been helping himself to his wares and changed him into a goat."

Simon bleated loudly and bared his teeth at the boy.

"Oh, all right," the boy grumbled. "I'll untangle the wretched rope. Even as a goat you think you can order me around." He bent down by the wagon wheel and took hold where it had knotted. "It was stupid, really," the boy said, and I wasn't sure whether he was talking to me or Simon. "The master wouldn't have noticed if some of the potions weren't quite filled to where they'd been before, but Simon took an entire bottle of poison. The whole thing." The rope was almost untangled and the goat took a few more bleating steps toward me.

I looked at him with horror. Could this animal really have once been the person I talked to yesterday? I couldn't detect any traces of a man in its narrow, fur-covered face or bulging eyes. Was the apprentice just teasing me?

The boy still worked on the rope, his hands loosening the tangle. "Even then, the master might not have noticed one missing bottle, but Simon should have known better than to pinch his divining mirror."

I took a sharp breath. It was my fault then. I'd insisted that Simon give me the mirror—but what about the poison? He hadn't given me that. It had been some sort of love potion.

Then I remembered what the wizard had said when I'd first approached him. He'd told me he was out of love potion.

So what had Simon given me?

I took a step back, my heart beating hard. Why would Simon want to poison me, a virtual stranger? It didn't make sense. He must have accidentally given me the wrong bottle.

The rope came free from the wagon wheel and the goat lunged toward me. I only stayed out of his reach by stumbling backward. He strained toward me, bleating, then stuck his tongue out trying to lick me.

I took another step back while the apprentice laughed. "Well, look at that. Simon seems to have taken a fancy to you."

Suddenly I understood why. Simon knew if he licked me we would switch enchantments. I'd become a goat and he would be free.

I didn't bother to say good-bye to the apprentice. I turned and ran from the wagon, the goat's bleats still ringing in my ears. My feet slipped on the uneven slope of the land but I didn't slow my pace.

What if Simon got loose? How fast could goats run? I sprinted the rest of the way to the stables.

I reached the doorway and leaned against the inside of it,

gulping in air even though it smelled of manure. The stable boy approached me tentatively. "M'lady?"

I peered around the door. Nothing was pursuing me, at least not yet. "Will you get my horse ready? I need to leave at once."

His eyebrows drew together and he gazed past me to see what I'd been looking at. When he didn't see anything out of the ordinary his attention returned to me. "Will Tristan be leaving too?"

So he hadn't left yet. Still, I didn't have time to look for him.

"Not right now, but after I'm gone, I'd like you to find Tristan and tell him I left. I'll wait for him at the place where we first met. Can you remember that?"

He nodded.

"Hurry with my horse and Tristan will double whatever money he usually gives you."

The boy's eyes lit up at that, and he gave me a quick bow. "Yes, m'lady." He left me in the doorway while he fetched the bridle and took it to my horse's stall.

I moved farther inside the stable. I was hidden to the outside, but certainly Simon and the new apprentice had seen where I'd gone.

The stable boy led my horse out of the stall, put a blanket on his back, then heaved the saddle on top of it. In my mind the words "hurry, hurry, hurry" tumbled over each other.

He adjusted the saddle, then worked on tightening the straps. Honestly, horses took longer to get ready than teenage girls.

If Simon managed to escape from his rope, he'd dash into the stable looking for me. How could I fend off an animal who only needed to lick me in order to transform me into a goat?

I grabbed a riding stick off the wall, held it out in front of me like it was a sword, then went and peered out of the door again. I could see the wagon plainly enough, but I didn't see the apprentice or the goat.

"M'lady?"

The stable boy's voice made me jump. I turned and he peered at me with a questioning expression. "M'lady, why are you holding the riding crop so?"

"Just in case I'm attacked by a goat."

His eyebrows drew together but he didn't speak.

"I have a fear of goats," I said.

The stable boy proved not to be the Black Knight, because my tongue did not burn out of my mouth. Still, as I climbed onto my horse—it was finally ready—I chastised myself for slipping up and lying. I had to be more careful about that.

My horse trotted out of the stable and across the ground toward the gate. As I passed by, I looked over my shoulder at the wagon. The apprentice was nowhere in sight, but Simon stood by the side of the wagon, the rope in his mouth and his jaw going in circles. He was trying to chew through it.

I knew he wouldn't be able to catch the horse, and I was too high up for him to touch anyway, but I wanted to be as far away from him as possible. As I rode out of the castle I became more and more convinced that Simon had given me the poison on purpose.

Chapter 18

I didn't let my horse stop and meander along the trail this time, and perhaps the horse sensed my urgency, because I only had to spur her on a few times. Before long the path led us into the forest. When I'd ridden through last time, the trees had seemed fresh and welcoming, like a national park or a summer camp. Now the birdcalls set me on edge. I kept thinking of how Tristan had held his sword across his lap as we'd ridden, and the way his eyes scanned the trees.

I scanned them too, unsure of what I was looking for. The wind through the trees set off hundreds of leaves that whispered in my direction.

Eight miles, I kept telling myself. It was only an eight-mile ride. It had taken us about two hours to travel the road before, and that was partially because my horse kept stopping for snacks. I'd be able to make it back faster.

Halfway through the forest, two men on horses appeared

out of the trees in front of me. They stopped on the trail. I waited
for them to pass or go ahead of me, but they didn't. When they
turned sneering faces in my direction, I realized with a sick thud
in my stomach that they were waiting for me.

Each wore ragged gray clothing. One man had a nearly
toothless grin, even though he couldn't have been more than
thirty. The other had a scar that ran from one eye to his
chin, making his face look like it was creased and about to
fold over.

"What 'ave we 'ere?" the scarred one said. "A lady without
an escort. Foolish, indeed." He took a long knife from under
the folds of his clothes and held it up for me to see.

I pulled the reins, trying to turn my horse around, but as I
looked over my shoulder I saw that another horse had come
out of the forest behind me. Its rider, a man equally frightening
and even dirtier than the first two, held onto a stick as thick as
a baseball bat. I was trapped between them.

"You'll be getting off your 'orse now," the dirty one said.

Fear wrapped itself around me like a searing blanket. I
couldn't breathe. I just stared at the man while my horse whinnied and took nervous steps sideways.

The scarred man spit on the ground. "Off the 'orse. Be a
good girl and we won't hurt you."

I didn't believe them. Once I was off my horse I'd be power-
less. I clutched my riding stick harder and tried to think of
options. Then I remembered: I was invincible.

I hadn't ever wanted to test the enchantment. Still, what
choice did I have? I looked the scarred man squarely in the
face. "Out of my way."

He put the knife to his lips as though about to use it to pick
at his teeth, then waved it in my direction again. "You'll be
giving up your saddlebags too. And your jewelry."

I nudged my horse forward. "Out of my way!"

His expression twisted with anger. He leaned forward in his saddle, and pointed his knife at me as though about to thrust it into my chest. "Do as I say now!"

At that moment the world slowed, grew sharp. I could feel the wind blowing strands of my hair around my shoulders and insects buzzing above my head. As the scarred man came toward me, I could sense every breath he took. It didn't seem difficult at all to knock the knife out of his hands with my riding crop. It was as easy as smacking a fly with a fly-swatter.

It didn't matter that the toothless man was coming at me with another knife. He too moved in slow motion, like a man walking through water.

I hit him on the side of his shoulder and he flew off his horse, screaming. He landed in the bushes by the side of the road, causing the branches to wave in leafy surrender.

I heard the man with the stick coming up behind me. I knew exactly where he was without even looking. I turned and saw the stick swinging toward me. I tapped it with the riding crop and it flew from his hands.

The man cursed, but he didn't waste time trying to fight with me anymore. He turned his horse and galloped back into the forest. The scarred man only waited another moment before following after him. Even the toothless man, who'd just managed to extract himself from the bushes, ran after them. I heard him crunching and crashing through the foliage as the world slipped back into its normal realm.

The now riderless horse stood on the pathway in front of me and I reached over and grabbed the reins as I rode by. Because hey, who doesn't want a free horse? I only regretted not knocking the other two into the bushes as well.

As I trotted off toward the inn, the forest once again

seemed a warm and welcoming place. And better yet, I felt confident and powerful. I *was* invincible.

. . .

I arrived at the inn dusty, tired, and hungry. It was frustrating not to have cell phones, not to be able to call Tristan and say, "Where are you?" and "By the way, a goat is out to get me and I was assaulted by thieves in the forest, and now I have an extra horse."

Then again, I couldn't tell him about most of it. He might be just as eager as Simon to switch enchantments.

I shared some cooked eggs, cheese, and gritty wheat bread with the inn's dog, then went to my room and looked out the window for Tristan's horse.

He didn't come.

Did he not care that I'd left? Did he want to stay at the castle fawning over Princess Margaret and telling stories at the king's table?

I ordered a bath, gave the innkeeper's wife my dress to clean, then sat in a big metal tub of steaming water. It felt luxurious against my skin but eventually it grew tepid and I had to get out. I pulled on my Snow White dress, combed out my hair, then went downstairs to try and dry it out by sitting near the hearth.

A crowd of half a dozen men had gathered around one of the tables. A large man with a pointy red beard sat with a mug of ale in one hand, speaking to them. At first I thought he was a storyteller, but as I drew closer I heard his voice. "If none can defeat the Black Knight—and I'll not claim as much until I've fought him myself—then it stands to reason that your king will give Margaret's hand to the man who has rid the land of his other foes. And that," he said, raising his mug as though offering a toast, "is what I shall do."

A rumble of approval went through his audience. One of the crowd called out, "How will you kill the ogre?"

The man with the pointy beard took a drink, then shook his head slightly. " 'Tis bad luck to speak of a thing before it happens. But I will tell you this: on the morrow I'll go to King Roderick and pay my respects to him and his daughter. Then I'll go up to the caves and destroy the wretched monster. When I come back to this inn we shall all feast, and I will tell you the story of my victory."

One from the crowd raised his mug and said, "Here's to Sir William—may he cleanse the land of the murderous beast!"

Another man said, "To the safety of our cattle and our children!"

The rest of the crowd raised their glasses and cheered, one by one adding in their toasts. I sat by the hearth and shivered.

Where was Tristan? Unless he killed the cyclops tonight, it might be too late. It didn't look like he'd even come today. The sun was nearly across the sky.

Perhaps Princess Margaret was detaining him.

I watched the fire crackling and felt nothing but cold and miserable. I'd come to help Tristan, hadn't I? And I was invincible now, so who had a better chance to kill the cyclops? Then I could just hide the thing until Tristan could come and take credit for slaying it.

But helping him meant helping him marry Margaret, and I didn't like her. She was conceited and mean and she'd tried to shut me up in her room for who knows how long.

My mind wandered away from Princess Margaret and back to Tristan. Tristan, who looked so good rugged and mussed and wearing a tunic. He had a new confidence about him, a sense of purpose, as though here in the past he'd found himself.

Margaret didn't appreciate how smart he was or the way his blue eyes seemed to look right into you. She would only ever see him as a page, a servant. So why should I do anything that made their wedding possible? I sat there for a while longer, but I didn't see another way. I'd come to help Tristan. I had to face the cyclops tonight.

. . .

I traded the thief's horse for a sword. I wasn't sure if it was a good trade or not, but since I hadn't paid for the horse I figured it didn't matter. Being invincible could prove to be profitable.

I got directions to the caves from the innkeeper's wife, who didn't seem to think it was odd that I was asking. Perhaps she thought I was asking in order to avoid the place. Instead, I rode out of the village and directly up into the hills where the cyclops lived. The sun had begun to dip down in the sky, and I pushed my horse to a gallop in an attempt to outrace it.

We rode to where the forest grew dense. The caves were somewhere beyond these trees—cold, dark mouths in the landscape. My horse whinnied nervously and twitched her head from side to side as though trying to shake off the bridle. I wondered if she could smell the cyclops from here.

I left her tethered to a tree by the main path. I may be invincible, but she wasn't. It was safer to leave her here until I'd finished my business. I didn't worry about her being stolen. I doubted any thieves hung out in the cyclops-infested part of the forest.

I made my way on a path that had already been overtaken by clumps of grass. It had been a while since people willingly rode through this part of the forest.

The night air pressed against my face and neck, and when I approached the caves my back tingled as though someone was watching me. I wished my senses would sharpen the way they did when the thieves had come so I wouldn't have to worry about tripping over tree roots and rocks, but all my senses remained normal. Apparently it only worked when I was in danger.

I gripped the sword in one hand, nearly using it as a walking stick. My feet made scuffing sounds against the dirt and fallen leaves. I could make out the opening to one cave in front of me and another farther off. Should I go inside and search them?

I heard a sound slithering through the trees to my side. I turned, searching the forest. It grew louder. What at first seemed like a strange wind was actually a voice. "Mmmaaaiiidddeeennn. I smell mai...den..."

I held the sword up and looked over its tip into the shadowy darkness. Any moment the world would grow slow. My eyes darted between the trees looking for movement.

Nothing. Nothing. And then a large shape, slinking toward me, hunched over as though he were about to pounce.

"Perfumey," he said in a nasally voice. "Stinking perfume filling my forest."

The cyclops came closer. I could make out his misshapen head. His greasy black hair looked human, but the similarities ended there. The top half of his face was a gigantic bulging eyeball that stared, unblinking, at me. The bottom half was a mouth so filled with teeth that it didn't look like he could close it. His lumpish brown nose wiggled up and down like a rabbit's.

He swayed his head as he walked toward me, and I realized why his stare was so intense. He had no eyelid over his eye. I clasped the sword harder, waiting for my senses to sharpen.

The cyclops circled around me. "Methinks she isn't lost. A maiden with a sword. Why does she come, the tasty maiden?"

I held out my sword more as a shield than as a weapon. "I've come to kill you. Sorry, but it has to be done."

The cyclops tilted his head back and laughed. Then he snorted. Then he laughed again. His bulging eyeball jiggled in his head.

I held the sword steady. "I know I don't look dangerous, but that doesn't matter. I'm enchanted and no weapon will hurt me, nor any man defeat me in battle."

Apparently he didn't believe in enchantments, because this made him laugh even harder.

"I'm sorry to have to kill you," I said, trying to dampen his humor. "Perhaps you could just surrender and beg for the king's mercy . . ."

Where his fingers should have been he had claws, which he tapped together menacingly. "The maiden can't kill me."

"I will."

"Foolish, foolish maiden," he snickered. "Your magic is nothing. I have no weapons and I'm not a man."

I took a step back from him. My heart knocked against my ribs. Could he be right? Is that why my senses hadn't sharpened yet? Why hadn't that occurred to me before?

The cyclops ran toward me. I screamed and held the sword out, hoping that the cyclops would impale himself as he jumped on me. Instead, he batted away my sword with one hand and knocked me aside with the other. I flew through the air and smacked into something hard, probably a tree. The breath went from my lungs, and everything went black.

Chapter 19

My ribs hurt when I awoke, which didn't make sense until I realized the cyclops was carrying me under one arm. His grip was painfully tight around my torso. I pushed against his arm, trying to get free, but he held me fast.

"Stupid two eyes," he hissed. "Squinty little two eyes never pay attention to magic. Only see the part they want to see. Bad vision, they have. Very bad vision."

"Let me go!" I yelled. I tried to scratch his arm, but his skin was like plastic. I didn't even leave a mark.

"Shall I eat her, the stinky maiden?" He shook his head and grunted. "She'll likely taste perfumey bad."

"Very bad," I said. "You should let me go."

"Maybe I should just break her pesky bones and save her for later. I might get very hungry later."

I gave up trying to loosen his grip on me and just tried to twist so that my ribs weren't quite as compressed. "I'm sure something better will come along. A pig or a deer . . ."

"Unicorn would be tasty," he said, and he dropped me on the ground.

I tried to crawl away but he stomped a foot onto my dress, pinning me in position.

"Maiden will sing," he hissed.

"Sing?" Then I remembered the legend that maidens could tame unicorns by singing to them.

"Sing now!" he yelled so loudly that he probably scared away any animal within a mile radius.

I couldn't think of a single song. The words all fled my mind. I couldn't even think of a tune to hum while he was leaning over me, clicking his claws together.

He sniffed at my face. "Perhaps if I rub her with leaves she will taste better."

"Happy birthday to you," I sang with a trembling voice. "Happy birthday to you. Happy birthday, awful cyclops monster thing. Happy birthday to you."

"Louder," he said.

So I sang louder. My voice wavered and cracked and mostly went off-key, but I yelled out the birthday song, then moved on to "La Cucaracha" and the alphabet song. When I'd reached LMNOP, the Cyclops straightened and sniffed the air.

"Something is coming," he said. "It smells horsey."

I stopped singing and looked, but as soon as the tune died in my mouth, the cyclops turned and growled at me. "Sing more!"

I sang again. The moment he took his foot off my dress I planned on bolting through the forest. Hopefully he would be more interested in catching the unicorn than pursuing me. And hopefully the unicorn would stab him with its horn and then run away.

"TUV," I sang, but then I stopped. A bright light pierced through the darkness, a beam from a flashlight. It went directly into the cyclops's large eye, blinding him. Unable to shut his eye, he turned away in pain, moaning, stumbling with both arms flung in front of his face.

"Run here!" Tristan yelled, but I was already on my feet, heading in his direction. When I reached him, he barely looked at me, just thrust the flashlight into my hand and said, "Try to keep this trained on his eye."

I had expected the cyclops to flee from the light into the darkness of the forest, but he didn't. He stayed where he was, roaring in anger. I shone the flashlight beam directly at his head, but he'd turned his face backward and tried to walk toward us while keeping his eye away from the light. One of his arms swung out in our direction as though trying to scratch us.

The cyclops, I realized, was not used to running away from people and didn't plan on doing it now.

Tristan walked toward him, a spear in one hand and an object I couldn't discern in the other. Some sort of cylinder.

"Don't get so close, don't get so close," I repeated, even though I knew Tristan couldn't hear me over the roars of the cyclops. Tristan walked around to the cyclops so that he faced the monster. I was afraid the cyclops would lunge at Tristan since he no longer stood in the protection of the flashlight beam. But before the cyclops could take a swipe at Tristan, Tristan held the object up and squeezed it. A stream of liquid shot out from the object and went directly into the cyclops's eye.

The monster screamed again, louder and fiercer this time. So loud that the forest seemed to shake. He clutched at his eye with his clawed hands and stumbled backward, out of the beam of my flashlight.

The cyclops's screams suddenly stopped. I searched for him with the flashlight, and when I found him, I understood why. He lay motionless on the ground. Tristan's spear stuck out of his chest.

It was only then, after I knew the danger had passed, that I began to shake. My hands trembled so much that the flashlight beam jumped up and down. Tristan walked toward me, appraising me. "Are you all right?"

"Yes."

He reached me, and once he was satisfied that I wasn't injured, the concern in his expression turned into anger. He put one hand to his temple, then held it out in my direction. "Okay, is there some reason you keep trying to kill yourself, some sort of death wish I should know about?"

"I wasn't trying to kill myself," I said, my words tumbling together. "Sir William told everyone in the inn that he was going to kill the ogre tomorrow, and I didn't think you'd make it back in time, so I had to try and take care of it myself."

Tristan looked at me like I'd lost my mind, then walked past me. I swung the flashlight beam after him to see what he was doing. A few feet away from me, his sword stood upright in the ground. He pulled it out with one hand, then strode past me to the cyclops.

"I was trying to help you, you know," I called after him.

"And I've had enough of your help. If you 'help' me any more you'll get us both killed."

I took two steps toward him. "I know you don't believe me, but I have an invincibility enchantment. I fought off three thieves on the way to the inn with nothing but a riding crop. How do you explain that if I'm not invincible?"

He'd reached the cyclops, but turned back to face me. "Three thieves?" A look of frustration crossed his face. "Did it even occur to you before you took off from the castle that it wasn't a good idea to go running around the forest by yourself?"

"The point is," I said firmly, "I beat them off, which proves that I've got an invincibility enchantment."

He put one foot on the cyclops's chest and tugged at his spear, trying to remove it. "Men here aren't used to ladies who fight back. You probably just took them by surprise and spooked them off." He gestured toward the cyclops as if presenting me evidence. "You weren't invincible against this thing."

"I didn't take into account that the cyclops wasn't human."

"Yeah, well, once again, that's where paying attention in school could have helped you."

I put one hand on my hip in disbelief. "Oh, you mean back in health class when they taught us what to do in case of a cyclops attack?"

"World Lit. *The Odyssey.*" The spear broke instead of coming free, and Tristan tossed it aside in disgust. He wouldn't be able to reuse it.

I didn't say any more about being enchanted. What was the point? He refused to take what I said seriously.

"Hold the beam on the cyclops's head," he told me.

I did, but couldn't watch when I realized what Tristan was about to do. I heard the *thwack* of his sword and shuddered. A minute later Tristan walked back to me carrying the cyclops's head by the hair.

He handed me his sword to hold, then took the flashlight from me and strode into the forest. I walked beside him, keeping my gaze averted from what he held in his hand. We walked for a few minutes in silence, following the beam from the flashlight. With more stiffness in my voice than I'd intended, I said, "Thanks for saving my life."

"You're welcome."

We took more footsteps in silence. I tried to match Tristan's quick pace without tripping on any rocks or tree roots. "So how did you find me?"

"When I reached the inn, I asked the innkeeper's wife where you were. She didn't know, but said you'd questioned her about the location of the cyclops's caves. After that, it was just a matter of hurrying as fast as I could to get things ready, cursing a lot, finding your horse and your sword along the way—did I mention cursing a lot? And then I followed the sound of your voice."

"What did you squirt into his eye? Acid?"

He shook his head. "Acid is hard to come by in the Middle Ages. It was actually watered-down shampoo. I'd forgotten how much it can sting your eyes until you brought it here."

So that's what he'd been holding. My Pantene bottle. "You mean you shampooed the cyclops to death?" The shock of the evening had taken its toll on me and I laughed out loud. "Well, that should make for an interesting story to tell at the king's table: Tristan and the Shampoo Bottle of Death."

He grinned, but didn't look at me. "Don't make me laugh. I'm still mad at you."

"I know you are, Tristan. You've been mad at me for the last eight months."

He didn't answer me. For the rest of the way to our horses, we didn't speak at all.

· · ·

We rode slowly back to the inn. Tristan rode in front of me, doing his best to light the way with the flashlight while my horse followed his. I spent a lot of time shivering and looking up at the sky, heavy with stars. How in the world could they be the same stars I'd seen back in my world? Everything else had changed.

Once we'd arrived at the inn, the priest rang the church bell to let the villagers know there was important news. Several of the men made a bonfire in the middle of the street. Then everyone crowded around for warmth while Tristan told them of my rescue and his daring triumph over the monster. In the story, Tristan said I'd gone to the forest searching for him because I thought he went to fight the cyclops. I had been worried when he hadn't returned and feared he might be lying wounded somewhere. Which I suppose sounded better than saying I went because I was foolish.

He left the shampoo out of it altogether, much to my disappointment, but did say he had temporarily blinded the cyclops with his magic lantern. Then he flipped on the flashlight and shined a beam of light into the crowd. They shielded their eyes and gasped, and were just as fascinated by the magic lantern—wanting to see and touch it—as they were by the cyclops's head. Which they also wanted to see and touch. Even the little kids had to come up and poke the thing in its face like it was some sort of elaborate Halloween mask.

I couldn't look at it without getting the dry heaves.

After everyone was done gaping at the head, the innkeeper took it, put it in a burlap sack, and locked it in his wine cellar for safekeeping. Then Tristan and a bunch of the menfolk went to the inn and the innkeeper brought out all sorts of food in celebration. Tristan paid for it, which I thought was backward, but everyone kept clapping him on the back and calling him the king's new son-in-law, so I guess they figured he could afford it. Even Sir William, who'd been downright put out during the bonfire, became more cheerful when the food was passed around.

It looked like the feasting could go on for quite a while. I didn't have much of a stomach for food—nearly being killed and then spending the evening with a decapitated cyclops head will do that to you. Besides, I didn't fit in here with these people. Not like Tristan did. I went up to my room.

I knew I wouldn't be able to sleep, and I didn't even want to try. I pulled the blankets around myself and sat on the bed, leaning against the wall. I'd left the door open so I could listen to the sounds from downstairs. I wanted to hear people chatting and laughing. Happy noises. It kept at bay the dark images of the day that kept darting through my mind. The goat lunging at me. The robbers' leering faces. The cyclops as he rushed toward me, and the feel of his claws holding me tight as he dragged me through the forest. My ribs still hurt.

"Savannah?" I saw a silhouette in the doorway and recognized Tristan.

"Yeah?"

"Why are you sitting in the dark?"

"Because I'm too twenty-first century and if I can't flip on a switch then it's too much trouble to light a room."

He hesitated, one arm on the door frame. "I want to talk to you about tomorrow."

I figured he didn't want to do that in the dark so I got up and walked toward the door, but he disappeared and came back with a torch that had been in the hallway. We met just inside my door. He put the torch into a hanger, then leaned against the wall looking at me. "In the morning I'm going to the castle to take the proof of the cyclops's death to King Roderick. Did you want to come with me?"

"No."

He nodded as though expecting as much. "That's fine, but you have to stay here. In this room." His blue eyes turned intense as he emphasized the point. "I don't want to come back and find you're off trying to help me slay the dragon, okay? I know they're fun magical creatures in all those fantasy novels back home, but here they're more like huge flying crocodiles. That have bad tempers. And shoot flames out of their mouths. And eat people. In fact, they don't like to eat raw meat so they cook their food inside their mouths, often while listening to it scream. Do you understand what I'm telling you?"

I turned away from him. "I understand perfectly. You think I'm incompetent."

"That's not what I said."

But it was too late; the stress of the day finally crescendoed in my mind. I was trying so hard to do things right and nothing had gone the way I'd planned. Even coming here felt like a mistake. Tristan didn't want my help. The tears didn't have time to well up in my eyes. They just came, spilling out onto my cheeks.

He walked toward me, a sigh on his lips. "Don't cry."

I wiped the tears off my cheeks but they were just replaced by others. Then I started sobbing.

"Savannah." He said my name softly, partially with exasperation, but with something else too. Forgiveness maybe. He put his arms around me and I lay my head against his chest. The scratchy wool of his tunic pressed roughly against my cheek. I didn't care that it felt like sandpaper or smelled of the bonfire smoke. I wound my arms around his waist.

The tears kept coming but breathing was easier.

"It's okay," he said, and then said it over and over while stroking my hair. "You're not incompetent. Hey, you're the one who brought the Shampoo Bottle of Death with you." His fingers lingered over a lock of my hair and he brought it up to his face. "Not only will it disable monsters but it makes your hair smell good too."

I didn't answer him. I couldn't.

"Look, I'm sorry I yelled at you before," he said, and he let out another sigh. "It's just . . . you belong back in high school. Back with the cheerleaders, and the track team, and the mall. Safe things. Things that don't eat girls. You don't realize how dangerous all of this is. It's some sort of game to you."

"No, it's not."

He ran his fingers across the back of my hair. "Why did you come back to the Middle Ages to help me?"

I lifted my head up to look at him. "I had to. It was the right thing to do."

His expression was unreadable, serious. He nodded slightly but I had no idea whether my explanation satisfied him.

"I didn't mean to send you here," I said. "I was just upset about the whole Hunter thing and not thinking clearly."

"I know," he said.

"And okay, a lot of times I don't think clearly, but I'm trying."

"I know," he said again. His hand moved from my hair down my back. Which, by the way, suddenly made it hard to think clearly.

My voice came out just above a whisper. "I'm really not looking for a prince."

"Good."

He was so near, and it was so comforting to have his arms around me. I didn't want him to move away from me. "What does Princess Margaret's hair smell like?"

"Cough medicine."

It bothered me that he actually knew the answer to that question. "Is that where you were all day? With her?"

He looked up at the ceiling as though trying to make an accounting of his time, but he didn't let go of me. "I was talking to members of the king's guards who've dealt with the dragon before, practicing archery with the other knights, and yes, part of the time I was trying to pump Princess Margaret for information on the Black Knight."

That shouldn't have bothered me, but it did. "Did she tell you anything useful?"

"Not really. She's upset about something. I didn't catch the whole conversation between her and Lady Theodora, but apparently whoever it was who stood her up yesterday still hasn't come by to beg her forgiveness."

"The Black Knight?"

He shrugged. "Who knows?" His hand was back on my hair, twisting strands of it between his fingers. Quite distracting.

I said, "Your future fiancée wouldn't let me out of her room."

He showed no alarm at this news. "She thought you were sick. You told her yourself that you were."

"I don't trust her and I don't think you should either, even if she is demure . . . and has a nice dowry."

"You don't need to be jealous." He tightened his arms, pressing me closer to him. "Some girls don't need to bribe guys into liking them."

He bent down to kiss me, and I tilted my face up to meet his lips. I wanted more than anything to kiss him, to feel like he cared about me that way. It felt like triumph, like acceptance. Then with a thud to my heart, I remembered what a kiss would do and pushed him away.

He stared at me, surprised, and I could only stare back at him, wide-eyed and breathless. I still had more than five days left until the switching enchantment wore off and I'd just come close to forgetting everything and making myself a permanent resident of the Middle Ages.

"I'm sorry," I said. "It's just that . . ." Did I tell him or not? I hadn't wanted to tempt him with the knowledge of how easy it would be for him to get rid of his enchantment, but he wouldn't take advantage of me, would he? I could trust him. He'd risked his life to save me from the cyclops . . . Of course he'd needed to kill the cyclops anyway . . .

I'd waited too long. Tristan supplied his own ending. "You're still getting over Hunter?"

I hated lying to him, but it was the safest way. I nodded. "I need a little more time before I can get involved with anyone." Five days to be precise.

I heard someone walking down the hallway and waited for them to pass before I finished talking to Tristan. But they didn't. They walked right to our door. I heard the innkeeper say, "This here be your sister's room."

And then Jane and Hunter walked in.

From the Honorable Sagewick Goldengill
To Madame Bellwings, Fairy Advancement

Dear Madame Bellwings,
    Due to the limitations of the Memoir Elves, there appears to be an essential gap in this narrative. Will you contact Leprechaun Relations and ask them for details regarding the transportation of Jane Delano and Hunter Delmont back in time to the land of Pampovilla?

Yours,
Professor Sagewick Goldengill

From Clover T. Bloomsbottle
To Professor Sagewick Goldengill

Dear Professor,

Some blokes up at the Roadside Tavern said you wanted to know my part in how those two mortals ended up in the Middle Ages. Well, after a series of unfortunate circumstances, I found myself in the land of the Yanks. I made a pact with a mortal girl and she said she'd mail me back to Ireland. Aye—but never trust a mortal—it was just a trick. She trapped me in the box so her sister could find me and demand me gold.

So there I was, trusting as you like, when I heard the tape ripping off the box. Then, sure enough, there were two gigantic heads peering down at me.

"What is that?" the lass asked.

And the lad said, "I think it's alive."

I at once told them what's what. "You can't have me gold, so don't even ask."

Well, the two of them took to staring at me some more and the lad said, "I think it's supposed to be a leprechaun."

The lass blinked at me. "A leprechaun? Magic is real?"

Ah, the arrogance of mortals! "Of course magic is real," I told her. "You think just because you don't see something that it isn't real? When was the last time any of you saw gravity or electricity? You don't appreciate magic when you see it, and that's why you mortals see so little of it."

The lad looked down in the box as though he hadn't heard a single word and said, "Why is Savannah mailing a leprechaun to Ireland?"

So I told them, "I promised I'd help send Savannah to the Middle Ages if she'd send me to Ireland. I did my part of the bargain. She's there, isn't she?"

Well, you've never seen such hysterics. The lass started gasping and clenching the side of the box so hard I thought she'd tip me gold right over. "Savannah can't go running around the Middle Ages! She'll catch the plague or something. What is she doing there?"

To tell you the truth, I couldn't remember myself. What are the affairs of mortals to the likes of us? Just one mess after another. So I scratched my beard and said, "It had something to do with a prince. She wanted to go to some fancy dress-wearing thing you mortals all do when you're in love."

The sister started a-gasping again. "A wedding? She wants to marry a prince?"

But I can't be expected to keep track of foolish young girls' wishes. I said, "I expect she'll be there for no more than a few months. Unless she gets stuck there altogether or killed. Sometimes that happens to the more foolish mortals."

The lass let out a shriek, and repeated, "She's doomed! I'm never going to see Savannah again!"

I hated to see the poor thing so distressed and technically I owed them a favor, as they opened the box that I'd been shut in. So I told them I'd use me magic mirror to check in on Savannah and tell them how she fared. Right generous of me, and I don't mind saying so.

A few minutes later I set their fears to rest. "Your worries have been for nothing," I told them. "Helped kill a cyclops, she did. True, it almost ate her, but she made good bait. The cyclops was so distracted with her that the other fellow was able to kill it. And all's well that ends well."

The lass proved to be of a weak constitution, for she nearly swooned—had to sit down, right there on the floor.

The lad said, "How do we get Savannah back?"

"Get her back?" I asked. "Why would you want to do such a thing when she went to all that trouble to get there?"

The lad got angry then. Pointed a finger at me and said, "If you won't help her, we're not taking you anywhere. You can just wait here for her to come back. If she ever does."

Well, I had to do something then, even if leprechauns have no power to send people to other places. I told them, "If you relinquish any claim on me gold—not that I'd give it to you anyway, so don't even ask—I might be able to call in a favor. Several years back I taught a fairy chap how to spin straw into gold. He still owes me something for that one, he does. I could have him send you back for a bit. That way you could talk to your sister and convince her to come back."

Perhaps it was dishonest for me not to tell them about the contract, and they may have been under the false assumption that all they would have to do to come home was to convince Savannah to ask her fairy godmother to send them all back. I may have even told them that fairy godmothers were akin to angels, just

waiting to bless the lives of the deserving. But I ask
you, since when have the mortal folk been honest with
us? It's never been their way. Deeds for deeds, I say.

I called me friend Rumpelstiltskin, and he sent
them back right quickly, he did.

Yours,
Clover T. Bloomsbottle

Chapter 20

Jane and Hunter looked as they had on many school mornings: jeans, tennis shoes, and backpacks on their shoulders. But streaks of dirt smudged their clothes, and the knee of Jane's jeans was torn. They looked tired and frazzled, and seeing them made it seem that the world had suddenly ripped open, mixing old with new, blending the centuries together.

Tristan turned to me, a look of accusation darkening his eyes. "You sent them here too?"

"I didn't!" I said, then turned to Jane. "What are you doing here?"

Frustration flashed across her face. Her eyes had a panicked look, a loss of composure that wasn't like her. She dropped her backpack onto the floor. "That's how you greet me? I've just spent the last two hours wandering around a forest in the dark—which I'm sure was your leprechaun's idea of a joke—and we never even would have found the village if it hadn't been for the church bell and the bonfire. And I kept falling down, and my jeans are ripped, and now we've finally found you and you ask me what I'm doing here?" Her voice spiraled in volume. "This is the Middle Ages, Savannah. This is not a safe place for a teenage girl. It's dangerous. It has the plague, and wars, and—"

"One less monster." Hunter took a step toward Tristan. He held up his hand to give Tristan a high-five. "Way to go, dude. They're making up songs in your honor downstairs."

Jane didn't take her eyes off me. "Mom and Dad are going to flip out about this. I don't know what you think you're doing here, but you've got to come home. Right. Now." Jane folded her arms and finished her lecture with an aggravated breath.

"So you're admitting that I'm not crazy," I said.

"What?" she asked.

"You thought I was crazy when I told you about the leprechaun and the Middle Ages. But you opened the package and found out the truth, didn't you?"

"Okay," Jane said, cutting me off. "You're not crazy. Now will you please come home?"

"Trust me, I want to come home but I'm here until Tristan can leave."

As calmly as if he were discussing the weather, Tristan added, "I can't leave until I become a prince."

"You? You're the prince?" Jane's voice took on an agitated edge and she turned in my direction. "You're not going to get married, are you?"

"Not to each other," I said and couldn't keep my lips from pursing. "Tristan wants to marry Princess Margaret."

"I don't *want* to marry her," he said. "It's all part of the deluxe prom package Savannah ordered."

Then I had to explain to Jane and Hunter how my fairy godmother had misunderstood certain statements I'd made and had sent Tristan back in time to become a prince. He still had two tasks left before he could achieve that goal and return to our time.

"Kill a dragon?" Hunter said as though he both envied and feared for Tristan. "Can you do that?"

"I've got to."

Jane shook her head, disbelief seeping into her tone. "But your leprechaun told us that all you had to do to come home was to ask your fairy godmother."

"Oh, well, that just means you were duped by a leprechaun," I said.

Hunter cocked his head and looked at me narrowly. "Your fairy godmother won't help you at all?"

"My fairy godmother won't even take my calls. She's sort of a teenage, airheaded shopping diva who didn't pay attention very well in fairy school."

Jane sat down on my bed and rubbed at her forehead wearily. "Well, that figures."

I followed her with my gaze. "Meaning?"

"They must match fairy godmothers to people by type. You pretty much just described yourself."

"I did not," I said. "I'm not . . ." I ran through the list of qualities I'd just said, deciding which one to protest first. *Shopping diva*, okay that was sort of me. *Didn't pay attention in school* . . . um, ditto for that one. I wasn't an airhead though, was I?

I thought of all the ways I'd messed things up in the last two days and wasn't sure. Still, I folded my arms. "I am not like her." Which was true. I always return my phone messages. "And besides, I didn't ask you to come. So if you don't want to be here why don't you just call your responsible, punctual fairy godmother and leave?"

"Because I didn't get a fairy godmother," Jane said. "I got a creepy little man who may in fact have been Rumpelstiltskin.

The leprechaun said your fairy godmother would take all of us back when you asked." Jane let her hands fall to her sides in exasperation. They were smeared with dirt and tiny scratches ran across them. "How could you mess up a wish from your fairy godmother?"

Tristan spoke, and his voice had a calmness to it that almost didn't belong in the room. "What did you bring with you?"

"What?" Jane asked.

"You knew you were going to the Middle Ages. You must have brought along things you were going to need. Savannah brought supplies. Things to barter. What's in your backpacks?"

It was more of a point than a question and Jane blushed at the reprimand.

Hunter said, "We only have our schoolbooks. We didn't think we were going to *stay* here." He thrust his hands into the pockets of his jeans. "I thought fairies were supposed to be good and do nice things for people."

Tristan picked up Jane's backpack from the floor, took it to the bed, and unzipped it. "In the original fairy tales, fairies were often seen as mischievous, dangerous tricksters. They did things like steal children. Smart people didn't trust them."

I let out a grunt. "Where were you with that information when I needed it?"

He dumped Jane's books out onto the bed. Without cracking a smile, he said, "Sitting in my room trying to work up the courage to call you." Then he put Jane's pens and pencils into one pile and her books into another. The notebooks he handed to me. "Paper is valuable. We'll be able to barter with these at least." He pulled out a makeup bag, opened it, and shook his head. He tossed it back on the bed along with her cell phone, then walked over to Hunter and took his backpack from him. "Anything in here that could be used to slay a dragon?"

"Paper. Pens. And my lunch."

"Well, at least you'll have one good meal in the Middle Ages then." Tristan took the backpack and looked through it anyway. While he did he said, "Savannah, your job tomorrow is to take Hunter and Jane to the market and buy them clothes so they fit in."

I said, "It takes days, sometimes weeks, to make clothes."

"Buy them off someone's back if you have to. I'll be gone all day at the castle. They'll want me to tell the story of the cyclops over dinner, and besides, I should practice my archery some more. According to everyone at the castle, the only way to kill a dragon is to shoot a poisoned arrow into its throat. It's a small target, but it's the only unarmored part. If I miss, the dragon is likely to swoop down and barbecue me."

A tremor went through me. I hadn't really thought about Tristan fighting the dragon. But now that he was planning it, I couldn't help but picture him standing underneath a monstrous dragon with only a bow and arrow for protection. Little waves of panic spread across my chest.

Tristan went through the contents of Hunter's backpack with a shake of his head. "What I really need is a small hand-held missile. How come no one carries those in their backpacks anymore?"

I knew he was joking, but still I said, "Could we make one?"

Jane and Hunter looked at me with that condescending expression smart people get when they think you're being an idiot, so I said, "Didn't the Chinese have rockets in the Middle Ages?" After all, I'd seen the movie *Mulan*. Hey, for a cartoon character, Shang was hot.

"They did," Tristan said. "But I have no idea what sort of fuel they used."

"Besides," Hunter said, "the body of a rocket has to be perfectly cylindrical or it won't fly straight. The chances of hitting a dragon's throat are slim."

"What about cannons?" I said. "Didn't they have those in the Middle Ages?"

Tristan calmly refilled Hunter's backpack. "They had trebuchets, which worked more like catapults—great for hitting castles, but not so accurate at hitting moving objects." He looked over at me, and his voice softened as though he appreciated my worry. "Trust me, people here have tried lots of ways to kill dragons—poisoning their food, drugging them. An arrow to the throat is the only thing that's worked."

I went and sat on the bed, just so I could be near him. "That's because the people here haven't considered everything. But we're from the twenty-first century. We know what's possible."

Jane shook her head. "Knowing what's possible and being able to replicate it are two entirely different things."

And so there was Tristan standing alone underneath the dragon again, and no one seemed to be bothered by this except for me. I poked at the blanket on the bed with irritation. "If you're not going to use your knowledge, then what's the point of being smart? Anyone could shoot a bow. I could do it."

"But you're not going to," Tristan said with more forcefulness than he needed. To Hunter he added, "Your job tomorrow is to make sure Savannah stays out of trouble."

"Could we feed it explosives?" I asked. "You told me it cooks its food inside its mouth."

"They didn't have explosives in the Middle Ages," Hunter said.

"But that doesn't mean they didn't have the ingredients," I said. "What's dynamite made out of? Or gunpowder?"

Tristan tilted his head back, his eyes narrowed in concentration. "She's right. Gunpowder was made from natural components. Fertilizer is one of them and they have plenty of that here. What are the other ingredients?"

Hunter leaned forward. He snapped his fingers trying to remember. "Saltpeter. The colonials made it during the Revolutionary War. It's part potassium nitrate and you mix it with something..."

I looked at Jane to see if she knew the answer, but she was turning pages in her history book. "Black powder," she said. "Developed in China in the ninth century...spread to Europe between the thirteenth and fourteenth centuries."

Tristan's brows furrowed with concentration. "But what are the ingredients?"

Hunter picked up his chemistry book and flipped through the pages. To himself he said, "What reacts with potassium nitrate?"

Black powder. I never even remembered hearing about it in history class, but I had plenty of practice guessing for tests. "It's got to be something black," I said.

Tristan's gaze shot over to mine and he smiled. "Charcoal. It's mixed with charcoal."

"And sulfur," Hunter said. He turned the book around and pointed to a bunch of letters, numbers, and arrows that meant nothing to me but made the other two say, "Ahhh."

Now everyone leaned together, making a semicircle around Tristan. "What about the ratios?" Hunter asked.

"We'll have to experiment," Tristan said. "I'll see how much charcoal and sulfur I can buy from the castle alchemists."

"Do we know how to make saltpeter?" Jane asked.

The guys looked at each other and laughed.

"What?" I said.

"That's the fertilizer part," Tristan said. "It's basically what happens when you combine a decaying material and urine. Your basic dung heap."

I sat up straighter. "How do you guys know this sort of thing?"

Tristan shrugged. "You hear it once and you never forget it."

"Gross," I said.

"Yeah, but you'll never forget it now," Tristan said.

I held up one hand. "For the record, I refuse to be in charge of the saltpeter."

Which is how I was put in charge of buying a pig. Tristan figured we could tie bags of black powder to a pig and put it near the dragon's lair.

We talked long into the night about who was going to do what, and what supplies we'd have to buy, and the fact that we needed to buy more horses for Hunter and Jane. It grew very late and even the villagers downstairs went home. Then Hunter went to Tristan's room and Jane stayed in mine. I scooted over so she had room on the bed to sleep.

I thought it would be awkward being in the room alone with her. We hadn't really talked, not normally anyway, since Hunter broke up with me, but I fell asleep before she even climbed into bed.

. . .

I slept in past sunrise and Jane slept even longer. She didn't even blink her eyes open as I walked around the room dressing. I put on the first dress I'd brought since my Snow White one had gotten dirty while I'd been dragged around the forest by the cyclops. I gave it to the innkeeper's wife to wash. Hopefully I'd be able to find something for Jane before she got up.

I had wanted to see Tristan before he left, but the innkeeper told me he'd gone at first light. I wondered if he'd gotten any sleep at all last night. I hadn't been able to tell him good-bye, which bothered me more than it should have.

He'd be gone all morning long, telling his story at the castle and being knighted by the king. At least I knew he wouldn't be spending much time with Princess Margaret. He wanted to get back to the inn and get things ready as soon as possible so he could go to the dragon's lair.

Celebrating aside, everyone figured it would be best to try and kill the dragon today instead of giving Sir William a chance to exhibit his archery prowess and shoot it first. Or as Jane had put it last night, "Anyone ever heard of William Tell?"

Sir William had said he was going up to the castle to pay his respects to the king and Princess Margaret today, but after that, it only made sense that he'd go after the dragon. Both he and Tristan needed the reward money that would enable them to challenge the Black Knight.

I hadn't said much about the Black Knight to the others last night, but that didn't mean I hadn't thought about him. I'd been so frightened when I'd gone to fight the cyclops and the enchantment hadn't worked. Had the Black Knight already figured out that his enchantment was gone? Did he realize I was the one who had taken it?

The thought made my insides tighten. What if my dream was right and he and I were meant for each other? Could we be?

Then I felt horrible for thinking things like that while Tristan was going off risking his life in order to undo the wish I'd made. And he'd nearly kissed me last night, and what's more, I'd wanted him to.

So which one of them did I have feelings for—the tall, powerful, mysterious one who was also a fantastic kisser, or the one who'd held me so tenderly last night told me that everything would be okay, and then stood up to Jane for me?

I bought horses for Jane and Hunter, then went to the tailor to see if he had a dress ready for me. He didn't, but I was able to buy one of the tailor's wife's dresses. It was worn and plain, but at least Jane wouldn't stand out in her jeans. Getting clothes for Hunter proved harder. He was taller than most of the men in the Middle Ages, which limited the people I could barter with for clothes. I didn't want to trade with a peasant, or Hunter would spend his entire time in the Middle Ages being treated like a servant.

Before he left for the castle, I was able to convince Sir William to trade me a pair of leggings and a tunic for my last two necklaces. I knew it was a bad trade, but I was desperate, and besides, it made him less ticked off about Tristan killing the cyclops before he'd had a chance.

I looked at my dwindling supplies and wondered how much longer we'd be in the Middle Ages. If it was much longer, I'd have to find some more thieves to rob.

Hunter spent the morning procuring saltpeter. This basically meant he went to all of the dung heaps in the village and scraped off a white, salty-looking layer that had formed on top. The stables proved to be a gold mine for this.

Jane and I went to the butcher to buy a pig. I ended up feeling sorry for all of them and made Jane choose one. She told me it wouldn't matter to the pig whether it was eaten by a person or a dragon—and besides, it was hypocritical to feel sorry for the pig when bacon was one of my favorite foods. But I still made her do it.

She chose the biggest one. It looked like it weighed as much as I did, had a torn ear, beady eyes, and a nasty disposition. I called him Mr. Ogden, after my geometry teacher.

Tristan came home at lunchtime, and then he and Hunter went out behind the inn and tried different ratios of saltpeter to charcoal to sulfur to see what exploded the best. They came inside not much later—their faces black with soot and their eyebrows singed—and told us that a ratio of 6 to 1 to 1 worked out very well.

It was midafternoon when Tristan and Hunter loaded Mr. Ogden onto a cart. It was odd to watch Tristan and Hunter getting the horses ready, working together. One was the guy I'd kissed about a month ago, and the other was the guy who I'd nearly kissed last night. I couldn't help but compare them. True, Hunter was taller and had broader shoulders, but watching him no longer made my heart flutter around in my rib cage. Instead I found my gaze being drawn to Tristan. There was just something endearing about Tristan's shaggy blond hair and light blue eyes. Maybe it was because he'd never cheated on me. Everything with him was a sky full of possibilities. Besides, I liked his dry sense of humor and the way he was so protective of me. He kept telling me over and over that I was to stay at the inn—as though he was sure I would insist on coming with him to the dragon's lair.

I did insist, but only once.

"You might need help along the way," I told him.

He looked at me, his eyes firm. "That's why I'm taking Hunter with me. You're staying at the inn until we come back." He mounted his horse and took hold of the reins. "It's only a ten-mile ride to the lair. If all goes well, we'll be back by night-fall. Then we'll be able to rest for an entire day before we go up to the castle for King Roderick's celebration tomorrow night."

Everyone of importance in the kingdom was going to be there. Everyone in town who could walk or ride would go up for it. Tristan was convinced the Black Knight would show up there and he wanted to be ready to face him.

Now I watched Tristan put a bag of black powder in his own saddlebag and another in Hunter's. His tanned hands moved so confidently. His perfect profile showed his determination.

I looked at the saddlebags and then at the pig. "But what if things don't go as planned with the dragon?"

Tristan smiled at me as he mounted his horse. "Then you can find another date to prom. I'll understand."

I should have smiled back at him, but I couldn't bring

myself to. A knot of worry wound around my insides, pulling tight.

Hunter stood by his horse, but before mounting it he gave Jane a hug. She buried her face in his shoulder and he kissed the top of her head.

Momentarily I was stung with their betrayal all over again. They were so easy about hugging each other. How often had they done it while Hunter was dating me?

I pulled my gaze away from them and noticed Tristan watching me, his eyes serious, evaluating.

I blushed and wasn't sure why. "Be careful," I said. Part of me wished I had hugged Tristan, but it would have been awkward beforehand and was impossible now. We hadn't been alone at all since he'd tried to kiss me, and it felt like both of us were waiting for an answer to a question that hadn't been asked yet.

Hunter mounted his horse with more ease than I'd expected and the two of them rode off, with Mr. Ogden bouncing in the cart behind Tristan.

Chapter 21

Jane and I wandered around the village killing time. We hardly talked at all, but I could tell by the way she had to stay in constant motion—tapping her foot, fiddling with her dress—that her thoughts were circling around Hunter. I knew it was hard for her to keep all that anxiety inside. She wasn't talking about him because she thought it would be painful for me to hear about her feelings for him.

After two hours had gone by, a lot of the villagers crawled up on their roofs in hopes of seeing the dragon in the distant sky.

Tristan had explained the way of dragons to us before he'd left. Dragons were slow moving and awkward while walking because their wings and tails dragged on the ground—thus the name, dragons. That's why they always stayed put in their lairs unless they were hunting or frightened. If startled, they took to the air at once, where they had the advantage of height and speed at their command.

So when Tristan and Hunter got close enough to the

dragon's lair that it could smell the pig, we should be able to see the shape of the dragon take off into the sky.

As the villagers climbed the inn's roof, I heard tidbits of conversation, people discussing Tristan's odds of success like it was a football match.

"The bloke's no archer. He hasn't a chance."

"I hear he has magic. Something to do with a pig."

"Pig magic? Can't be powerful. I reckon he'll be dead before we can toast his victory over the cyclops on the morrow."

All of it made my stomach turn. Still, I wanted to see the events for myself. I'd rather see it firsthand than have to ask the villagers what they'd seen. I left the inn and headed for the church. It had the highest roof and was the only one in the village that wasn't thatch.

Someone had pushed a ladder against the side, and several people—including the priest—were already on top.

Jane followed me up, all the while telling me that we shouldn't be up here because there were no building codes in the Middle Ages and the roof was likely to collapse. Luckily, I'd had practice ignoring her.

I took a seat next to the priest. He was reciting something in Latin; I hoped it was a prayer for Tristan. I pressed my arms around my knees and stared in the same direction that everyone else was looking. Jane sat next to me. We didn't talk.

The sun kept creeping across the sky. Certainly it had been long enough, hadn't it? The villagers had stopped their noisy chatter and were looking above the tree line in earnest. Now their predictions were given in hushed tones, perhaps out of respect for us. "Did misfortune befall them before they reached the lair?" one asked. "Perhaps they've turned back," another said.

"Or the dragon killed them without ever having to take flight."

Jane looked dully at the horizon. Her voice was no more than a whisper. "This is my fault."

I turned to her, surprised. "Your fault?"

"If I hadn't taken Hunter away from you, then you wouldn't have wished for a prince to take you to prom. You'd be going with him and he'd still be alive." She looked blankly at the sky, the spirit drained from her.

"He's still alive," I said.

She shook her head. "We haven't seen the dragon take flight. That means it was never frightened. He didn't . . . I shouldn't have . . ." She let out a ragged moan. "I made Hunter come here."

I took her hand, trying to keep her worry from spinning out of control. "Tristan has been living here for eight months. He knows how to take care of himself. He won't let anything happen to Hunter."

She squeezed my hand. Her breathing came in labored spurts. "You really think so?"

"If we never see the dragon in the sky, it only means they thought of a way to kill it before it took flight. They're probably already on their way home and they'll laugh once they see us all up here on the roofs." I glanced down at the ground. "Or they'll yell at us because they didn't have building codes in the Middle Ages and sitting up here is dangerous."

Her grip on my hand loosened. "You're sure?"

I didn't have time to answer. The crowd around us gasped. My gaze shot to the sky, and there in the distance was the outline of a dragon, wings beating, rising above the trees. It was too far away to make out any detail. I could just see the enormous wings, long neck, horned head, and the tail that curled slightly as it flew.

The priest beside me broke out into a new chant. Latin words tumbled over one another in loud succession. I squeezed Jane's hand back. The dragon paused in flight, its wings only moving slightly as it hovered, then it swooped back down-ward.

None of us breathed. None of us spoke. We waited. I said my own prayer, repeating Tristan's name over and over again in my mind.

The dragon rose back up above the tree line and I could make out the shape of something in its mouth. Four legs stuck out—was it the pig? It looked too big for a pig. The legs were too long. Then I realized what it was. A horse.

Something had gone wrong.

I squinted at the dragon. Had there been a rider on that horse before the dragon grabbed it? Was there one on it still? I couldn't tell. A slow moan came from my mouth, a moan I couldn't stop.

The dragon tilted up his head and the entire horse disappeared into his mouth. The next moment a blast of light appeared where the dragon's head had been. A clap like thun-der went through the sky, and the dragon plummeted straight down, leaving a trail of black smoke to show where it had been.

The crowd around me lifted up their arms and cheered. Some even stood up and clapped, yelling, "Long live Sir Tris-tan, the brave! Sir Tristan, the mighty dragon slayer!"

Jane turned to me, her face flushed with excitement. "They did it. The dragon ate the pig."

I couldn't speak. I didn't know what to say, or if I should say anything.

"Look at you," she said with a relieved smile. "You were as afraid as I was. You're white as a ghost."

"Am I?" I told myself that I was wrong, that it had been the pig and not a horse, but my stomach still felt like it had torn open. Tristan and Hunter had both left with bags of black powder in their saddlebags. Had the dragon discovered them before they had a chance to tie the bags onto the pig?

Which horse had it been? It had been so far away—but the shape had seemed dark. Hunter's horse had been dark brown, Tristan's a lighter color. Besides, Tristan's horse had a cart attached. There had been no trace of that in the sky.

The priest said, "Everyone must get down so I can ring the bell. Ten rings—the death of a monster!"

Another cheer went up, and the villagers headed for the ladder. The discussion now turned to the castle feast. What dancing and eating there would be!

I wanted to yell at all of them to stop it, that they didn't know what they were talking about, that something horrible had happened. I didn't. There was no point in frightening Jane. No sense in telling her I thought Hunter wouldn't return to us.

We climbed down from the roof and walked back toward the inn. "What should we do while we wait for the guys to come back?" Jane asked me.

I shook my head, unable to speak.

"Maybe we could help the tailor sew. My dress really isn't nice enough for a castle feast. Do you think we could get a dress done by tomorrow night?"

I wasn't planning on going to the castle at all, but it wasn't the time to mention it. "I think we should be here when . . ." My throat clenched and I had to force the rest of the sentence out, "When the guys get back."

She shrugged in agreement. "I suppose they might worry if we're not here."

She looked so relaxed now, so happy. I thought of how she'd clung to Hunter when they said their good-byes, and how she'd nearly fallen apart up on the roof while we waited for the dragon. If Hunter didn't come home, if all her worries formed into a hard, relentless reality, how would she cope? How would we tell his parents when we went back home?

My throat clenched again. I wanted Hunter to be okay so

badly, but I wanted it for her sake, not mine. She looked at me questioningly. Instead of saying anything I walked over and hugged her. We would do this again, I knew, when one horse returned.

She hugged me back. "I really am sorry about everything. I never meant to hurt you about Hunter." As though offering me proof she added, "We both came when we found out you were here. We both wanted to get you back."

"I know," I said. "It's all right. Sometimes things happen when we don't mean them to."

She laughed, and it turned into tears—tears of relief that I'd forgiven her. Then I was crying too, but for a different reason.

Finally she stepped away from me. "Look at us—we're a mess. What will the guys think when they get back?"

I wiped my face and didn't answer.

She said, "I think I'm going to go lie down while we wait for them. I hardly slept at all last night, what with the time change and the worry. Now suddenly I'm exhausted."

"You should sleep," I said. "I think I'll walk down the trail a little ways to meet them when they come."

Tristan would have told me it wasn't safe to go off on a trail by myself, but Jane just watched me for a moment, then gave me a half smile. "You like Tristan, don't you?"

"Yeah."

She nodded, still smiling. "I thought so. He's gotten really cute, hasn't he?"

"Yeah," I repeated, then watched her turn and walk into the inn with the smile still on her face.

• • •

As I walked down the trail, I kept thinking about the dragon. In my mind I saw it fly through the sky with the horse in its mouth, again and again. The more I walked, the more I realized

I couldn't be sure the dragon had eaten the darker horse. It was so far away, anything would look dark, wouldn't it?

Which meant I didn't know which rider had been attacked.

It was Tristan's quest; he would have insisted on going first. He would have made Hunter stay behind and wait someplace safe. All along I'd wondered how to comfort Jane, but I was the one who needed to be comforted.

My pace turned from walk to jog. It wasn't fair. I'd already lost Hunter and now I'd lost Tristan too. I pushed myself to go faster. I needed to know for sure. I ran as fast as I could, my feet pounding into the ground, each step bringing me to a future I didn't want to face. Cold air rushed by my face, the trees hurried by. But before long my lungs burned and my feet slowed even though I didn't want to let them, and still there was nothing on the path in front of me but emptiness.

I kept going, now sure I knew the answer to the question I'd asked myself earlier—between the Black Knight and Tristan, I cared about Tristan more. Much more. Otherwise it wouldn't hurt so much knowing I wouldn't see him again.

It shouldn't have been Tristan, I thought. And then I hated myself for wishing death on Hunter. Even after he'd just broken up with me I hadn't wanted him dead. And now that he'd come back to the Middle Ages to help me, I was hoping it was his death and not Tristan's that I'd seen.

I couldn't run any farther. My legs were giving out. I sat down on the edge of the trail, breathless, my clothes clinging to me with sweat, and I waited for someone to come.

None of this was Jane's fault, it was mine, and I was a horrible person because I wanted to see Tristan's horse come down the path. I wanted Tristan to live. I wanted to run my fingers through his blond hair and feel his blue-eyed gaze on me. I wanted to kiss him.

I sat there for more than an hour. I called Chrissy, hoping

there was something she could do. She never came. Finally I quit trying and just put my head on my knees and cried.

Then I heard horse hooves. One set. It might be someone else, I told myself, but I knew it wasn't. I stood up and walked to the path, waiting to see which horse would appear around the bend in the road. I kept my gaze down so I would see horse hooves first, not a face.

The rider came on a dark brown horse. Hunter's horse. I lifted my eyes and saw Hunter holding the reins.

Chapter 22

I stared at Hunter and couldn't speak. Surprise flitted across his face and then concern. *He doesn't want to tell me,* I thought.

"What are you doing here?" Hunter asked. "What's wrong?"

I staggered toward him, my hands balled into fists. "Where's Tristan?"

And then I saw him. He sat behind Hunter on the horse. He leaned around to look at me, and although his face looked pale and drawn, he gave me a smile. "I'm okay, Savannah."

If he had been on the ground I would have hugged him. I was tempted to pull him off the horse and do just that. Instead I just stood there, trembling and staring at him.

"What's wrong?" Hunter asked again. "Where's Jane?"

I tried to pull myself together. I let the fear and the worry drain away from me. "She's fine. She's back at the inn sleeping. I just came because we were watching from the church roof and when I saw the dragon eat a horse—"

Hunter's voice took on an incredulous tone. "So *you* were worried and came out to meet us, but *Jane* went to sleep?"

"She thought it was the pig. I didn't have the heart to tell her differently."

Hunter laughed and turned toward Tristan. "See, I told you it was pointless to make *me* sit in front." Then to me he said, "Tristan wanted to make sure that Jane saw me first, so she wouldn't think I'd been eaten. He thought she'd be worried sick by the time we reached the village."

I looked at Tristan and he returned my gaze with serious eyes. Right then I understood that it hadn't been Jane he was worried about, but me. He thought I'd want to make sure that Hunter was alive.

I took a step toward them and shook my head. "I knew it was Tristan's horse." I kept looking at his eyes, trying to see if Tristan realized what I was saying, but I couldn't tell. His gaze remained serious.

"How did the dragon get a horse?" I asked. "What happened to the pig?"

Hunter shrugged. "You'll be happy to hear that Mr. Ogden is running free somewhere."

Tristan nodded. "It was harder to get to the lair than we'd thought. It's all rocks and undergrowth once you get close. Not a good place to drag a cart."

"We made too much noise," Hunter said. "Before we'd even gotten to a place where we could tie the black powder to the pig, the dragon was roaring and bearing down on us. It went straight for Tristan, and nearly got him, too. He dove off his horse at the last second. Hurt his arm on the way down."

For the first time I noticed that Tristan held his left arm close to his body. "I don't think it's broken," he said. "Just jammed."

"When the dragon grabbed the horse, the cart snapped

right off," Hunter said. "And last we saw him, Mr. Ogden was hightailing it through the forest."

"I'm mad it got my horse but I'm happy we had enough black powder in my saddlebag to do the job," Tristan said. "Two quests down, and one to go. We've got the paw of the dragon inside Hunter's saddlebag. We'll take it with us to the castle."

I looked at the saddlebag and noticed it had turned dark with moisture. "Great," I said, and then turned my gaze before I started gagging.

Hunter looked back at Tristan. "Do we have room for Savannah on the horse? We ought to get going again."

"I can walk back," I said. "It isn't that far."

Tristan gave me one of his stern looks. "You shouldn't walk in the forest by yourself at all. I'll go with you."

But Hunter was already dismounting. "Not with your hurt arm. You need to get back to the inn and ice it. I'll walk with Savannah."

This solution didn't appear to make Tristan happy, but he didn't argue about it. He just nodded in my direction, took the reins in his right hand, and rode past us down the path.

. . .

There are many awkward places to be alone with your exboyfriend. Meandering through the forest in a medieval fairy tale gone wrong is high on the list. We hadn't walked for two minutes before he was apologizing again about the way things had ended and for hurting me.

I would have loved to tell him that he hadn't—he'd never meant that much to me to begin with—but it's hard to pull off that sort of aloofness when a guy knows you wished for a prince to take his place as your prom date.

Finally I just came out and said, "Look, Hunter, I appreciate the apology, but you can stop now. I know it's only been a few days for you since this happened, but I've been in and out of the Middle Ages for the last month. A lot has happened since then and I'm over you." I didn't add that I'd just been hoping for his death.

"Oh," he said with surprise. "Well, good. That will make things easier between us." And it did, immediately. He visibly relaxed and the conversation felt almost normal as we walked. "So what did you do here for a month?"

"I learned to appreciate the twenty-first century."

"Really? I think it's pretty cool here—well, except for almost getting eaten by a dragon."

"Two words: indoor plumbing."

"But they've got awesome weapons here—look at this." He unsheathed a sword that had been by his side and I recognized it as the one I had unsuccessfully tried to fight the cyclops with. "Tristan gave it to me. I hope I get to take this home with me."

I should have known Tristan wouldn't give it back to me. Apparently he didn't want me anywhere near a sword.

"And we get to ride horses," Hunter said.

"And smell like them too."

The time passed quickly as we walked and before I knew it the village was back in sight. I didn't know when we'd ever be alone again so I said, "Hey, Hunter, I'm really glad you didn't die back there."

He laughed like I was joking, but it was the truth.

• • •

We found Tristan sitting at a table in the inn. He had his arm in a bucket of water. "It's the closest thing I could find to ice. Feels cold enough anyway."

I sat down beside him, but he didn't look at me. When I'd first come in, Tristan's gaze had ricocheted between Hunter and me as though searching for something, but now he was pointedly ignoring me.

"When I go to the castle tomorrow, I'll see if there's a wizard around with some healing potion. I can't face the Black Knight with only one arm working."

With the mention of wizards I remembered that I hadn't told Tristan about Simon and the poison. I'd been so occupied with the cyclops, Jane and Hunter's arrival, and then the dragon, it hadn't crossed my mind at all.

"About wizards," I said. "You were right when you told me they couldn't be trusted. Do you remember that red bottle I had when I went to meet with the Black Knight? The wizard's apprentice, Simon, told me that if I drank it, the Black Knight would do anything I asked—but it was poison. The next day when I saw the wizard's cart, he had a new apprentice and Simon had been turned into a goat because he'd stolen a bottle of poison."

For the first time since I'd sat down beside him, Tristan looked directly at me. "You're sure?"

"Yes. Somewhere out there is a goat who wants me dead. That's why I'm not going with you to the castle tomorrow—if he licks me, I'll turn into a goat."

"If the wizard licks you?"

"No, the goat."

Tristan looked at me blankly. "Why don't you just start at the beginning and tell me exactly what happened during each of your meetings with the wizard."

I tapped one finger against the table. "I can't. Not for another four days."

"Why not?"

"I can't tell you that either, but the point is, I don't want to go to the castle because that plotting little goat may still be there."

Tristan ran his hand through his hair and turned to Hunter. "Did any of that make sense to you?"

"Nope."

Tristan nodded philosophically. "Just checking."

"There's one more thing I meant to tell you," I said.

"Am I going to understand any of it?" Tristan asked.

I leaned closer to him. "I bartered a gold hibiscus ring to Simon. Then the same day I saw it on Princess Margaret's hand."

Both Hunter and Tristan waited for me to continue. When I didn't, Hunter shrugged as though trying to guess my meaning. "So you think Princess Margaret bought the ring from him?"

"Why should I know about that?" Tristan asked.

I didn't have a good answer. "It just strikes me as suspicious."

Tristan took his hand out of the water, stretched his fingers, then balled them into a fist. "Well, you've never liked my future fiancée, have you?"

"And you refuse to think she's dangerous because she's pretty."

His gaze returned to mine. "That's not true. I think pretty women can be very dangerous."

I sat back in my chair with a *humph*. "She's sneaky and vindictive. I'd watch her if I were you."

He smiled over at me. "Oh, I will. I'll watch her very closely as we dance together tomorrow night."

After that, I went upstairs to check on Jane.

• • •

The next day Tristan slept in until midmorning. None of us woke him; we figured he needed the rest. After he got up, he hardly spoke to me and he watched my reactions every time Hunter said anything. I wanted to just tell Tristan, "By the way,

I'm over Hunter," but I didn't know a good way to work that into casual conversation, especially since Hunter and Jane were always around.

He planned to ring the bell for the Black Knight tonight when he went up for the king's celebration. It bothered me that I wouldn't be there for it, but then, perhaps that was for the best. I didn't want to see the Black Knight.

Tristan was going to challenge him to a javelin throw—something he'd done in track with enough success that he had a chance of winning. I wanted him to win desperately. All of this could be over soon. Maybe by this time tomorrow we'd all be back home eating ice cream and potato chips and trying to convince ourselves it had really happened.

Or maybe we'd just be at the wedding feast for Prince Tristan and Princess Margaret. This thought made me grit my teeth. I didn't want to think about what we'd do if Tristan lost.

I sat in my room and watched out the window as Hunter, Jane, and Tristan left for the castle. It was lucky for them, really, that I didn't want to go. After the dragon attack we only had three horses left.

By midafternoon most everyone in the village had gone to the castle as well. The only ones left behind were the young mothers with little children and the older people who couldn't travel the distance. I'd seen them waving good-bye to their kinfolk, asking that a piece of pie or a morsel of meat be brought back for them.

I stared out the window for a while after they left. It irked me to no end that Tristan had told me he was going to spend the night dancing with Margaret. *She* hadn't run up the trail until her lungs felt like they were going to burst, mourning his death.

Besides, he had nearly kissed me. Didn't that mean anything to him?

Okay, so I'd pushed him away and told him I wasn't over Hunter yet, and then Hunter had shown up. And maybe Hunter and I had both been chatting happily when we walked into the inn. But still.

I took out Jane's schoolbooks and read for a few hours. I didn't even mind that they were textbooks. They reminded me that there was a life beyond this one. And besides, reading textbooks makes a person smarter.

Before the light had gone, I wandered into the kitchen and decided to take a bath and wash my dress. I lugged buckets of water from the well, filled a metal tub that was kept in the kitchen, and then boiled enough water over the fire to turn the water in the tub warm. You know that saying, "A watched pot never boils"? I'm pretty sure that came from the Middle Ages. It took forever. When the water was finally warm enough, I climbed into the tub and relaxed, for oh, a good fifteen minutes until the water grew cold again.

When I got out, I wrapped myself in a towel—or at least, the medieval version of a towel—a stiff piece of linen that had probably been a tablecloth before it grew too stained to lay out anymore. I wore it while I washed my dress out and hung it up on a peg by the fireplace to dry.

I figured I might as well wear the towel all night. No one was around to see me anyway.

That's when I turned around and nearly bumped into someone.

Chrissy stood in the kitchen, this time wearing a white sequined ball gown. Her platinum hair was piled on top of her head in a bun, making her look older than the last time I'd seen her. She wore no sunglasses and the end of her wand glowed like a nightlight. Pale glitter covered her face. She smiled at me benevolently. "I am your Fair Godmother."

I let out a breath because she'd scared me. "Yeah, I know. We've already been introduced, Chrissy."

She shushed me, waving the wand in my direction. "I am trying to do this right. Don't mess me up."

"Do what right?"

"Shush, and you'll find out."

I was already in a bad mood and this didn't help. "You know, yesterday I called you, like, a hundred times. I thought Tristan was dead. Dead! Where were you when I was hysterical and I needed you—out shopping or still at a party?"

She lowered her wand and sent me a condescending look. "You know, even for a mortal, you're really ungrateful."

"Ungrateful for what? To be here? A cyclops tried to eat me not long ago."

She brushed off my comment with one perfectly manicured hand. "Did you think wishes were like kittens, that all they were going to do was purr and cuddle with you?" She shook her head benevolently. "Those type of wishes have no power. The only wishes that will ever change you are the kind that may, at any moment, eat you whole. But in the end, they are the only wishes that matter. Now then," she looked me up and down, from my wet hair to my bare feet. "I take it you aren't ready to go to the ball."

"I'm not going to the ball."

"Not like that," she said. "The dirty-sheet look just doesn't do anything for your figure." She waved the wand over me, and before I could begin to protest I wore a purple velvet gown with gold trimming. I took a step and my skirts swished around two sparkling slippers on my feet.

I felt my hair. It was in some sort of updo with a tiara snuggled into its curls. I shook my head at Chrissy. "What did you do that for?"

"It's my job as your Fair Godmother. It's all part of the Cinderella package you ordered during your first wish." She gave me a satisfied smile. "This really is some of my best work. It's a shame my ball gown professor isn't here to see this. Oh, and you'll need to be careful with those shoes. They're dancing slippers. The rest is just fairy magic. Now then—onto the transportation. What sort of vegetables do you have lying around?"

She opened the pantry door and I followed after her. "I'm not Cinderella anymore and I don't want to go to the feast—or the ball, or whatever you want to call it. I can't go. It's too dangerous." I wasn't sure if she'd be mad at me for getting rid of her enchantment, but I didn't see a way around telling her. "I took some switching potion a few days ago and I can't kiss anyone's hand, or who knows what sort of enchantment I'll end up with."

She picked up an onion and turned it over in her palm, surveying it in an unconcerned manner. "That's what gloves are for. Everyone wears them at these formal events." She walked to the kitchen door and stepped outside.

I followed after her, looking at my hands. Between my sleeves and the gloves I wore, none of my arm was visible at all. The only skin showing was my face and neck. Still, the thought of Simon frightened me. "That's not the only problem. The wizard's apprentice—well, actually he's a goat now, but he used to be an apprentice—tried to poison me. What if he's still around? He wanted me dead and I don't even know why."

Chrissy tossed the onion in the air. It arced away from the inn, then just before it hit the ground, it splashed open into an ornate round carriage with gold trimming in the shape of leaves. The doors on each side had golden handles and glass windows. Chrissy walked toward it. "Ah yes, the poison. You really haven't given that the thought it deserves, have you?"

"I've had other things on my mind. Mostly impending doom—thieves, cyclopses, dragons—and my ex-boyfriend dropping by."

Chrissy opened the door and leaned into the carriage, sniffing. "If you want my opinion, you should ask yourself why Simon would want to kill you."

"I have asked myself that. Unfortunately I don't have any good answers."

She wrinkled her nose. "Does this carriage smell like onions to you?"

I sniffed and nodded. It did. "So, do you know why he wanted to kill me?"

She waved her wand at the carriage and once again it was an onion lying on the ground. She tapped her wand against her dress, thinking.

I didn't want to disturb her in case she was thinking of the answer to my question, even though I knew it was more likely she was recalculating her carriage. Finally she turned and stalked back into the kitchen, but I stayed there trying to decipher the riddle.

Why would Simon want to kill me? I couldn't think of a reason at all. He didn't even know me. What possible advantage could he gain from my death, a virtual stranger?

Then the other thing I knew about him clicked into place. He had contact with Princess Margaret before he became a goat. I knew this because she somehow got my ring from him. The next thought made my heart pound harder. What if he hadn't given me the vial of poison at all? What if he had given me something else—just as he'd said—and he'd sold the vial of poison to Margaret?

Who would she want dead? If she was in league with the Black Knight, she'd want to kill the man most likely to defeat him—and that meant Tristan.

A painful gasp escaped my lips. I had to warn him. I had to tell him not to eat any of the castle food. Was it already too late? I had to leave right now. I ran toward the kitchen, but Chrissy was on her way out, grasping a turnip in one hand. "It isn't my fault your pantry isn't equipped with a pumpkin," she told me. "They should be standard at your basic inn. I can only work with what I've got."

"Does Princess Margaret want Tristan dead? Is that it?" I asked.

She threw the turnip into the air, waved her wand, and once again a carriage appeared. This one was not as round as the last and looked a little misshapen at the edges but otherwise appeared just as elegant. "I'm a Fair Godmother, not a private investigator. You'll have to figure out those sorts of things on your own." She walked to the carriage, peering inside. "But don't worry. Despite what you keep telling yourself, you are smart enough to do it." She opened the door, leaned in, and sniffed. When she turned back to me, a smile of triumph lit up her face. "No smell at all. Now, in you go while I round up some mice to turn into horses." As I climbed into the carriage, she looked back at the inn distastefully. "At least I know I'll have no trouble finding *those*."

Which is another thing about the Middle Ages: it had vermin galore. I probably didn't need to know how many mice were in the place where I was eating and sleeping, but I couldn't keep myself from looking.

After she went inside, mice flew out of the kitchen door. At first one, then two more, five, then seven—I was going to have to look more carefully at the inn food before I ate it—and finally twelve in all. As they hit the ground they transformed into beautiful white mares. Each shook its mane out, then trotted over to the carriage. Once near, the carriage put out tendrils that wound around the horses' necks, turning into harnesses.

Last of all, Scuppers, the scruffy inn dog, ran out the door. Before he'd taken two steps he transformed into a coachman wearing fine clothes—but still with scruffy pale hair. He also had a wild-eyed expression, like he was still partially dog. He bent his face toward my window and panted at me before climbing up on the carriage to take the reins.

Okay, that worried me in a driver.

Chrissy appeared at my window, holding the wand and beaming happily. "Everything is perfect and Prince Edmond is waiting for you." She let out a dreamy sigh. "He is such a babe."

"Are you sure you got the coachman right? He looks a little off."

She glanced up at the carriage seat and her voice grew stern. "Come back here, Scuppers." She snapped her fingers. "Right here. Now sit. That's a good dog." She turned back to me, her voice smooth and calm again. "He'll be fine. Besides, the mice know the way to the castle. Trust me, if they serve food there, the mice can find it." She stepped back and waved at me like I was on a homecoming float. "Have a good time! Fall in love! And remember, at midnight you'll be wearing nothing but a stained sheet and driving a turnip!"

I waved back and called out to her, "Thank you!" Really, for once it had paid off to have a fairy godmother.

• • •

The trip to the castle went by quickly, which was good since I was racing the sun across the sky. Even though Scuppers didn't do anything to actually drive the horses—every once in a while I caught sight of him leaning sideways over the driver's box, like a dog hanging his head out a car window—the horses raced up the road that led to the castle. They didn't seem to know how to do anything but gallop. Perhaps because mice scurry when they're trying to go somewhere. The sunlight was already fading and I hoped they still had their micelike nocturnal vision.

I caught a glance of my reflection in the window and barely recognized myself. Glittering makeup outlined two large eyes. Perfectly pink lips opened in surprise, and the tiara on my head sparkled among braids and curls.

I hadn't realized I was wearing jewelry, but amethysts and diamonds clustered on both my ears and throat. I looked exactly like the princesses of every fairy tale I'd ever read.

I touched the amethysts at my throat gingerly, each smooth stone emphasizing the irony of my situation. This is what I had wanted when I first wished to be Cinderella and now that I was actually getting it, I wanted nothing more than to go home with Tristan, Jane, and Hunter and live a normal life again.

The carriage hurried on. Finally, the castle came into view. The horses raced toward it without slowing even when we approached the drawbridge. I knocked on the carriage ceiling, hoping Scuppers could hear me. "Slow the horses!" I yelled.

He didn't. Instead he hung his head over the side of the carriage, his eyes wide and his mouth still panting. "The horses!" I yelled again. "Slow them down!"

His face disappeared. The horses didn't lessen their pace. From the window I could see that the peasants were having their own feast outside of the castle. A bonfire glowed in the yard while a hundred or so stood around it eating and drinking. Some danced while others sang and clapped out a tune.

We drew too close to the crowd and several people had to dive out of the way to keep from being hit. While fleeing, one woman flung her drinking cup in the air and it splashed onto the window as I went by.

"Sorry!" I yelled, but she'd already passed from my sight and I wasn't sure she'd heard me.

Moments later the carriage came to a lurching stop at the castle doors. A castle doorman opened the carriage and eyed me. Slowly, primly, he held out his arm to me. "Madame."

I took the doorman's arm and stepped out of the carriage. "Sorry about the quick arrival. I'm in a hurry to find Sir Tristan. Do you know where he is?"

The doorman gave me a curt nod. "You may inquire within as to the guests' whereabouts." He paused as he glanced at the driver's box. "Is your driver all right? He's acting rather addled."

"Addled" was the word they used for crazy in the Middle Ages. I glanced up at Scuppers. He was biting his shoulder as though he had an itch and hadn't thought to use his hands to scratch it.

"He'll be fine." As I turned and walked toward the castle, Scuppers jumped from the carriage, landing like he was in a game of leapfrog. He sprang up into standing position and took loping steps to follow after me. "Oh no you don't," I told him. "You're not coming inside."

He sniffed in the direction of the castle, licked his lips, and then whined.

"I don't care what you smell, you're not coming." The last thing I needed was a man-dog tagging along after me.

Scuppers whined again and took two quick steps toward the castle as though trying to get around me. I took hold of him by the lapel. "Bad dog, Scuppers. Now go back and wait with the carriage."

He lowered his head and whimpered, but then scampered back to the carriage.

The doorman watched him go with a questioning expression.

"He's not feeling quite himself tonight," I said, and I walked the rest of the way to the castle.

A doorman let me in. Another servant pointed the way to

the great room. He needn't have bothered; the noise of the crowd and musicians led the way. I went and stood in the line to be introduced. It wasn't until I was there that I realized who stood in front of me: my WSM and two wicked stepsisters from the Cinderella fairy tale.

Chapter 23

I stood behind them, hardly breathing in hopes that if I was quiet they wouldn't turn around and notice me. The fairy tale said Cinderella's stepfamily didn't recognize her, but things had never gone exactly like they had in the real fairy tales and perhaps this would be one of those differences. I'd never read a version of the story where Cinderella went and stood right by her family.

Hildegard grasped at her skirt and tapped one foot nervously. "No one will even look at us. Every noblewoman and princess within riding distance will be here."

WSM swatted Hildegard's hands. "True, but so will every nobleman and prince. Perhaps there will be some left over for us."

Matilda leaned toward her sister and snorted. "Perhaps Prince Hubert will take a liking to you."

Hildegard giggled but WSM sent her a cold-eyed stare that silenced her. "A prince is still a prince. I'd give either of your hands to him quickly enough."

Hildegard looked away from her mother and noticed me. Her gaze traveled over me and stopped on my face. She stared at me for a moment and then turned back to her mother.

I waited for her to tell WSM who I was, but instead she whispered, "It isn't fair, Mamá. No one will notice me at all!"

I let out a sigh of relief. A few minutes later a servant introduced me as Lady Savannah of Herndon, and I walked into the ballroom. I don't think a single person heard him. Between the musicians that played in the loft, the dancers that swept across the floor, and the crowds chatting by the food table, no one was paying attention to latecomers. I stood for a few moments trying to catch sight of Tristan's blond hair. I didn't see him, although I caught sight of Prince Edmond dancing with a young woman in the center of the room.

He looked exactly as I remembered from when I was Cinderella—tall and broad shouldered with glossy brown hair and chiseled features—straight out of a Hollywood leading-man catalog. He moved gracefully across the floor dressed in a purple tunic with gold trim. We looked like we'd coordinated our outfits, and I supposed Chrissy had.

I moved past him, glad he hadn't seen me, and looked for Tristan. Princess Margaret danced in the middle of the floor with some nameless nobleman. She wore a cranberry velvet gown and it gave me a guilty sense of pleasure that my dress was nicer.

I walked around the edges of the room, still searching. Every once in a while I noticed men staring at me with smiles on their lips, but I didn't recognize anyone. The thing that struck me the most as I walked through the crowd was how good everyone smelled. It wasn't just the perfume, the smell of the rich was the absence of stink.

I caught sight of Jane talking to Prince Hugh in one corner. She looked out of place in my Snow White dress—it was nicer than the clothes the peasants and servants wore—clearly a lady's dress, but not fancy enough for a ball.

As I walked up to her, she shook her head at Prince Hugh apologetically. I wondered where Hunter was. "Jane?"

She turned and her mouth opened with surprise. "Savannah, how did you get here?"

"Compliments of Chrissy. The inn is now short twelve mice and a turnip, and don't ask what happened to the innkeeper's dog." I gave a quick curtsy to Prince Hugh, then turned my attention back to Jane. "Where's Tristan?"

But Prince Hugh wasn't about to let me ignore him. "You're Savannah?" he asked incredulously. "The lady I spoke to on the stairs?"

"Yes," I said.

Jane gave an "oh!" of understanding, then turned to Prince Hugh. "You thought I was my sister—that's why I didn't know what you were talking about."

The prince's gaze ricocheted between us for a moment longer, adding up our similarities and differences, then he held out his hand to me with a smile. "Your sister tells me that she prefers not to join in the festivities, but I can see you came to dance. Would you do me the honor?"

He wasn't really giving me a choice, but I didn't take his hand. "I'd be happy to dance as soon as I find my friend. I'm afraid it's urgent."

A flash of annoyance went across the prince's face. "Sir Tristan is outside with his friend waiting to see if the Black Knight will answer his challenge. I doubt he'll come. It's bad form to fight during a ball. Any knight of worth is inside dancing."

He raised his hand to me again and this time I took it. Over my shoulder to Jane I said, "Tell Tristan I need to talk to him. Make him promise not to eat or drink anything. Someone may be trying to poison him."

She looked as though she wanted to ask more questions, but the prince had already pulled me away from her. She turned and disappeared into the crowd.

I was out on the dance floor and in Prince Hugh's arms before it hit me that I didn't know how to dance any medieval dances. It wasn't like modern times where slow dancing consisted of huglike swaying to the music. This dance actually had steps. I opened my mouth to tell him I didn't know how to dance, but as I formed the words I realized my feet were moving. I was dancing already.

I looked down at my feet and remembered what Chrissy had said about the shoes—they were dancing slippers—and apparently magic. Cinderella must not have known how to dance either, so her fairy godmother had to give her special shoes to help her out. No wonder the glass slippers didn't disappear when everything else did at midnight. Really, these fairy tales made a lot more sense now that I'd been here.

"You fear that someone is trying to poison your friend?" Prince Hugh asked. The smile on his face told me he found the idea amusing.

"Yes."

"Who?"

I couldn't very well tell him I suspected his sister and yet I couldn't lie. The Black Knight could be in this room. Prince Hugh had just said that any knight of worth was inside dancing. If he heard me lie, if I even did it in his presence, would my tongue burn? I looked around the room even though I knew I wouldn't be able to recognize him.

"You don't know?" Prince Hugh prompted.

"I don't want to discuss it."

His eyes searched my face and he nodded. "Every lady has

her secrets." He leaned a bit closer and added, "I imagine you
have several."

"I have my secrets," I answered.

He smiled at me and two perfect dimples formed in his
already perfect face. He surveyed me another moment and said,
"You look remarkably like your sister."

"And you look very much like your brother."

A bit of cynicism twisted his smile. "Yes, except he is more
handsome."

"That's not true at all."

"As long as Edmond wears the crown, he will always be
more handsome."

I hadn't thought of that. Prince Edmond would inherit the
entire kingdom. What did the second sons of kings do in the
Middle Ages? I'm not sure history class had ever covered this
topic but apparently whatever it was, Hugh wasn't pleased
with it. I felt a pang of sympathy for him.

"Jane is my older sister. She's always done everything better than me. She's a straight-A student." I realized that didn't
mean anything to him so I added, "She's the smart one."

He looked at me as though he didn't believe it, which made
me smile.

The song ended, and although Prince Hugh released me
from his arms, he didn't move from the dance floor. I supposed
that since we hadn't danced long, he wanted to dance a second
song as well. As we waited, Prince Edmond appeared at his
brother's side.

He nodded in my direction then turned to Prince Hugh. "I'm
afraid I must ask to cut in." Prince Edmond's attention turned
back to me and he sent me a dazzling smile. "I find I can't go
another moment without meeting this enchanting woman."

Hugh glared at him, which Edmond didn't see as he was

busy staring at me. Then Hugh said curtly, "Edmond, may I present Lady Savannah to you."

I curtsied, and when I looked up again Hugh was gone, making his way through the crowd.

The music started and Edmond took my hand and pulled me into dance position. I looked over his shoulder at Hugh's retreating back until I couldn't see it anymore.

I could feel Prince Edmond's gaze on me. He leaned toward me and spoke softly. "I'm quite pleased to make such a fine lady's acquaintance."

"Thank you."

We danced, and I was glad for the shoes that effortlessly moved me across the floor.

"From what part of the country do you hail?" he asked. "Do I know your parents?"

"You don't know them, your highness. I come from a land very far away."

I waited for him to ask me more questions about myself, dreaded it actually, since most of them I wouldn't be able to answer. But he seemed content to hold me in his arms and watch me dance. Another minute passed. "I daresay I've never seen the likes of your grace or beauty in my kingdom."

Right. He'd looked right at me over eight months ago and called me "serving wench." It made me wonder how much of beauty is in fact wealth or fashion or mystery. "Thank you," I said.

He smiled and his face took on a stunning glow. "You'll think this is foolishness, but last night I dreamed a fairy stood beside my bed and told me that tonight I would meet the woman who was meant to be my wife. The fairy said this woman would have to go suddenly, but she would leave behind a token so that if I searched hard enough, I might find her again." He looked at my feet, then gazed back into my eyes. "I won't tell you what she said the woman would leave—it's so silly—not the type of token a woman normally gives to a man..."

Okay, this was all going a little fast and in a direction I didn't want. I glanced around the room, more than ever wishing Tristan was somewhere nearby. "Your highness, I'm sure you'll meet many women tonight. And besides, you can't trust anything a fairy tells you. They're constantly getting things wrong."

He laughed and pulled me closer. "Ah, you're modest too. You'll do nicely as my bride."

Just like that? He was deciding to marry me after one dance? "You don't really know me at all," I said. "What if I'm not...smart or punctual?"

He twirled me effortlessly, then returned me to his arms. "When you're a queen, time bends on its knee to serve you, not the other way around. As for intelligence—in my opinion wives shouldn't be too smart. It only complicates things."

I laughed, then realized he wasn't joking. "But you might not like my personality..."

He leaned closer and flashed a set of perfectly white teeth. "Trust me, your beauty compensates doubly for any deficit in your personality."

At one point—well not too long ago, really—I would have loved to hear this comment. I would have even hoped it was true and not just charming. Now it seemed silly on his lips and altogether insulting. I didn't want someone who had to force himself to overlook my personality.

I glanced out across the room and noticed Tristan standing on the edge of the dance floor somehow managing to look both sleek and rugged—and utterly handsome. He watched me with his arms folded. This is when I realized I was a hypocrite, because suddenly I wanted nothing more in the world than for Tristan to notice how beautiful I was and to overlook all my deficits.

He looked at me not with admiration but with frustration, as though he wasn't happy to see me.

The dance ended, and I waited for Prince Edmond to walk me off the dance floor. Instead he took hold of my hand, raised it to his lips, and kissed my glove. "I'm afraid I must claim your dances for the rest of the night. No other partner can tempt me to leave you."

Cinderella and Prince Charming had danced the night away, hadn't they? Very inconvenient when I needed to warn Tristan that Margaret might be planning to poison him. "That's so sweet," I said casting a glance at Tristan. "But I really need to talk to Sir Tristan for a few minutes."

Prince Edmond was already pulling me farther away on the dance floor. "Sir Tristan can wait."

And Sir Tristan did. As I twirled the floor with Edmond, I saw him standing on the side of the dance floor, talking to one noble and then another, but his gaze kept returning to me, impatience darkening his expression.

The song ended and the next started. Still Edmond wouldn't hear of me leaving his arms. He told me my eyes were like brilliant jewels, my skin shone like sunlight over the snow, and my lips looked as soft as rose petals. He couldn't have been more romantic, and I just wanted to leave.

I spotted Jane and Hunter standing at the far end of the room, looking out of place among so many guests with fancy clothes. But Hunter held Jane's hand and she leaned in close, and both seemed oblivious to everything else going on around them.

I noticed the wizard talking to a group of men and saw Scuppers standing by the food table, gnawing on a cooked chicken leg. So much for obeying my orders to stay outside. Still, there was nothing I could do about it even if I had wanted to shoo him away. Besides, when you came right down to it, his table manners weren't all that much worse than those of other men I'd seen in the Middle Ages.

Prince Edmond talked to me of the kingdom and the crop predictions for the season. He pointed his father out to me, a middle-aged man who, despite the streaks of gray hair on his head, seemed to be made mostly of muscle. I wondered what the king did to stay so fit. As Edmond spoke, I nodded, smiled, and answered him halfheartedly.

My WSM and two stepsisters, as per the fairy tale, watched me sullenly from the side of the room, but showed no sign that they recognized me. It wasn't worth taking the time to gloat. I kept wondering how I was ever going to get away from Edmond long enough to talk to Tristan.

After another song Tristan apparently grew tired of waiting for me, and disappeared from the edge of the dance floor. When I saw him next he moved past me, towing Margaret in his arms. Margaret. He'd probably have been safer if I'd left him outside.

She smiled at him, but even from a distance I could tell it was a condescending smile. Why in the world he kept smiling back at her, I didn't know.

We danced two more songs. When I saw Tristan walk Margaret back into the crowd, I told Edmond I was thirsty and asked if he could get a drink for me. He obliged me and we walked off the dance floor. As soon as he went to look for a serving girl, I slipped through the crowd, making my way toward Tristan.

He stood by Princess Margaret and several other nobles. They were offering their condolences that the Black Knight hadn't responded to his challenge.

"Surely he's heard of your success with the cyclops and dragon and is afraid to face you," one man said.

Several agreed. A few suggested Tristan ring the bell

tomorrow and see if the Black Knight responded then. One added, "It's a fight I won't miss—when the Black Knight finally faces Sir Tristan."

I took hold of Tristan's arm to get his attention. "Can I speak with you for a moment?"

The men all stopped talking and bowed in my direction. Their eyes took me in and they smiled enviously at Tristan. I found the attention disconcerting, but I could tell it totally ticked off Princess Margaret. She pursed her lips together and glared at me.

Tristan said, "May I present Lady Savannah to you," then repeated the names of the earls and barons who stood nearby. I didn't try to remember them, I just smiled and nodded, then pulled Tristan away. As we walked toward the far corner of the room, I checked over my shoulder. No sign of Prince Edmond, but I was sure it wouldn't be long until he tracked me down again. Really, if Edmond insisted on being so attentive, I would flee long before midnight.

"You decided to be Cinderella after all," Tristan said tightly, eyeing my dress. "I thought you were through with princes."

"I came to warn you that Margaret may be trying to poison you. I'm not positive, but she could have bought the poison from Simon and I can't think of who else she'd want to kill."

"Oh." Tristan gazed back at me without concern. "Margaret *might* have bought poison and she *might* want to use it. Well, you obviously couldn't deliver that message without dressing in a ball gown and dancing with Prince Edmond for every song." Tristan reached over and pushed my skirt away from my feet. "You've even got the glass slippers. Perfect."

I yanked my skirt out of his hands. "Did you even hear me about Princess Margaret?"

"Yes, you don't like her. I understand that."

I tried again to make him see my point. "The poison that

Simon stole—think about it—if she's in league with the Black Knight, what else would she do with it?"

Tristan's blue eyes narrowed in on mine. "You just assume, of course, that she doesn't want to marry me. That she couldn't. Marrying me would be a fate worth killing for."

I blinked at him in surprise. "That isn't what I meant. I just don't want you to trust her. She could hurt you."

"She could hurt me? She's always been very nice to me." He looked upward as though considering the charge. "And not once has she set fairies on me to transport me to another realm."

"Tristan—," I started, but he cut me off.

"One time when she didn't know I was near, she told her lady's maid that she didn't care whether a man was lowborn or not. An ambitious man would rise to the top regardless. And I have. It's too bad you've been too wrapped up in fairy-tale princes to notice."

I took a step away from him, stung. "I came all this way to warn you. I don't know why I bothered."

His gaze ran up and down me. "You came all this way to meet up with Prince Charming. It's what you've wanted all along. I read your contract."

I felt my cheeks flushing. "Fine. Trust her. You'll see I'm right after you're dead."

"Well, it all becomes a moot point after that, doesn't it?"

Which is pretty much why it's impossible to argue with smart people. They pay more attention to what you say than to what you mean. I turned around so quickly my skirt twirled around my ankles, and I stalked off in the direction I'd come. I'd find Edmond again and dance with him until midnight. And I didn't care if Tristan spent the entire time dancing with Margaret. They deserved each other.

Chapter 24

I weaved through the crowd, but instead of looking for Edmond, I went outside onto the balcony. I wanted to be alone.

I walked past couples standing in the moonlight. The stars spread out in the sky above the green, untamed land below. I had to grudgingly admit that the Middle Ages was nice in that regard—everything green and wild. Even here at the castle, their pinnacle of civilization, thick vines crawled up the balcony's walls.

Looking at the romantic scenery made me feel even worse. I had thought that Tristan cared about me. Had all his feelings for me evaporated? Perhaps they hadn't been that strong to begin with. I should just leave and go back to the inn.

I'd only taken a few steps into the ballroom when Edmond found me. He carried two goblets, and after giving me one, took my free hand in his. He pulled me back toward the dance floor. "Come, let's quench our thirst and dance again. You've been away from my arms for too long."

We walked several steps until we came upon Tristan. His eyes flickered over my hand in Edmond's and his jaw grew tight. I nodded at him, said "Sir Tristan," and waited for him to move out of our way. He didn't. The next moment Princess Margaret arrived at his side holding two goblets. She offered one to Tristan without paying any attention to Edmond or me. "Are you thirsty, Sir Tristan?"

"No," I said too quickly.

I sent Tristan a wide-eyed look of warning, but he took the goblet from her hand just to spite me. "Thank you, your highness. You're as thoughtful as you are beautiful."

"A toast then." I held my goblet up and tried not to glare at him. "To love, and the things we do for it."

Edmond smiled and raised his own goblet. "Here, here."

Margaret raised her drink and clinked it into mine with a cold smile. Tristan reluctantly raised his own drink. His face was serious and he didn't take his eyes off of mine.

I slammed my goblet into his with such force that it flew backward, spilling the entire contents on his tunic.

He flinched, gasped, and took a step backward as the liquid ran down his shirt.

"Oh! So sorry," I said. "I'm horribly clumsy." To Prince Edmond I added, "It's one of those personality deficits you're going to have to overlook."

Edmond waved to a passing kitchen girl, but smiled at me. "It's already forgotten."

Tristan held his tunic away from his chest and sent me a dark look. "I haven't forgotten it."

I looked at Margaret to see if her facial expression showed any frustration. Had I just spoiled her plan to poison Tristan?

She took a linen napkin from the kitchen girl and dabbed at Tristan's chest without showing any emotion at all.

Edmond looked between his sister and me. "I've forgotten my manners. Have you met my sister, Princess Margaret?"

I curtsied awkwardly.

She turned from Tristan long enough to cast me a disdainful look. "We've met. Or at least I've met one of you. I hadn't realized before that you came in a pair."

"A pair?" Edmond asked.

Tristan said, "I think Princess Margaret is referring to her sister, Jane. They look very much alike."

Edmond's brows lifted in surprise and he scanned the room. "Two such beauties? It's impossible."

Princess Margaret finished dabbing at Tristan's shirt. "The other one is in the far corner in that horribly plain red dress."

We all looked in that direction except for Tristan. He took the cloth from Margaret and tried to absorb some of the liquid still dripping down his shirt.

Edmond narrowed his eyes in on Jane. "That's odd. I could have sworn Queen Neferia told me that damsel was her stepdaughter." He considered her for a moment longer, then shrugged. "But I should have known I misunderstood. If the queen had thought she was her kin she most certainly would have gone over to speak to her." He took a sip of his drink as though he'd already dismissed the matter, but I clutched my glass as one thought and then another crowded in on me. Just as this ball proved that the Cinderella wish was still in effect, Edmond's comment had shown me the Snow White wish was going on too.

Queen Neferia was here somewhere and she wanted to kill Snow White.

I looked around the room, searching, even though I didn't know what Neferia looked like.

It had been eight months since I'd been in the dwarfs' home and longer than that since Snow White had left Neferia's court. Neferia hadn't seen Snow White since then, but Jane, wearing her dress, looked enough like me to be mistaken for her.

Which meant Jane was in danger.

"Where is Queen Neferia?" I asked. "What does she look like?"

Princess Margaret twisted her goblet between her fingers. "Why the interest?"

I didn't have time to come up with a reason. "What color is her gown?"

Edmond nodded to the left corner of the room. "Black."

I turned and saw her. She stood tall and regal, with stunning, cold features. Her hair lay against her skin, shiny and dark as crows' wings. It matched her black velvet dress perfectly. She stood not far from Jane and Hunter, watching them.

Thank goodness for Hunter. At least Neferia wouldn't try to hurt Jane when he stood by with a sword hanging at his hip.

I shoved my goblet back into Edmond's hand. "Tristan, we've got to—" I didn't finish my sentence. As I spoke I saw Neferia take a spiced apple from her hand and place it onto a serving girl's tray. She bent over and whispered something into the serving girl's ear, then pointed toward Jane. "No!" I gasped, and headed toward her.

The music stopped, signaling a break for the musicians. Which meant that all the people left the dance floor and congregated directly in my way. I tried to weave my way around them, pushing past noblemen and ladies. "Pardon me. Pardon me." I said the words like a panicked mantra. Behind me, I could hear Prince Edmond calling my name, but I didn't turn around.

Jane and Hunter came into view again. The serving girl was already there, dipping into a curtsy and handing the apple to Jane. "I've been asked to tell your ladyship that the kitchen prepared this delicacy just for you, m'lady, in honor of your beauty."

Jane blushed and took the apple. "That's so kind. Tell the kitchen thank you for me."

"No!" I called, but she either didn't hear me or didn't realize I was calling to her.

She brought the apple to her lips.

I dashed the last few steps to her and grabbed hold of her hand. "Don't!"

Jane tried to pull her arm out of my grip. "Savannah, what are you doing?"

I didn't let go of her arm. "It's poisonous."

Jane looked at me and then at the serving girl, who stared back at us with startled disbelief. Jane lowered her voice but didn't let go of the apple. "Why would someone want to poison me?"

"Because you look like Snow White."

"No, I don't."

Instead of arguing about it, I snatched the apple from her hand, dropped it on the ground, then lifted my skirt and stomped on it with my foot. "Why. Don't. You. Ever. Listen. To. Me?" Little pieces of apple splattered onto the hem of my gown and my slippers, but at least I knew no one would eat it.

With a nearly emotionless voice, Princess Margaret said, "I take it the refreshments were not to your liking?"

I looked up and saw not only her but Tristan and Prince Edmond staring at me. Tristan's brows were drawn together in question.

Edmond looked at the smashed apples by my feet, then said, "Of course there may be some things in your personality that are harder to overlook than others."

I'd still been clutching my skirt, and now I let go and it fell

back into place like a curtain coming down at the end of a play.
"I'm sorry," I said, "but that apple was poisonous."

"Poisonous?" Princess Margaret took a sharp breath inward.
"You accuse us of poisoning our guests?"

"Not you; Queen Neferia. She told the serving girl to give
my sister that apple."

The serving girl nodded, her face white as though she knew
however this turned out, she was going to get in trouble.

Edmond held out a hand, prompting me. "And?"

They were all staring at me, even Hunter, Jane, and Tristan.
But how could I tell Prince Edmond that I knew what was
going to happen because of a fairy tale?

"She's already tried to poison Snow White three times."

Tristan exchanged a look with Hunter and Jane. They, at
least, now understood the situation. Hunter took a step toward
Jane and put one hand on the hilt of his sword. Then each of
them scanned the crowd.

Edmond and Margaret still gazed at me with skepticism
though. I said, "You can ask Prince Hubert. He knows. The
dwarfs Snow White lives with told him about it."

Prince Edmond nodded, as though finally able to make
sense of my distress. He snapped his fingers in the serving
girl's direction. "Go fetch Prince Hubert—I believe he's in the
barn." Then Prince Edmond stepped over to me and took hold
of my arm. When he spoke, his voice was firm—the way one
talks to a child. "You can't believe the things Prince Hubert says.
His mind, sadly, is filled with nothing but whimsy." He squeezed
my arm. "Queen Neferia, however, is our closest ally. It will not
do to have you insult her."

Edmond tried to propel me away, but I didn't move. "Queen
Neferia is evil. Is that really the type of person you should have
as your closest ally?"

Prince Edmond looked at me with surprise, although I had a feeling this was because I refused to move and not because of my accusation. "You needn't worry about politics," he said. "The wisest men in the land are my advisors. Your task is to do only what you have so well accomplished already; to stand by my side, a vision of beauty." He didn't wait for a response from me. Instead he snapped his fingers at a passing serving girl and pointed at the smashed apple near my feet. "Wench, clean up this mess."

I knew there was no point in arguing with him and besides, he didn't give me the chance. He started up a conversation with his sister about the musicians, pointedly changing the subject.

Hunter and Jane began a hushed conversation with Tristan that I only caught a few words of, just enough to tell they were talking about the sleeping arrangements at the castle tonight and whether Jane and I would be safe staying here with a homicidal queen in the vicinity.

I nearly volunteered that Jane could run off with me at midnight, but then decided that wasn't the sort of thing I should say in front of Prince Edmond.

After a few minutes of this, Prince Edmond looked toward the ballroom door. "Here's Prince Hubert coming in now."

Princess Margaret smiled over at me. "You say it was dwarfs that told him about Queen Neferia? I suppose that's a step up from the mice and doves he usually converses with."

The contempt in her voice prickled me even more than Prince Edmond's patronizing tone had earlier. I clutched my hands into fists. "No matter what Prince Hubert says, I have told you the truth about Queen Neferia. You can think what you want to about *him*, but *I* am not crazy."

I looked over at the door and saw a handsome, well-built man coming into the room. He carried a cat in his arms, but this wasn't what I noticed about him. The thing that caught my eye was the goat that trailed behind him.

. . .

Granted, it's probably not the best way to prove your sanity if you, for no discernable reason to those standing near you, suddenly let out a scream, push your way through the crowd, and crawl onto the refreshment table.

Quite a few people watched me do this with open mouths. During my scramble up on the table one of my slippers fell off my foot and tumbled to the floor. Prince Edmond looked at it, held up his hands, then turned away muttering, "I'm not picking that up. Someone else can get it."

So much for love at first sight.

Tristan looked at me on the table and yelled, "What are you doing?"

I didn't answer. I heard someone in the crowd say, "What's that goat doing in here?" And several people laughed and pointed at it running across the room while others moved out of its way. I looked around for something on the table to defend myself with but only found a ladle.

Then Simon saw me. He stopped so quickly he momentarily slid across the floor, his hooves scraping on the stone as he tried to adjust his direction. And then he charged toward me.

I realized the table wasn't going to be high enough to keep him away from me. Goats could jump up on things, couldn't they? That's why there was a whole breed of them called mountain goats.

"Tristan!" I screamed. "Help me!"

He wasn't far away from me, but he only looked at me in confusion.

Simon ran past Tristan. I watched him coming toward me,

his feet clipping faster and faster across the floor and his bulgy eyes training in on me. My hands shook on the ladle. How ironic that although I had the Black Knight's power of invincibility, I was going to be undone by a goat.

Simon rushed toward the table. I could see him getting ready to leap. And the next moment something shot out from under the table and rammed into him. A man. They both rolled onto the floor.

It took me a second to realize it was Scuppers. He must have crawled under the table to sleep and when he woke up and saw the goat charging toward him, he leaped out at it like any dog would.

Simon broke free from the scuffle, but Scuppers stood in the way of the table. Simon ran to the right and Scuppers bounded after him, hands over feet, making better time than any real man could have done. Simon darted toward the back of the room and Scuppers followed after him, his coat tails flapping as he ran.

Tristan walked up to me and picked up my slipper from the floor. He didn't hand it to me, which is when I realized I was still clutching the ladle tightly in front of me.

He tucked the slipper into his pocket and pulled out his sword. Raising one finger in question he asked, "Who exactly am I supposed to protect you from? The man or the goat?"

"The goat. The man is actually the innkeeper's dog."

Tristan turned to face the crowd, his sword raised. "And why am I protecting you from a goat?"

"He's actually Simon, the wizard's apprentice, and he wants to switch places with me so I'll be a goat."

"I see." I knew he didn't, but he didn't press the point. "Is there anything else you'd like to tell me about?"

A crack of light went off midway across the ballroom, as though lightning had struck the floor. The crowd cleared from the spot; the bright color of dresses and tunics moving to the edges of the room like a retreating rainbow.

Scuppers had the goat pinned to the ground. His mouth angled to get a hold on the goat's neck while it kicked and bleated. The wizard strode toward the two, arms raised, as though this would increase the volume of his voice. "Off, you foul beast! Begone! That's my goat and none shall touch it!"

Scuppers backed away from the goat, still on all fours, and let out a throaty growl of protest. The wizard bent down, picked up Simon, and flung the goat over his shoulder.

Then the wizard turned and headed toward the door, yelling, "This is the treatment I get from King Roderick's court? You take my animal and make sport of it for your pleasure? I shan't stay where a wizard isn't treated with respect. I shan't!"

The goat bellowed as he walked by me, his bulgy-eyed gaze never leaving my face. Then the door shut behind them and the two were gone. I dropped the ladle and it clanked onto the table. Deep tremors rumbled around inside of me and I was afraid my legs would give way. Tristan looked up at me, concerned. He held his free hand out to me, and I stepped down and flung my arms around him. I was just so glad that— instead of disappearing like Prince Edmond had—Tristan was still here. I pressed my cheek to his chest. "There's actually a lot I need to tell you about."

I knew he would probably push me away, what with his future fiancée milling somewhere in the crowd, but he didn't. He just wound his arms around me and let out a sigh.

From the middle of the room the king called out, "What is all this? Guests on the table, goats running around—and what is that man doing on the floor? Who invited him to my ball?"

I looked and saw Scuppers squatting on the floor, trying to scratch his ear with his foot. I nearly pretended that I didn't know who he was, but really, after he'd saved me from Simon he deserved better than that. I stepped away from Tristan. "He's my coachman, your highness. He's harmless really."

King Roderick's gaze swung over to me and when he spoke his voice rolled around me the way a river tumbles stones in its current. "I shall decide that for myself. Who are you, Madame?"

But before I spoke a single word, a page burst through the door. "Your highness, the Black Knight is outside the castle. He wishes to fight Sir Tristan."

Chapter 25

The exodus outside was immediate. The crowd let out a cheer as Tristan turned and headed for the door. He only gave me a backward glance and motioned for Hunter. "This is it."

I took two steps after Tristan and realized he still had my other slipper. I called after him, but with everyone else cheering and calling his name, he didn't hear me. I wobbled a few steps, then bent down, took off my remaining slipper, and put it in my pocket. I walked through the castle barefoot, knowing it would ruin my stockings.

Jane came up beside me. She looked over one shoulder and then the other. "So a wicked queen is trying to kill me and an enchanted goat is after you?"

"Yeah."

"Great party."

"We'll leave as soon as Tristan is done."

Jane slowed her pace and kept searching the crowd. "You should have told me about all of this before tonight."

"I didn't know I was still Cinderella or Snow White, let alone both of them, but we have more important things to worry about right now. Tristan has to face the Black Knight."

We made it through the front door of the castle, then followed what was left of the crowd across the grounds. The bonfire I'd seen earlier still glowed but it had been deserted by the peasants for better entertainment.

We passed through the castle gates. Torches cast their light over the crowd and shone on the form of the Black Knight. He sat atop his horse like a dark statue, with peasants and nobles alike making a large circle around the two combatants.

Tristan stood with his back to me, and after another moment my eyes found Hunter standing just at the edge of the crowd as well. King Roderick stood closest to the castle gate, as though he wanted to make sure his path was clear in case he needed to run from the knight. The castle guards surrounded the king, each one with his sword drawn. I didn't see the royal children at all and wondered if they didn't dare venture out when the Black Knight was around.

I felt a twinge of worry for the knight. He probably didn't know he wasn't invincible anymore, that he was in danger here. I wished I'd told him.

I'd missed the first part of Tristan's and the Black Knight's speech because I'd been slow coming out, and I stood on my tiptoes trying to see over the heads in front of me.

"You didn't accept my challenge of a joust," the Black Knight said, and his voice was as cold as the night air. "I see no reason why I should accept your challenge of a spear throw."

"Then we are at a draw," Tristan said. "I have promised Lady Savannah that I would not fight you with the sword or the lance. Chivalry prevents me from breaking my oath to her."

The Black Knight lifted his head. I couldn't tell where he

was looking—it could have been at anyone in the crowd, but I felt like he was staring at me.

"Lady Savannah made you promise such?" he asked, and muffled though his voice was, I heard an edge creep into it. "You think highly of the lady?"

"I do," Tristan said.

I backed several steps away, letting those behind me fill my spot. I wanted to shrink from the Black Knight's gaze; I wanted to disappear into the veil of the night.

I hadn't really made Tristan promise not to fight with the sword or lance and if the Black Knight asked me I wouldn't be able to lie. What would happen then?

The Black Knight's voice cut through the night toward me. "And she thinks just as highly of you?"

"Yes."

"A knight is lucky to have the affection of such a noble lady."

"Yes," Tristan said. "Do we have a contest or not?"

The Black Knight's helmet still looked out in my direction. I took two more steps backward, my heart pounding. I shouldn't have come outside. I shouldn't have let him see me.

Slowly, the knight said, "I think we can come to agreement about a contest—a contest of chivalry—and the same consequences would apply."

Tristan nodded. "Speak, and I will tell you whether I agree or not."

The Black Knight leaned down toward Tristan and lowered his voice. I was too far away to hear what was said, and yet in the murmur of words I was sure I heard my name spoken.

Me? They were going to involve *me* in their fight? I clenched the sides of my dress, simultaneously wanting to flee and refusing to move.

Tristan yelled, "I accept!" and the crowd cheered and clapped.

Tristan turned in a circle, searching the faces around him. "Where is Lady Savannah?" he called.

At once everyone looked around them. The Black Knight raised a hand and pointed in my direction. One by one people stepped out of the way, opening up a path for Tristan to find me.

"I didn't hear what they said," I called out, trying to find Jane's face among all the rest. "What is the contest?"

No one answered me, although several people laughed. Everyone stared at me.

Tristan ran toward me, but there was no concern in his expression, only happiness, triumph. Was the contest already over? Had he won?

I looked over at the Black Knight, but he wasn't moving, only calmly sitting on his horse, watching.

Once Tristan reached me he took hold of my arms and smiled at me breathlessly. I hadn't seen him so happy since before we'd come to the Middle Ages. "Kiss me," he said.

"What?" I tried to take a step back from him but he held onto me tightly.

"Just kiss me. Do it now."

But I couldn't. I would switch enchantments with him and be stuck in the Middle Ages forever. I shook my head.

Frustration filled his face. "Savannah, this is no time to be shy. The contest depends on it."

"What?" I asked again.

His grip tightened on my arms. "The Black Knight and I are having a contest to see who you will willingly kiss first. You have to kiss me or I'll lose."

I could feel the crowd pressing around us, watching, waiting, and yet I stood there unable to move or speak.

His eyes didn't leave mine and I couldn't break his gaze. I watched disappointment seep into his eyes with every second that passed. "Savannah," he said, and it was half question, half reprimand.

I whispered, "I'm sorry, I can't. I—"

Tristan dropped his hold on my arms. "You can't?" and it wasn't a whisper.

From on top of his horse the Black Knight laughed. All heads turned in his direction. All heads but mine. I looked at the ground and took shuddering breaths.

"She can't," the Black Knight called, "because she has already kissed me. On our first meeting, in fact; she begged me to kiss her. Ask her—I've given her truth potion and she cannot lie in my presence lest her tongue burn out of her mouth."

I didn't say anything, just felt my cheeks burning with shame. I wanted to explain but couldn't. I couldn't let an entire crowd know I'd taken a switching potion.

Tristan turned to me, his eyes blazing with anger. "You kissed him? You *asked* him to kiss you?"

I raised my gaze to his and at once felt scorched by his expression. "It isn't what you think."

"What I think?" he asked. "You told me you needed more time after Hunter. You said you were through with fairy-tale romances. What I think is that you're a liar. Now did you kiss him or not?"

It hurt to do it, but I nodded.

Even after his speech, Tristan still took a step away from me as though I'd struck him. The crowd at once murmured, pressing toward us and throwing words of scorn in my direction.

"Hussy!"

"The way of such a woman is wickedness!"

"The downfall of he who held her dear!"

I stepped toward Tristan, my hands out. My voice came out in broken spurts. "I'm sorry, but we'll think of another way to defeat him."

He shook his head. "Don't you understand?"

"Tristan—"

I didn't finish; the Black Knight spoke again. "And thus falls your most promising knight." He held his sword out to the crowd and yelled, "All of you will likewise fall if Prince Edmond does not accept my challenge soon. I tire of waiting. I give him a fortnight and no longer. Then I will return and you shall feel the wrath of the Black Knight." He nudged his horse forward, and the crowd parted before him. He called over his shoulder to King Roderick. "I leave it to the king to see that the consequences of Sir Tristan's challenge are fulfilled. If his head isn't posted outside the castle wall by tomorrow at nightfall I will consider it an act of war."

"What?" I yelled and then screamed, "No!"

I knew the Black Knight heard me. For a moment his head swung in my direction and he paused as he looked at me. I stepped toward him, half stumbling. "No!" I cried. "Have mercy!" But he spurred his horse on and rode toward the forest.

I turned back to Tristan, my head shaking, all of me shaking. "You didn't wager your life. Tell me you didn't wager your life."

His voice, his manner was bitterly calm. "It was the only way I could get the Black Knight to agree to his own banishment if he lost."

Above the rumblings of the crowd, I heard the king, his tone heavy with regret. "Guards, bring Sir Tristan to me."

I couldn't breathe. Everything looked dark and shadowy by the torchlight. The cold air grabbed at my throat.

The crowd at once erupted with protests. "It wasn't a fair fight!" someone yelled.

"It should be *her* head, not *his* that hangs on the castle wall!"

"We don't answer to the Black Knight!" someone else shouted.

Instead of moving out of the way, the people stood their

ground, blocking the way of the guards as they tried to come for Tristan.

I put my hand on Tristan's arm. "You have to run." I looked around the courtyard. "My carriage—I have twelve fast horses, at least they'll be fast until midnight—"

He didn't move. "And what will I do when the Black Knight seeks revenge on all of these people? Where will I run to then?"

"They'll be able to handle the Black Knight. He's not invincible anymore."

Tristan still made no move to leave. His jaw was set. He looked at the progress of the guards through the crowd.

I tugged at Tristan's arm to get his attention again and kept my voice low so only he could hear me. "That's how I stole his invincibility enchantment. I drank switching potion and now I'll switch enchantments with anyone who kisses me this week." I knew he didn't understand but I went on trying to explain, trying to redeem myself. "I kissed him, but I did it for you."

Tristan nodded but still didn't look at me. I wasn't sure if he believed me or not. "I remember that day. You were worried you'd end up being the Black Knight's downfall. Ironic, isn't it?"

The guards were making headway through the crowd. They yelled and pushed people out of the way, their swords gripped in tight fists. No one was putting up much resistance anymore. The guards would be here soon.

I reached over to Tristan's waist and pulled his sword from its sheath. I held it in front of me, my senses already growing sharp. "I won't let them take you."

He let out a sigh. "You don't know how to use that. Put it down before someone decides to chop it out of your hands."

I didn't.

Tristan reached out and took the sword from me. I could

have stopped him. The world slowed as his hand came toward mine, every moment crawled by. I saw not only his hand reaching for the sword, but the guards and the crowd before us. One of the guards had his sword pointed at Hunter, was yelling at Hunter to drop his weapon. Another had just grabbed Jane by her arm.

I realized I could save Tristan, but I couldn't save them all. If I stood here and fought for Tristan's life, Hunter and Jane would lose theirs.

So I let Tristan take the sword.

The world still moved in slow motion. I put my hand on Tristan's shoulder and leaned in close to him. I pushed myself up on my tiptoes and kissed his lips.

At once the world sped up, crashed around me, with noise and motion.

But Tristan looked with wonder out at the crowd and I could tell his new senses had already kicked in. "What's happened?"

"You're invincible now. They can't hurt you."

The guard who had grabbed Jane held his sword at the base of her throat. Her eyes stared at us, wide and frightened. "Drop your sword!" the guard yelled to Tristan.

Tristan held his sword upright. "Let her go first. Let all of my friends go."

The guards were circling us now; several came around behind us. King Roderick walked toward us but stopped behind the protection of the guards. "You're not in a position to make demands."

The sword swayed in Tristan's hands. He looked from Jane to Hunter and then at King Roderick. "You don't have to fear the Black Knight anymore. He's no longer invincible. I can defeat him for you. Isn't that what you really want?"

The king rubbed his forehead wearily. "We've already seen

how you defeated the Black Knight. Don't make us take the lives of your friends as well as your own."

To me, Tristan whispered, "How fast am I?"

"Not fast enough to save them both," I said.

Tristan lowered his sword slightly. "Give me your word that you'll let them go, and I'll throw down my sword."

King Roderick conferred with two of the guards near him. I wondered why he needed to talk to them about it.

"Don't trust him," I said. "After we're gone, escape. We'll meet in the forest at the cyclops's caves."

Tristan shook his head. "I just need to explain my power to them. If I save them from the Black Knight, they'll make me a prince."

"You don't have to be a prince anymore," I said. "I do. I kissed you, so we switched enchantments." It hurt to say the next words and they cracked in my throat. "Chrissy will probably show up in a day or two to take you back home. Make sure you take Hunter and Jane with you."

Tears flooded my eyes and I hated myself for crying instead of taking my consequences as stoically as Tristan had earlier. It only made it worse to see the alarm in his blue eyes.

He bent over and brushed his lips against mine. "There—now you have your power back. I won't let you be left here forever."

The tears came harder this time because he'd tried to sacrifice himself for me. I should never have been worried before that he would kiss me if he knew how easy it was for him to get rid of his enchantment. "It only works one way. We can't switch back the same enchantments."

The king called over, "Lay down your sword and we will release your friends. You have my word."

Tristan didn't look away from me. "I won't let Chrissy leave you here," he said and dropped his sword.

Immediately the guards flanked him, pointing half a dozen swords at his chest and head. One of them yanked me away from Tristan. He dragged me roughly farther away from the castle gates. "Get her coach ready!" he yelled to someone, though I couldn't see who he was talking to. "Her ladyship is leaving."

He bent his head toward me and sneered at me with rows of crooked teeth. "Her ladyship, the viper. You cost a good man his life this night. I hope you're satisfied with who you've been kissing."

I didn't answer. It was hard enough to see where I was going in the dark and little rocks and pebbles bit into the soles of my feet. I grabbed my skirt with my free hand and tried to hold it up so I wouldn't trip.

The guard went on berating me so loudly that I didn't realize Jane and Hunter were behind me until we were quite a ways from the castle gates and two guards pushed them in front of me.

Jane's hair was mussed and her shoulders heaved up and down from crying. Blood dripped from the corner of Hunter's mouth and he held one hand over his stomach as though in pain. I looked from them to the guards. "What did you do to them?" I demanded.

My guard pulled me a step farther, his foul-smelling breath close to my face. "Nothing that I won't do to you if you try and fight me." He didn't let me go the way Jane and Hunter's guards had. His grip bit into my arm.

My coach pulled up in front of us. The horses pawed and panted as if they knew something was wrong. Instead of Scuppers, one of the guards sat on the box seat.

"What did you do with my coachman?" I asked.

The guard jumped off the box seat and held the reins out to Hunter. "He ran off like a frightened dog when he saw us coming for him. Your other man will have to drive the coach."

Hunter winced, but he managed to climb up on the box seat and hold the reins. "Don't worry," I told him. "The horses know the way. It will be all right." I tried to sound confident. Jane and Hunter didn't know yet that we had a plan and a meeting place. They didn't know Tristan was going to be fine. I wanted to show them that I wasn't worried, which was hard because my voice trembled anyway.

Once Jane saw that Hunter had made it up onto the box she opened the coach door and climbed inside, leaving the door open for me. I stepped toward the coach but my guard jerked me back. "Not you," he said, and the next moment he pushed some bitter-smelling rag against my mouth. "We said we'd let Sir Tristan's friends go. You don't count as a friend anymore, do you?"

One of the guards slammed the coach door shut, then smacked the lead horse on the flank. The horses raced off down the trail, hauling the carriage behind them. I struggled to get away, but my last vision of them was Jane's hands pressed up against the window and her mouth opened in a soundless "No!"

Chapter 26

I clawed at the guard's hands, trying to move them away from my mouth. I kicked at his legs, but with my long dress and bare feet, I didn't do any damage. The other guards converged around me. One held a rope in his hand. "The king still has need of you," he told me. "Doesn't want us to kill you. It would be a regrettable thing if you struggled so much while we tied you up that we broke your neck."

I stopped fighting after that.

They tied my ankles and wrists together, and even though I had stopped struggling, they still gagged me. "It's best for folk not to know we still have you," the guard told me. "It looks bad for a king to go back on his word to a knight—aye, and one who's given his life for the kingdom, at that."

I didn't like the way they talked of Tristan as though he were already dead. It made my heart pound even harder than it already was.

One of the guards picked me up and heaved me over his

shoulder. The other guards took off their cloaks and draped them over my head and back. They walked me back through the castle gates and with each heavy footstep I felt the guard's shoulder jabbing into my stomach.

Then the guard stopped. I heard voices yelling but they sounded far away. The guard dropped me off his shoulder and without being able to put my hands out in front of me, I hit the ground with a painful thud. The cloaks fell from around me and at first I just saw boots. Pairs and pairs of guard boots running toward—I strained my neck to see better—running toward the stables.

A horse emerged from the stables. The rider was young and handsome, with blond hair blowing around his shoulders. Tristan. I tried to call out to him but only managed to make a muffled noise. The guards had reached him. With a raised sword, he knocked away one weapon and then another from the men who ran up to him.

"Over here," I tried to yell to him. I tried to catch his attention but I was just a dark mound lying in the shadows.

Tristan kicked a guard, who sprawled into the others. Without a glance in my direction, he spurred on his horse and rode across the grounds and out the castle gate, leaving me behind.

• • •

The guards took me to the king's chamber. I struggled all the way there, hoping to catch sight of Edmond or even of Hugh, hoping they wouldn't let their father hurt me.

But I didn't see them.

I was dropped in a corner by an empty fireplace and left to sit there, bound, on the cold stone floor. I strained to hear voices in the castle around me. I wondered where Jane and Hunter had gone. I hadn't been able to tell them they were supposed to go to the cyclops's cave. Would they go back to the inn? And would Tristan look there for them when they didn't show up at the cave? When they finally found one another and Tristan discovered I was still at the castle, would he come for me? He wouldn't know where to look and the castle was so big.

Chrissy had always been so late showing up, but she'd been right on time to send me to the ball as Cinderella. What if she'd already come and taken the rest of them home? What if there was no one left who could save me?

I thought of the Black Knight then; I'm not sure why. Perhaps because it seemed like the sort of thing fairy-tale knights would do—rescue damsels who were tied up in castles. The idea left me with no hope though, just sourness. I couldn't forget the way he'd tricked Tristan and then demanded his death, the way he'd just looked at me and ridden by when I'd begged him for mercy.

If the others had already been taken back home, well, I was just going to have to work on saving myself.

I pulled on the ropes, twisting my hands. The ropes didn't give, not even an inch. I scooted over to the hearth and tried to find a sharp edge that I could use to cut through the ropes.

That didn't work either. So much for saving myself. In a low muffled voice, I tried to call out, "Chrissy!"

Silence. Nothing.

"Chrissy!"

Still nothing. It occurred to me that in the story of Cinderella the fairy godmother never came back to check on Cinderella, not even when the messenger came and her stepmother locked her in her bedroom. Really, what was the point of having a fairy godmother if she was never around when you needed her?

I laid my head back against the wall, trying to breathe as normally as possible with a gag stuck in my mouth, and wondered what the king would do with me. Perhaps he just wanted to punish me for ruining his best chance to get rid of the Black Knight.

I shivered and tried not to think of that possibility.

The stroke of midnight came and went. I knew because my dress turned back into a towel. Which was just one more reason that I didn't want to face the king. But eventually I heard voices on the stairs. Angry voices, like gears grinding into overdrive. Moments later King Roderick and Prince Edmond strode through the door. Edmond stopped just inside the doorway. He folded his arms and stared at me grimly.

King Roderick marched over to me, still panting from the climb. He raised his sword to my face. For a moment I thought he would slash me with it. I held my breath and shut my eyes tightly, but he only cut off the gag, then bent down and moved it away from my mouth.

After he'd straightened up he regarded me with fierce eyes. "You have many things to explain." He took a step back from me, resting his sword at his side. "You are an enchantress?"

"No." My mouth was dry and the word fell from my lips like chalk.

"But you are full of enchantments or your fine gown and jewels wouldn't have disappeared."

I felt my cheeks go hot. "That's not an enchantment, just some fairy magic for the evening. Something I wished for long ago." I looked at Edmond, trying to see any sign of kindness in his face, but all of his earlier admiration for me was gone. He watched me with narrowed eyes.

King Roderick waved his hand in my direction as though erasing the subject. "I'm not concerned with fairy trinkets. Those mean nothing now. What I want is the identity of the Black Knight. You will tell us who he is."

"I don't know who he is," I said.

"Pity. Then we'll have to do things another way." His grip

tightened on the hilt of his sword. "Because you will help us to identify him."

"How could I—"

But he didn't give me time to finish. He bent down and grabbed my chin. "The Black Knight said you couldn't tell a lie in front of him or your tongue would burn out of your mouth. This is true?"

I didn't answer, just gulped. I was beginning to understand what he wanted.

Still grasping my chin, King Roderick said, "I will drag every nobleman, farm boy, and merchant from the entire kingdom into this room. One by one you will lie to them. And when your tongue burns out of your mouth, we will know who the Black Knight is."

He let go of my chin and turned to his son. "Tell the guards and the scribes what I want them to do. We'll start with the castle household and move on from there. How many guests do we have staying the night?"

"Enough to keep us busy till daybreak," Edmond said.

"Start with the guardhouse."

They walked toward the door, making plans. They'd almost gone before I called out, "Edmond!"

He paused at the doorway and looked back at me.

"Edmond, don't do this." I pulled at the rope around my wrists, even though I knew it was pointless. "Just hours ago you wanted to marry me."

His gaze ran over me with cold calculation. "And you're just as beautiful now as you were in jewels and a gown. It's almost enough to make me think that I could overlook your odd behavior at the ball." He shook his head slowly. "But you kissed the Black Knight—my enemy. And *that* I could never forgive."

The door shut with a thud. I was left alone in the room, my heart beating as quickly as if I'd just run a mile.

I had to get away, but I'd already tried and I couldn't. No, I had to figure out who the Black Knight was so I didn't have to lie to men until my tongue burned away. There had to be clues. He said he was young and handsome. What else did I know about him?

He was a knight. Knights needed help getting in and out of their armor so he had to at least have one other person somewhere helping him . . . and he was a good kisser. That probably wasn't helpful. What else?

My mind was blank except for the panic that gnawed at the edges of my thoughts. I didn't know enough.

Back at the inn, Chrissy said I was smart enough to figure it out—okay, actually she'd been talking about the stolen poison, and I hadn't figured that out either.

The poison . . . For a moment it took center stage in my mind. Who had Simon stolen it for? Perhaps Queen Neferia— she had an apple to poison. But she could have bought it right from the wizard. Why would she have needed Simon to steal it and sell it to her?

No, it had to be for someone else, which led me back to the first suspect, Margaret. She was involved with both Simon and the Black Knight. But how and why?

The three of them circled in my mind. If she was in love with the Black Knight, why not just leave with him? No one could stop her. Tristan had said he'd heard her tell a lady's maid that she didn't care if a man was lowborn as long as he was ambitious.

Certainly he was ambitious enough. He kept challenging Prince Edmond. But if he was trying to take over the kingdom, why didn't he just challenge the king? Wouldn't that have been the thing to do? Even if he killed Prince Edmond, he wouldn't be king. Roderick still would be.

Did he have a grudge against Edmond? There had been that whole matter of the peasant rebellion he'd put down.

And how did Simon work into all of this? Did he just have a business arrangement with Margaret—selling her stolen potions—or was there something more to it? My mind jumped at the thought—could he be the Black Knight? He was young and handsome. He had access to magic and was stealing things from the wizard, so he might have been able to come up with the invincibility enchantment. Margaret could be in love with him. He was around the castle enough to form an attachment with her. It all fit . . . except that he was a goat now.

Oh, and I guess he wouldn't have stood there and let the wizard give me the switching potion if he was the Black Knight.

But . . . he hadn't had a choice about that. It was the wizard who sold me the switching potion, and Simon hadn't looked happy about it at the time. If he was the Black Knight—no, he wouldn't have cared if I'd taken switching potion if he'd been the Black Knight because he would have known not to kiss me—but if Simon was in league with the Black Knight, then he would have been worried about me taking away the knight's enchantment.

This seemed to fit, to make sense. After all, the Black Knight had truth potion on him when I'd met him. He had to be working with some wizard. And Simon had sold me a vial of something and told me to drink it when I saw the Black Knight. Poison would have taken care of any threat I'd posed.

The knowledge spun around in my mind, fear mixing with excitement. I'd been right the first time. The poison had been for me.

So they were both in league with the Black Knight—
Margaret and Simon—but who was he?

The door swung open. A guard came inside, followed by
King Roderick. My time was up, and I still hadn't figured out
who the Black Knight was.

The king had his sword drawn; the guard didn't have one. He
stood at attention, looking stoic and uncomfortable at the same
time. King Roderick motioned to me. "Well, be quick about it.
Tell a lie and let's see what happens."

"I'm not going to sit here and lie until my tongue burns away."

The king stepped toward me, examining my face. "I assume
you meant that as a lie, because you *are* going to sit here and
do just that."

I fingered the fireplace stones beneath my fingers, wishing
I could break the rope. "You're a tyrant."

"I'll take that as a lie and not an insult, but why don't you
try one more time just to make sure that Henry here is not the
man I'm looking for." He lifted his sword, held its tip against
my cheek, and moved it down to my neck slowly, precisely. He
didn't mean to draw blood, not yet. When he spoke, his voice
was deceptively soft. "You will do as I say, or you'll lose much
more than your tongue tonight."

"Ask your daughter who the Black Knight is. She knows."

The blade pressed harder against my neck. "More treason.
You will not speak ill of my daughter. She knows her place. I
suggest you learn the same."

It was then that I remembered something about fairy tales.
Hansel and Gretel, the smallest billy goat gruff, Puss in Boots—
they never conquered through strength. It was always through
outwitting those who were stronger than they were.

I drew in a careful breath. "I have a better way to help you
find the Black Knight, but you'll have to untie me first and give
me some clothes."

The king shook his head. "I think that's too subtle of a lie. Why don't you say something along the lines of, 'I am a spotted bird.' Try that one, and let's see what happens."

I leaned forward, trying to show him I meant it. "I can find him for you."

"You said you didn't know who he was."

"I don't, but I still can identify him. He kissed me, after all. You don't think he did that without taking off his helmet, do you?"

The king let his sword fall back at his side and took a step away from me, considering. "How will you find him?"

"Bring all of the nobles, any man who is rich at all, to the ballroom."

"And how do you know he is a rich man?"

"When he kissed me he didn't smell bad. He's wealthy enough to bathe regularly."

The king nodded, pleased with this information. He walked to the guard, sniffing. "Well, Henry, it looks like you're innocent by that account. Go tell all the guards to assemble our fine guests in the ballroom." He turned back to me. "I'll have clothes sent to you, but I warn you, if you try to escape, if you cross me in any way, I'll cut off your fingers and use them as chess pieces. Do you understand?"

I nodded and shivered again. "Will you let me go once I've found him for you?"

He smiled at me. "Of course." But even though I didn't have any truth potion, I knew he was lying.

I had to find a way to escape.

Chapter 27

King Roderick sent me a pale linen dress that probably belonged to Margaret. He also sent in three husky washerwomen to cut my ropes and make sure I didn't escape while I dressed.

I changed quickly, wishing I had shoes. Tristan had my other slipper. Still, I couldn't bring myself to leave the remaining glass slipper on the floor where it lay. I put it in my pocket. After that I walked to the ballroom, flanked on both sides by guards.

With every step I took I tried to think of ways to escape. It was too dangerous here in the heart of the castle. I'd never be able to make it outside without the guards cutting me down, but once inside the ballroom there was that terrace—the one with the balcony. If I could climb down the vines, perhaps I could lose them in the dark.

Of course, getting over the castle walls would present another problem and I didn't really have an answer for that.

A guard opened the door and I saw dozens of men standing in a line against the wall. They still wore their finery—silk and velvet tunics, splashes of color against the gray stone walls, but they no longer seemed festive. Their swords had been taken from them and they stared at me silently. King Roderick paced back and forth in front of the men with his sword drawn. Prince Edmond and Prince Hugh were also there, swords hanging at their sides, as though they would contend with anyone who crossed the king. While they spoke to each other, Hugh glanced over at me with a cold stare. I supposed that Edmond had told him what I'd done.

Princess Margaret stood near them, her arms folded tightly across her chest. Two crimson patches of color flushed on her cheeks when she saw me. I wondered if the king had told her of my accusations.

The king saw me and motioned me over. "Here they are. Take a look. Which one is he?"

"I need to ask each of them a question," I said. "It will take a few minutes." Instead of giving the king time to protest, I walked to the first man at the end of the line. He didn't have the height to be the Black Knight, but still I said, "Answer me yes or no. Are you the Black Knight?"

His voice was clipped with indignation. "No."

I moved to the next man. "Are you the Black Knight?"

He shook his head. "Of course not."

The king came up behind me, hands on his hips. "This is how you're going to identify him? You expect one of them to tell you yes?"

"One of them will tell me the truth. Be patient."

The king turned away from me, cursing, but he didn't stop me. I went down the line asking the same question. Each time the answer was no.

I listened to them, but half my mind was still trying to piece together what I knew. If Princess Margaret was in love with the Black Knight, they could have run off together long before now . . . so maybe it was Simon she loved. Back when I first met her, she had been waiting for someone who hadn't come, and Simon wouldn't have been able to meet her after he was turned into a goat.

Margaret wouldn't have been able to marry Simon without her father's permission, so perhaps the two of them had devised a plan with the Black Knight. Maybe Simon was supposed to defeat the Black Knight to win Margaret's hand. But why hadn't they done it before now? Why wait? There was still something about the Black Knight I was missing.

I came to the last man in the line. "Are you the Black Knight?"

He shook his head. "I'm certainly not."

The king strode up to my side, his lips set in an angry grimace. "And what was the point of that exercise besides wasting my time? You don't know whom he is at all, do you?"

But I did. It had all just clicked into place. I understood what it was the Black Knight wanted.

"I haven't spoken to everyone in the room," I told the king and walked slowly toward Prince Edmond and Prince Hugh. Part of me was sorry to reveal him, but he'd ordered Tristan's death. I couldn't forgive him for that.

I stopped in front of Prince Hugh. "Are you the Black Knight?"

He folded his arms and scoffed at me. "You think you can insult me by asking such a question?"

The king came toward me, and I could tell he was in agreement with Prince Hugh. The king grabbed my arm and dragged me several feet away from his son, but I didn't stop talking. I had to say it all now. "You wanted to be heir to the throne so you invented the Black Knight and had the wizard's apprentice make an invincibility spell for you. In return you told him he and Margaret could marry when you came to power. After the Black Knight killed Prince Edmond, he would disappear. Or better yet, you'd have Simon dress in the armor and you'd vanquish him yourself. The people would love you for it."

The king stopped dragging me across the floor. He turned back to Prince Hugh, his eyes considering his son again.

I said, "He is the Black Knight."

Margaret stepped toward me, but her eyes turned to her father. "Are you going to let her live after speaking such treason? She kissed the Black Knight. She can't be trusted; she's in love with the enemy."

I turned to Margaret. "And you're in love with a goat. That's why Simon hasn't come to see you. The wizard found out he'd stolen potions and turned him into a goat."

Margaret flinched as though I'd hit her. The color poured out of her face and she held her hand to her lips. "No," she said.

The king watched her and then his eyes narrowed in on Hugh. "Is all of this true?"

Hugh shook his head and he tried to smile. "Lady Savannah is a liar."

The king loosened his grip on my arm, and I took advantage of his uncertainty and stepped away from him. "Sometimes I am a liar, I admit it. I used to have an enchantment that, whenever I lied, a reptile would grow on my tongue. It happened more often than I liked. But then, luckily, I took switching potion and when I kissed the Black Knight, I switched enchantments with him. Now instead of invincibility, if he lies a reptile will come out of his mouth. So I'll ask you again: are you the Black Knight?"

Hugh took several quick breaths. His eyes locked on mine. "I don't need to answer your charges."

Edmond drew his sword. "Yes, you do."

Hugh looked between his brother and his father, and he shook his head. "You don't believe her, do you? Who is she? What are her credentials, that you should believe her?"

I took another step away from the king and toward the window. "Why shouldn't they believe me? I can't tell a lie in the presence of the Black Knight or my tongue will burn out of my mouth."

King Roderick gripped his sword harder. He slowly raised it. "Answer the question."

Hugh held up the palm of his hand, pleading, but his other hand was near the hilt of his own sword. "She is trying to trick you!"

Which proved to be a lie. Hugh grimaced, then coughed, and a long gray snake slithered out of his mouth and dropped to the floor. The room was silent for the length of a gasp.

Then Edmond lunged toward his brother with a yell.

Hugh sidestepped him and drew his own sword. "Whether I have the invincibility charm or not, I can still beat both of you with a sword. Stay back."

I didn't know how long the three of them would stay occupied or who would win. At that moment I didn't even care. I ran to the terrace and climbed over the balcony.

The vine cracked when I stepped on it, and for a moment I thought it would give way and I'd fall to my death. I clung to the branches, waiting, but it held firm. I figured I wouldn't give it a chance to change its mind and moved my feet downward along the vine until I found another foothold. Little branches and twisted knots cut into my feet and hands, making me move even faster.

I had to get down. I had to get down. I had to get—I saw a light down in the courtyard, not far away from where I would land. And not a torchlight—it was the unmistakable beam of a flashlight. "Tristan!" I called, probably too loudly since I didn't want to let any of the guards know where I was.

The flashlight beam momentarily swung over to me, and I heard the clang of swords, the yell of men. I squinted in the direction of the light and saw Tristan. He was on foot and fighting four of the castle guards.

He had come back for me, just like I'd hoped.

I hurried to find the next foothold. How far away was the ground? Eight feet? Ten? I shifted my weight downward, ignoring the pieces of bark that bit into my hands.

Below me, Tristan knocked the swords away from one guard and then another. Still he managed to hold the flashlight steady with one hand as he fought with the other. With a kick to the chest, he sent one guard flying into two others. In between all of this, he slowly made his way toward me.

"So," he called over to me when he was close enough that he didn't have to shout. "Any particular reason you're hanging from the castle vines?"

"I'm escaping," I told him. "What brings you here?"

"I'm rescuing you. Hold on a second." He knocked the last guard's sword to the ground. The man held up his arms in a manner of surrender, backing up slowly, then turned and ran into the darkness.

Tristan walked over to me and offered me his hand. "You're almost to the ground. Just a few more steps."

I took his hand and jumped down the rest of the way. I wanted to hug him, but instead he pulled me along the grass. "We need to run to the wall."

But my feet stung from where the vines had cut into them and I couldn't think of running barefoot across the grounds. I slipped my hand out of his, reached into my pocket, and put one slipper on my foot. "Please tell me you still have the other one of these."

He took my other slipper from his pocket, then knelt down and placed it onto my foot. "I guess I'm your Prince Charming tonight."

I smiled back at him. "Thank you."

He stood up and took hold of my hand again, already pulling me forward. "Now we've got to run."

We went across the grounds and Tristan turned off the light so that we'd be harder to spot if the guards were planning another offensive. I hoped Tristan's senses were still working and he could see through the darkness, because I couldn't. Everything was dark shapes. It was like running blind.

Tristan took me to one of the towers and we hurried up the stairs. When I started to slow, he tugged me along. "Come on, this is just like track practice. Pretend we're running up the bleachers."

We reached the level of the wall, and I saw he had a rope hooked to the side.

I peered over the wall. It was a long way down. In the dark, I couldn't see the ground at all.

"You can do this," he told me, and put my hand on the rope. "There are knots along the way to help you get footholds. It's easier than climbing the rope in PE."

It was wonderful, really, how well school had prepared me for life as a medieval fugitive.

I went down the rope first, trying to ignore the fact that my hands were stiff from the cold, and it was hard to get a foothold in dancing slippers. Finally I reached the ground. In moments Tristan was beside me again, holding my hand and guiding me along the wall.

We came to where he'd tied a horse to a post beside the wall. Tristan untied the horse and helped me up, then mounted the horse himself. He turned on the flashlight then, trying to light the way for the horse as it walked toward the forest.

I tucked my arms around Tristan's waist, but looked back at the castle. By the dim light of the torches on the wall, I could make out figures, people watching us. "They can see us," I told Tristan. "Shouldn't you turn off the flashlight?"

He shook his head. "It doesn't matter if they see us now. They won't be able to surround us—and if they come after us, their horses won't move any faster in the dark than ours. Besides, I think they've figured out that I'm invincible." He put his hand over mine and gently squeezed my fingers. "You can stop worrying. You're safe as long as you're with me, and I'm not letting you out of my sight again."

I leaned against his back, just like I'd wanted to do on our first ride, but I couldn't stop worrying. "Where are Jane and Hunter?"

"Safe," he said.

I wanted to ask more, but Tristan was busy trying to hold the flashlight steady with one hand and guiding the horse with the other. I'm not sure how much having the flashlight actually helped. The horse seemed to be spooked by the beam and kept stopping and jerking his head as though trying to get away from it.

We probably could have walked through the forest just as quickly ourselves, but I was glad we didn't have to. I was tired and the frigid night air pushed through my dress and swept across my face. I shut my eyes, enjoying the warmth of Tristan's back.

I didn't remember falling asleep, but suddenly Tristan was dismounting. "Let's make camp here. We're both tired and not making much progress. It'll be easier in the daylight."

"Here?" I asked, because it was nothing but dirt, trees, and bushes.

"I'll start a fire."

I wrapped my arms around my chest and didn't get off the horse. "Won't that give away our position?"

"They won't be able to see the smoke in the darkness and the forest should hide the light from the castle. The only people who will know we're here are those that are close by. And if any of them attack, I'll be able to take care of them."

I slid off the horse, still muddled with sleep, and helped him gather up twigs and branches. We also piled up handfuls of dry leaves. Finally, after a very long time of rubbing sticks together, he coaxed a small fire to life.

Then I sat on the ground, my hands wrapped around my knees, and wondered where we were heading. Not to the inn— the king's guards would look for us there. Tristan sat down close beside me and didn't speak. I could tell from his posture that he was as tired as I was.

"Where are Hunter and Jane?" I asked.

He didn't answer, which made me panic.

"You said they were safe. Where are they?"

He looked at the fire, not me. I could see the flames reflected in his eyes. "I found them on the roadside. Their horses had turned into mice, and the carriage into a turnip. They were trying to decide what to do. Hunter had been hit pretty hard. I guess he put up a fight back there at the castle. Jane was worried that he might have broken ribs.

"They told me what had happened to you, and I told them that I had the invincibility enchantment. I figured I'd go back, rescue you, and then meet up with them again."

He stopped talking for a moment and I had to prod him to continue. "And?"

"Then your fairy godmother came. All of a sudden she was there like some magical stewardess telling us she hoped we'd enjoyed our visit to the Middle Ages. She said the terms of my enchantment no longer applied and she'd take me back home with Jane and Hunter."

He glanced over at me. "Jane didn't want to leave you, but Hunter wouldn't go unless she did, and she thought he needed to see a doctor."

"They left?" I asked. Part of me felt glad—they should have never come in the first place, and now it was even more dangerous for them to be here. Jane should be home, where it was safe. But another part of me was devastated. I'd never see her again.

I felt tears pressing against my eyes but didn't want to wipe them away. That would just draw attention to them. I looked into the fire instead. "When is Chrissy coming back for you?"

"She isn't." He took hold of my chin and brought my face around to his. "I told her I wouldn't go home without you." His thumb caressed a line across my jaw. "Savannah, you came back to the Middle Ages to help me. You gave up any chance to go home so I could escape from the guards. How could I leave you here alone?"

My voice had nearly fled altogether, but I managed to say, "You shouldn't have stayed just because you felt obligated to me."

"I didn't," he said, and he leaned over and kissed me.

I kissed him back, thankful for the warmth of his arms. And really, I'd been wrong to ever think he wouldn't kiss as passionately as the Black Knight.

Chapter 28

I'm not sure what time we fell asleep, only that it was very late. Eventually I felt the sunshine drifting through the treetops in patches. A part of my consciousness registered that birds were chattering in the branches around us, but I didn't want to wake up. I was still too tired. Every time the fire had died down, one of us had to get up to throw more wood onto it.

Besides, I felt perfectly safe with Tristan sleeping just on the other side of the fire. He was invincible.

As I drifted into another dream, I felt lips brush against mine. I smiled and opened my eyes, already thinking of what I would say to Tristan.

Only it wasn't Tristan. I was looking directly into Hugh's face.

I let out a startled gasp and sat up, my heart pounding and my head still dizzy with the remnants of sleep.

Beside me, Tristan sat up, reaching for his sword. Before he pulled it from its sheath, Hugh said, "It won't do you any good. I've already kissed her."

Tristan paused. "You what?"

Hugh stood and looked down at us with a triumphant smile. He still wore his clothes from the ball, although they were rumpled and stained. He had an air of weariness about him, and I wondered if he'd walked all of this way. "Didn't you know she had the invincibility charm?" he asked Tristan. "She stole it from me, and now I've stolen it back."

To me he said, "You should have understood how it worked before you told anyone you had it. It only sharpens your senses when your enemy has a weapon pointed at you." He held up his hands, showing me they were empty. "I don't have a weapon, so I was able to sneak up on you without detection."

He walked over to our horse as though we no longer concerned him. "It was thoughtful of you to make it so very easy to find you. What with the light pointing the direction you went last night and then the smoke showing your location this morning." He patted the horse's mane. "Thoughtful of you to provide me with a horse too. I suppose it was the least you could do after you turned my father and brother against me."

He turned back to us, his gaze suddenly chilling. "Of course, that doesn't mean the two of you won't pay for what you did to me, because you will."

He walked slowly back toward us, picking up one of the sticks we'd gathered for the fire. As he gripped it he looked at me. "You were a fool to choose him—he's nothing but a storyteller. I would have come for you. I wouldn't have let my father hurt you."

He may have meant it, but I didn't regret choosing Tristan. I glanced at Tristan to see what he would do, but he was only gazing at Hugh patiently.

Hugh held out the stick, making it into a weapon, then

turned to Tristan. "What will you do now, page? If you don't draw your sword, I will strike her. Draw it, and it will only make your end come more quickly."

Tristan stood up slowly, faced Hugh, then pulled his sword from the sheath. "Do you feel anything happening?"

Hugh took a step away from him. A flash of uncertainty crossed his expression.

I stood up but made sure to stay near Tristan. "You don't understand magic either, Hugh. If you did, you'd know that you can't switch the same enchantments."

Hugh took another step backward, this time as though he'd been knocked by a fist. His eyes had a wild look to them and his voice came out strangled. "I still have the same enchantment?"

"No. I switched with Tristan last night. Now he has the invincibility enchantment and you—well, you can't go home until you're a prince."

As soon as I spoke the words, a stream of sparkles swooped down from the sky. Like thousands of little fireflies, they encircled Hugh and lifted him from the ground.

He put his hands out as though trying to swat them away. "What's happening?"

"I think you get to go home now," I said. Then the lights drew together and he was gone.

Tristan and I stood looking at the empty space for a few seconds, checking to make sure he'd really left. At last Tristan lowered his sword. "Well, they're going to be happy to see him back at the castle."

I nodded. "I think so."

Then we both laughed and Tristan wound his arms around me. He laid his head against my hair, holding me close. "You still smell good."

"Better than cough syrup?"

"Way better than cough syrup."

The lights came again, a shower of sparklers this time, and then Chrissy stood before us.

She wore a tropical blue swimsuit and a pink terry cloth cover-up, and she smelled of suntan lotion. She took her sunglasses from her nose and slid them on top of her hair. "Okay, I'm saving myself the fifty voice mails you'll be sending me shortly and taking care of this right now." She tossed her blond hair over her shoulder and held up her hand to keep me from speaking. "I already know you no longer have that can't-go-home-until-you're-a-prince enchantment. So what will it be, are you happy with your prom date now, or are you going to claim that I still messed up your wish?"

I held onto Tristan's hand tightly. "I'm very happy with my prom date."

"Good." She smiled at me, satisfied. "All that anxiety you had over the dance and what everyone at school would think of your date—I hope you've learned that you can't let people in high school hand your happiness to you."

I nodded.

"I'm the one with the wand," she went on. "Leave it to the professionals."

"What?" I asked, because it wasn't what I'd expected her to say at all. But I don't think she heard me. She flicked her wand in our direction and the next thing I knew, we were standing in my bedroom.

• • •

Tristan turned in circles around my room. "Wow," he said.

I let out a sigh of relief. "We're back in the modern world." Just because I could, I walked over to the light switch and flipped it on. "Look, electricity."

His eyes kept roaming around my room. "You have a ton of clothes."

"Not really," I said, and shut my closet door. I hoped he wasn't referring to all the clothes sprawled over my bed and thrown across the top of my dresser. In truth, it did seem like an overabundant amount. Everything in my room seemed luxurious now. Even Princess Margaret hadn't had such nice things.

"I need to call my parents," Tristan said.

"What are you going to tell them?" I asked.

Which was the reason he didn't call them right away. I gave him a haircut first, then he showered, and I gave him a pair of my dad's sweatpants and a T-shirt.

I also called Jane's cell phone to let her know that I was home and to find out how Hunter was, but she didn't pick up. And then I remembered that she'd taken her cell phone to the Middle Ages.

Yeah, so Jane probably wouldn't be answering that anytime soon.

After Tristan was clean, shorn, and standing in my kitchen, I helped him with his story. "You leaned out of your window and fell out. Head injury. You wandered around for two days and don't remember anything."

"Wouldn't my window have been left open if I fell out of it?"

I looked at him and sighed. "It's not going to matter what you tell them. They'll know something odd happened to you—you've grown at least an inch and filled out. You've got scars on your arms. Plus you've turned into this total hot guy."

He took my hand and squeezed it. "I saw myself in the bathroom mirror. I don't look that different."

"Yes, you do," I said, because it was true.

He shook his head. "You just see me differently now."

I knew he was wrong, but the funny thing was that when he went home—he gave me a blow-by-blow description later—his parents only noticed the new haircut. They thought that's why he looked so different.

He ended up telling them this very creative tale about how he'd snuck out of his house Saturday night because he was going to come to my window and ask me to prom in the moonlight like Romeo and Juliet, but in the dark he'd gotten lost and accidentally fell into someone's underground cellar. When he finally came to, he realized that the owners must have locked the cellar without realizing he was in there. It took him an entire day of banging on the door before someone heard him and let him out.

And the haircut? He'd trimmed his hair himself before he came to see me because he wanted to look his best.

Tristan wasn't sure they completely believed him, but that's the thing about being the responsible honors-kid type of guy. Your parents are willing to cut you a lot of slack. They were so happy and relieved to see him that they overlooked the minor details.

Not long after Tristan left, Jane called from the ER to check and see if I was home. She cried when she heard my voice. "I just knew your fairy godmother wouldn't leave you stranded at that castle."

Uh, right. I thought it was entirely possible that not only could Chrissy have left me stranded there, but decades could have passed before I crossed her mind again. The one thing I had learned from all of this was that magic shouldn't be meddled with and that fairy godmothers were an unreliable bunch. Okay, technically that's two things. Plus, I'd also learned that Tristan was a total catch, so I guess that's three.

Hunter had X-rays taken and he didn't have any broken

ribs. He told the doctors and his parents that his injuries had been from a car accident, but since his car didn't have a dent anywhere on it and he also had a huge bruise on his cheek from where one of the castle guards had punched him, this story was somewhat suspect in nature.

I was just glad I didn't have to lie to anybody about all of it. Even though the reptiles-on-my-tongue enchantment was gone—Chrissy had said it would only be there until my wishes were complete—I still got a sick, watery feeling in my mouth whenever I even thought about lying.

Tristan went back to school Tuesday morning, and despite his assurances that no one would notice a difference in him, people did. Perhaps it wasn't his looks so much as it was his walk and his new air of confidence. Or, as he told me, life looks different when you're invincible.

Prom night came, and Tristan and I doubled with Jane and Hunter. Jane spent her own money to buy back my prom dress for me, and I did her hair in a style that rivaled Cinderella's. It felt nice to be friends again, the way we had been before.

The dance took place in a local hotel conference room, not a castle; and rock music blared over the speakers instead of musicians playing in a loft. But it still seemed more magical than my last ball had.

I danced with Tristan nearly every song and felt like I'd never get tired of having his arms around me. Toward the end of the night they announced the prom royalty. Hunter was crowned prom king. They made him come up to the front of the room and put a spiky crown on his head.

Tristan nudged me while we clapped for him. "So do you still think a crown makes a guy look hot?"

"Actually, I think I'm more into sleek-looking suits right now." I ran my fingers over the arm of his tuxedo and gave him an appraising stare. "You know, sort of that James Bond cool look."

"Uh-huh." He finished clapping and took hold of my hand. "I guess I should be glad you've only recently gone for the spy look, or for the last eight months I would have been somewhere dodging bullets, wouldn't I?" Then he tilted his head. "You're not talking to your fairy godmother anymore, are you?"

I laughed and squeezed his hand. "Don't worry. You're safe."

From the Honorable Master Sagewick Goldengill
To the Department of Fairy Advancement

To the Honorable Department,

I am in receipt of student Chrysanthemum Everstar's extra-credit report and have reviewed it thoroughly. Although I approve of the results Miss Everstar was able to achieve, I found her methods lacking. I recommend she has more practice before admittance to GM University.

I'll have Madame Bellwings give her another assignment.

Yours,
Sagewick Goldengill

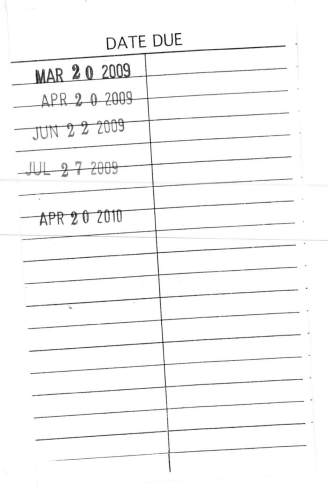